Entirely YOURS
RACHEL LEWIS

Editing: Sadie (Dot The i Edit)

Cover Text and Layout: S.R. Clark (@srclarkdesigns), Kelsey Bowman (Let's Get Lit Studio)

Cover Illustrations: Isabelle Diaz (@procastle_studios)

Copyright © 2025 by Rachel Lewis

All rights reserved.

No part of this book may be reproduced in any form or by any electronic or mechanical means, including information storage and retrieval systems, without written permission from the author, except for the use of brief quotations in a book review.

This novel is entirely a work of fiction. The names, characters, and incidents portrayed in it are the work of the author's imagination. Any resemblance to actual persons, living or dead, events or localities is entirely coincidental.

ALSO BY
Rachel Lewis

The Bardot Siblings Series

Yours, Unexpectedly (Book 1)

Merrily Yours (Book 1.5)

AUTHOR'S NOTE

Hello my wonderful readers!

Thank you, thank you, thank you for taking a chance on me and my books! Whether you've been here from the beginning or you are just now picking up a copy of one of my books, I'm so grateful that you're here.

A few things before you embark on your journey back to Sassafras! I like to include content warnings and a list of spicy chapters, not because I think you should skip these chapters, but because I firmly believe everyone should have the opportunity to decide what they are comfortable reading before diving in. Always do what is best for you!

Content Warnings:
—On page explicit sexual content (see Dicktionary below!)
—Emotionally abusive/narcissistic ex (referenced on page to the past relationship)
—Loss of parent and grandparent (past, not on page)
—Pregnancy
—Swearing

Dicktionary:
—Chapter 3
—Chapter 10
—Chapter 11
—Chapter 26

—Chapter 33
—Chapter 37
—Chapter 46

xo, Rachel

PLAYLIST
Available on Spotify

This playlist is meant to be enjoyed as you read, but it also has great vibes in general! With Jules being a musician, the music adds an extra layer to the book. There's one song for each chapter and I hope it gives you an immersive reading experience! Happy listening!

1. Neon Moon—Brooks & Dunn
2. Can't Fight The Moonlight—LeAnn Rimes
3. One Night—Griff
4. Close To You—Gracie Abrams
5. Signs—Ethan Dufault
6. Keep It Up—Good Neighbours
7. I Fall Hard—The Strike
8. Roses—Matthew Parker, Sajan Nauriyal
9. first night—elijah woods, JESSIA
10. Back in My Arms—Carlie Hanson
11. Vulnerable—Selena Gomez
12. invisible string—Taylor Swift
13. Automatic—Fly By Midnight, Jake Miller
14. Oh shit…are we in love?—Valley
15. Fall Into Me—Forest Blakk
16. Nothing Seems To Matter Now—VICTORS
17. Till We Both Say—Nicotine Dolls
18. We'll Figure It Out—Smithfield
19. safety net (feat. Ty Dolla $ign)—Ariana Grande, Ty Dolla $ign

20. Pasta—New Rules
21. Jolene—Dolly Parton
22. playing house—phem
23. Stuck On You—Meiko
24. Big Plans—Why Don't We
25. Surrender—WALK THE MOON
26. Big Energy—Latto
27. Shower—Becky G
28. You've Got a Friend—James Taylor
29. Sugar, You—Oh Honey
30. This Will Be (An Everlasting Love)—Natalie Cole
31. Good Enough—Carlie Hanson
32. Are We a Thing—Leidi
33. I Want To Be Alone With You—Wishes
34. Forever Young—Bob Dylan
35. Say Love—James TW
36. Fake—Lauv, Conan Gray
37. party 4 u—Charli xcx
38. Dance With Me—Tones And I
39. Day Dreaming—Jack & Jack
40. Bad Liar—Selena Gomez
41. 8 Letters—Why Don't We
42. Lost Without You—Fly By Midnight, Clara Mae
43. Crazier Things (with Noah Kahan)—Chelsea Cutler, Noah Kahan
44. Lovers On The Moon—AJ Mitchell
45. Hey Stupid, I Love You—JP Saxe
46. Somebody To You—The Vamps, Demi Lovato
47. Long Run (feat. Nina Nesbitt)—Deacon, Nina Nesbitt

*To anyone who wasn't ready but did it anyway.
I see you and I'm so proud of you.*

Chapter One
TO BE DETERMINED
Thea

NEON MOON
Brooks & Dunn

Brooks and Dunn croon about broken dreams and neon moons over the speaker of The Dusty Barrel, serenading me like they do most nights. Surprisingly there are a few country music bars in the greater Boston area, though, The Dusty Barrel claims to be the oldest and where I felt the most at home after moving from middle-of-nowhere Texas several years ago. The floors are sticky, everyone is cast in a faint red tint from the beer-themed, neon lights, and there's always at least one old man with a cowboy hat on, talking about "The good ol' days."

It has a *Coyote Ugly* vibe—without the misogyny.

Okay, maybe it has *some* of the misogyny. I've been known to hop up on the bar if I need some extra tips.

I've liked it here well enough, but tonight is my last night before I move again. It's time for me to get back to small-town life—I want somewhere slower paced for Chloe, my four-year-old, to grow up. She's only known Boston streets and apartment buildings full of strangers. It's easy to be invisible here, but

Chloe deserves to be visible. I want her to experience what it's like to really feel known. A feeling that is always present when everyone knows your name, who your first kiss was, and what your order is at the local burger joint.

A feeling I thought I hated until suddenly it was missing.

I'm also more than ready to get my hands on the keys to my new dance studio. A dream I've had since I was barely old enough to reach the barre is finally coming to fruition, thanks to money my Grandmother left when she passed away and years of scraping pennies together... hence the dancing on bar tops. I will admit, I didn't think it would come together quite this soon, but here we are.

I wipe down the counter and busy myself pouring another beer when my eyes snag on *him* for what feels like the hundredth time this evening. It's always pretty quiet around here after the holidays, January is notoriously slow, which is why he immediately caught my eye when he walked in. Though, I think I would have noticed him even if it was packed tonight.

"TBD" is what I've been calling him in my head. One: because it is *to be determined* what I want to do with him. And two: because he's *tall, brooding, and dark* with two sleeves of tattoos winding around what I can see of his tanned forearms and full, luscious locks of mahogany hair, pulled back into an effortless messy bun that would've taken me three hours and several rounds of tears to execute. A wistful sigh leaves my parted lips.

He's here alone and has been for the past hour. I know this because I kept waiting for someone to join him, and yet no one ever did. No ring that I can see either, not that everyone wears one. I can't decide if I should go say hi or keep awkwardly staring at him from across the bar.

While attempting to make up my mind, my inner monologue goes something like this: *Thea. Get your ass over there and talk to the deliciously hot man that you will never see again. What's the worst that could happen?*

Then I say to myself: *Well, my dearest Thea, there are many terrible things that could happen. One, he could be a serial killer. Two, he might say no. And three, he says yes and you will continue to be a disappointment to yourself and those around you.*

I know, it gets dark real fast. Then I chastise myself for being too hard on myself and that cycle repeats over and over again, presumably until I'm dead.

I realize I'm in one of these thought spirals when TBD lifts his hand—the smallest of waves, accompanied by a furrowed brow. Fuck. *Fuck!* Have I been watching him this entire time?!

Staring dumbly, I think through my two choices: walk over to him or duck behind the bar and pretend like I'm not here. As much as I want to choose option two, I buck up and head toward him.

"Hi. So sorry about that, I think I blacked out for a second… Low blood sugar probably…" I ramble. I'm actually a fairly put together person—I have a child for fuck's sake—but this man is making my brain do pirouettes. And those pirouettes seem to be executed by Pre-K dance students.

He chuckles and it's somehow… melodic? I'm unsure how that is even possible. Then his grin hits me full force, and he has fucking dimples. They look just like Chloe's. I've always fallen head first for dimples, and it dawns on me that I'm quickly losing a battle against my already thinning restraint.

"Well, that's better than why I thought you were staring at me," he says.

"Why did you think I was staring at you?" I'm curious now, another negative trait. Always too curious *and* too willing to sleep with men who have dimples. Okay, so it was just the one other one, but still.

"I had a run-in with a feral chipmunk on the way here, and I was worried the little guy had messed up my hair," he deadpans.

I feel my eyes grow three times their size because, little known fact, I am terrified of chipmunks. We don't have them in

Texas, at least not the part of Texas I'm from, and I vividly remember the first time I saw one after moving to Boston. I thought maybe I'd channel my inner Disney princess and try to befriend what had to be the cutest little creature I'd ever seen. That desire lasted until the fucker took a chunk out of my finger, and I had to get a tetanus shot.

Needles are another thing I hate.

TBD must sense my terror because he immediately holds up both hands to console me. "No, I'm joking. That did not actually happen. Sorry, are you a big fan of chipmunks? No creatures were harmed on my walk here."

I take a deep, cleansing breath like the therapist I follow on social media taught me. "I am the opposite of a fan. A hater? I'm a hater of chipmunks," I reply.

"Obviously…" He grins. I decide I like his teeth. Maybe I'd let him take a chunk out of my—nope! Don't go there, Thea.

We stare at each other for one beat… two. He really is just *so* pretty. I find my gaze wandering to his forearms. They're covered in black lines that I now realize are flowers. All different kinds winding up and down both forearms. Music notes twine in between the blooms and come to a stop at his wrists. He catches me staring—again—and holds out his arms for me to inspect.

"I like them," I murmur. Talking about the tattoos and his forearms, if I'm being honest. God, when did I get so horny?

I spot a rose wrapping around his left wrist and reach out to graze the ink before I can think better of it.

"I've always had a thing for roses," he says, eyes trained on where my fingers meet his skin. I feel them burning into me. "Not sure why," he continues. "My mom tried to plant rose bushes a few times throughout my childhood, but most of them didn't really stick."

"Roses are fickle things," I muse, my finger still following the lines around his wrist.

"You sound like you know from experience." He looks at me

with his dark, soulful eyes, sending a little shiver down my spine and causing an inconvenient heat to grow in my stomach.

I huff a laugh. "Yeah, well—" I"m cut off by my manager yelling from down the bar.

"Thea! Can you grab more towels from the back?"

"Yeah, sure," I call at the same time TBD says, "Thea… That's a pretty name."

He says it with such genuine care that I stumble a step on my way to the back. Before I push through the door I turn to him, rushing out, "Don't go yet! Please. I'll be right back."

He nods and those dimples pop out.

I press through the swinging door into the back room before immediately turning on my heel and poking my head back out. "Also…" My smile is sheepish. "What's your name? Since you know mine."

"Jules," he replies. "People call me Jules."

"That's a pretty name," I echo, loving the way he dips his chin to hide his smile. "Be right back."

After I've located some towels, I head back to the front, drop the towels behind the bar, and beeline back over to my new friend, Jules. Playing hard to get has never been my forte.

"So…" I start, elbows making their way onto the counter to cradle my chin. "Come here often?"

The corner of his mouth quirks. "In town for a gig actually."

"A gig?" If this guy is a musician then he's hitting the trifecta that makes up my own personal kryptonite—tattoos, dimples, talent.

He nods, taking a sip of his beer. My eyes follow as he licks a stray droplet from the corner of his lips. "I play violin with a band occasionally. Only when they need an extra or their normal guy is out."

"Didn't feel like taking advantage of the groupies after?" I cringe. *The groupies? Who am I?*

He rubs his knuckles across his mouth, hiding a smirk. "Not really my scene."

I give a disbelieving laugh at that. "But a northeastern version of a honky tonk is?"

"Honestly, my hotel is across the street, and I wasn't quite ready to go to bed yet." He says everything like each word is thoughtfully picked out of his brain in just the right combination.

Because of that, a picture of Jules in a bed suddenly flashes into my mind. I can feel the heat creeping up my neck—the telltale signs of a blush that my pale skin is unlikely to conceal. Jules clocks the red spreading across my chest but is kind enough not to mention it. "So where are you from if not Boston?" I ask, quickly attempting to divert his attention.

"A sm—" The sound of glass shattering cuts him off and nearly makes me jump out of my skin. Apparently we aren't going to get through a conversation uninterrupted tonight.

I whip around and see the new girl—my replacement—has just dropped a tray of dirty beer pints, leaving her surrounded by shattered glass. She meets my eyes, and I can tell she's about to cry, which simply won't do.

"Shit." I grab the broom and dustpan and rush over to begin sweeping up. "It's okay, babe. No one even noticed," I joke. She doesn't seem quite ready to joke about the situation, however. A lone tear drops from her eye and she purses her lips, head shaking.

Standing to meet her gaze, I whisper, "Do you know how many glasses I've broken during my time here?"

Her watery eyes look into mine, and she shakes her head again. "Dozens," I reply. "Tim finally took pity on me and found someone else to bus the tables. I think he realized it would save him money in the long run if I stayed behind the bar." I smirk. "Now come on, let's clean up and go take your fifteen."

Thirty minutes later, I've finally gotten the new girl, Sophia, calm and have resigned myself to never seeing TBD again—it would be my luck that he's already left or moved on to some other person at the bar. Turns out Sophia is newly pregnant, and her baby daddy is just as shitty as mine. I felt like I needed to reassure her that, while everything might not turn out "alright," and it definitely wouldn't be easy, she has someone she can call and vent to when needed.

Raising Chloe is hard, but it's also the best thing that ever happened to me. However, becoming a mother at nineteen was not in my life plan. I honestly wasn't sure if I would ever have kids. I was planning on dancing for Ballet Boston until I retired, probably in my late thirties, and opening my own studio, but never really thought beyond that.

After fluffing Sophia's hair and refilling her water bottle, I slide out of the back and immediately look over to where Jules was seated.

My heart instantly drops out of my chest. He's gone.

Chapter Two
FAMILY GROUP CHATS
Jules

CAN'T FIGHT THE MOONLIGHT
Leanne Rimes

Normally after a gig in Boston, I go straight back to Ben's apartment. Sometimes he'll try to talk me into going out with some of his work friends, but usually I'm so peopled-out, I want to get back home as quickly as possible.

Ben moving back to Sassafras really makes me second guess taking gigs in Boston anymore, though. Since he's not here, I had to stay at a hotel which feels so sterile and also cuts into my pay... I really need to find somewhere to play closer to home. And then, of course, the one time I don't have Ben with me, I got back to the room and could not fall asleep.

That's how I found myself shutting down a western-themed bar across the street from my hotel.

When I walked in earlier tonight, *she* immediately caught my eye. She's tall and lean with long blonde waves cascading down her back. A skintight black shirt is tucked into even tighter jeans, which flare out enough for bright red boots to peek out from the bottom. She's wearing minimal jewelry and—most importantly—no ring. When her eyes locked onto mine for the first time, the sparkling green momentarily took my breath away.

She's a fucking bombshell. A muse.

I almost went back to the hotel to grab my notebook. She makes me want to write, which I haven't done in a while. My siblings would definitely make fun of me for the way I'm ready to wax poetic about this woman.

And then I caught her staring at me, and I knew I had to talk to her.

She opened her mouth and not only is she a bombshell but she's cute as hell, too, with a light accent that sounds almost southern. I can't tell if it's real or a part she plays at work.

Then she disappeared into the back for thirty minutes with the poor woman who broke that tray of glasses, and I didn't know what to do with myself. I closed my tab, fiddled with my now empty glass, refused the male bartender who kept asking me if I wanted another, and finally got up to shake some of the nervous energy off of me.

I wash my hands in the dingy bar bathroom sink and then proceed to pace in front of the mirror. I'm not this guy, but I want to spend more time with her.

Against my better judgement, I pull out my phone and text the family group chat. It's almost 2 AM, so I'm not sure if anyone will even answer.

> Anyone up?

TWIN

The better question is why are YOU up?

BB

I'm up, pregnancy insomnia is real.

> Hypothetically, if I wanted to bring a girl home - how would I go about that?

> **BB**
>
> Home? Like to Sassafras?
>
> **TWIN**
>
> HOLY SHIT, no Bexy
>
> Jules wants to bring a lady friend back to his hotel
>
> The first time I'm not in Boston with you and THIS happens??
>
> I shouldn't have texted
>
> **BB**
>
> Oh my god, hell yes. I need one of you to find a woman ffs
>
> Is she pretty?
>
> What's her name?
>
> Want me to FaceTime?
>
> **TWIN**
>
> Just pretend to be me, I have way more game than you
>
> I'm turning on my do not disturb

I pocket my phone and push the door open to head back to my place at the bar. What I see stops me in my tracks. Thea, looking so... sad. She's staring at my empty seat, unaware that I'm staring at her.

Her brow furrows, and she seems to be having a silent conversation with herself. She tilts her head, rolls her eyes, and then covers her face with both hands. I see her shoulders rise on a big inhale, and I know I should go over there, but I'm mesmerized by every movement of her body.

Only when she drops her hands and turns back toward the back room do I make myself known.

"You're back," I say, projecting my voice so I can catch her attention over the bar noise. I know she hears me because her whole body freezes. When she turns back toward me, her smile is luminous.

"I thought you left," she says, a hint of that sadness still remaining. Almost like she's used to being forgotten.

"Just ran to the bathroom." I gesture over my shoulder. "Honestly, I was beginning to think *you* had snuck out the back."

The corner of her mouth lifts. "I had to help Sophia," she says by way of explanation.

"Of course," I reply as if I know who the hell Sophia is. "You guys are closing soon, right?"

She nods.

"Can I—I mean, would you like me to walk you home? Or… something." *Not creepy at all, Jules.*

Her face screws up again, the slope of her nose creating a crease that I'm dying to reach out and smooth. "I drove. It's fucking freezing in Boston."

"That it is…" I reply. "I could walk you to your car?" I'm trying not to sound as desperate as I feel.

Her eyes narrow. "Are you a serial killer?" she blurts. "I watch a lot of *Dateline*."

The laugh bursts out of me. "What? No! I don't even like to kill the bugs that find their way into my house. We can FaceTime my sister—she'll vouch for me."

That answer seems to satisfy her because she visibly relaxes and says, "I always wanted a sister."

I'm about to tell her she can have mine when she leans over the bar and props her head in her hands. Her full lips fall into a pout, and I have to tear my eyes away.

"Here's the deal, Jules. I like you—you're funny, hot as fuck, and tonight is my last night here. You can walk me to my car if you want, or…"

"Or…?" I ask.

"You said you were staying across the street?" I nod. "No wife or girlfriend?" She pauses. "Or boyfriend? I don't judge."

"No, ma'am," I reply with a barely concealed smirk.

She pushes off the bar. "Then let me finish shutting down while you decide where you want to walk me." Then she fucking winks.

Chapter Three
TOTALLY NORMAL ONE-NIGHT STAND
Thea

ONE NIGHT
Griff

This is probably a mistake.

Actually, it's definitely a mistake.

I've never been as forward with someone as I just was with Jules.

But I can't seem to make myself care.

I was surprisingly distraught when I thought Jules had left without saying goodbye. Luckily, it seems like he's not ready for our night to end, and neither am I. Dad has Chloe taken care of so it's not like I need to rush home anyway. And selfishly, I want to do something for myself. Something that feels good. Tomorrow I can go back to being responsible.

Tonight, I want to be reckless.

As I'm cleaning up behind the bar, I can feel Jules' eyes on me. I convince myself I can be casual. People have one-night stands all the time! No one I know personally, but surely it happens. And maybe it'll be nice to not get so attached, like I did before.

It'll definitely hurt less.

I walk over to Jules, and the unmistakable hunger in his eyes sends a shiver down my spine. "I'm going to grab my jacket, and I'll meet you by the door?"

He nods but doesn't say anything. He seems like the type that doesn't talk unless he has something really important to say, spending most of tonight observing the world around him. Observing *me*.

I get my coat and wave goodbye to Tim and Sophia, who are headed out the back door. Tim has been a good boss, but he's not a sentimental guy. He gave me a pat on the back when I turned in my two weeks notice, and that's about as much affection as I've ever seen him give anyone.

I, however, tend to be overly sentimental. I meet Jules at the front door, pausing to take the bar in one last time. It's not like I'm moving that far away, but this place has felt like a home away from home since I started—back when I had to leave the ballet company at sixteen-weeks pregnant because I was starting to show.

The neon beer signs, the hodgepodge of photos up on the walls, the worn-down dance floor where Chloe took some of her first steps—it all carries memories, both good and bad.

I feel Jules' hand slide across the small of my back, as if he senses I need some comfort in this moment. "You ready?" he whispers.

As ready as I'm going to be. "Lead the way, TBD."

He raises a single brow at me but doesn't ask any questions, so I don't give him any answers.

We walk out of the bar and cross the deserted cobblestone street. I'm usually exhausted by the end of a shift, but the thrill of what I can only describe as a crush—God, it's been so long since I had a crush—has me wide awake.

Jules' hand drops away from my back as he reaches out and opens the door to the small hotel lobby. It's plain but tidy. There's an older woman working the front desk—well, she's sleeping at the front desk. We stride right past her and go straight to the elevator.

I watch Jules slide his hands into his pockets, leaning against the wall as we wait. His forearms are on full display, corded and muscular. My eyes track up his arms to where his button-down shirt covers, and I give myself a moment to imagine what he looks like underneath. The elevator dings, my eyes popping up to his smug smirk. Oh, he knows exactly what he's doing to me.

Once we are inside, Jules pushes the button for the eighth floor and turns toward me. "We don't have to do anything you aren't comfortable with," he says. "I'm fine if you just want to talk or watch a movie. I—" He scrubs a hand across his trimmed beard. "I would never pressure you, Thea."

It's the way he says it that makes me decide to kiss him. So much conviction, like he actually means what he says. A trait I've found that's hard to come by in most men.

So, I step closer to him and angle my face until my lips are just a breath away. "I know," I breathe just before my lips meet his.

Now, it's been a while since I've kissed anyone that wasn't four years old with peanut butter and jelly smeared across her cheek, but holy shit is kissing always like this?

Jules' lips are soft, his stubble tickling my skin, creating the most delicious sensation. I'm enjoying it so much that it takes a few moments for it to dawn on me that he's not really moving. I pull away suddenly, my face on fire as I realize that maybe his way of getting out of doing anything physical tonight was telling me that we could just talk or—oh God, watch a movie.

I can't watch a movie with him now that I've made a complete ass of myself! I have to get off this elevator.

"I'm so sorry if that's not what you wanted." I panic-press the lobby button, which does absolutely nothing since we're already heading up. "I think I completely misinterpreted…" My sentence trails off when I look at Jules, and he's glowing in the elevator light, like some sort of sex god.

He prowls toward me until my back is pressed against the wall. The elevator dings, alerting our arrival to his floor, but Jules completely ignores it. Both of his hands come up to push my hair behind my ears before trailing to the back of my neck.

"I think you are," he whispers, tilting my head back. "Exactly what I want." His lips meet mine again, and I fucking *melt*.

Vaguely, I'm aware of the elevator doors beginning to close and Jules sticking his foot out to stop it. His hands slide down my back, over my ass, to my thighs, urging me to jump. I'm slightly taller than average but so is he, so my legs easily wrap around his waist.

I'm instantly aware of something else that feels larger than average as Jules starts walking us out of the elevator and down the hall, his lips staying connected to mine, further confirming his sex-god status.

We stop in front of a door about halfway down the hall. Keeping a solid hold on me with one hand, he reaches into his back pocket, pulls out the keycard, and kicks the door open.

"You. Are. Perfect," he whispers into my neck as we walk into his hotel room, each word punctuated with a nip to the delicate skin there.

I groan. "You aren't drunk, are you?" I don't know why I feel the need to double check everything with this man before letting him just have his way with me.

"The only thing I've had to drink was the beer that I sipped for nearly two hours while I worked up the courage to talk to you," he replies.

"Oh."

His dimples pop. "Yeah… 'Oh.'"

And then he lays me out on the bed, pulling back slightly to look at me.

I still have my puffer jacket on, but I didn't bother to zip it since we were only walking across the street. As I sit up, Jules falls back on his knees. I remove my jacket and then think, *Why the hell not?* and start to take my shirt off too.

"Wait," Jules says, stopping my hand.

"You really know how to kill a girl's confidence," I huff.

"Thea," he sighs, shaking his head. "I really want to do it myself." Another *Oh* moment. This is new and I'm glad it's only one night—I can't afford to get used to this.

He runs his hand under my top, slowly guiding it up over my shoulders, pulling it all the way off. I am suddenly very grateful for the Thea of yesterday who was too tired to do her laundry which forced the Thea of today to wear the slightly uncomfortable, but very hot, lacy bra that lives at the back of my underwear drawer.

I think Jules is also grateful, judging by the look he's giving me. He could get me pregnant off of that look alone.

And while that obviously won't happen tonight, I'm officially ready to start practicing. I get up on my knees to face him, feeling slightly lightheaded—probably a result of the pure lust pumping through my veins.

"Sit up against the headboard?" I ask.

He pulls me in for a searing kiss, thumbs grazing just below the wiring of my bra, but ultimately complies with my request. Once he's settled back against the pillows, I straddle him, seating myself on his lap, grinding down in an attempt to get a little bit of friction where I desperately need it.

In a flurry of movement, Jules rips his shirt off too, pressing our chests together. I get a brief look at the tattoos that continue across his chest and the single gold chain that hangs loosely around his neck.

Kissing along the top of my breast, he toys with the clasp behind my back. "May I?" he whispers before biting gently through the cup.

"Please." I bite my lip, a move Jules tracks, eyes hooded, before unhooking my bra and pulling the straps off my shoulders. His movements are quick and sure, telling me he's just as eager as I am.

As soon as it's been completely removed, he leans in and gets to work.

And, holy hell, does this man know how to work me. He nips and kisses and licks every inch of skin he can reach while simultaneously reaching down and undoing the button on my jeans. He toys with the waistband but leaves them on and continues tracing his fingers down to my fire-engine-red boots.

"And these fucking boots," he mutters. "I want these on my shoulders later." I moan and grind down onto his erection, the seam of my denim rubbing perfectly over my clit. There's something so erotic about the fact that we are dry humping, only naked from the waist up, my nipples rubbing against his chest in a way that shoots heat straight to my core.

I wish there was a better mirror in here because I bet we paint quite the picture.

Jules' tongue meets mine, all at once soft and coaxing, and then strong and demanding. I'm lost in him. So lost that I'm hardly aware that the lightheadedness hasn't gone away.

Then I think back to the last time I ate, which, I realize, was the granola bar I shoved into my mouth during my fifteen minute dinner break. Fuck.

"Fuck," I say, out loud this time before unceremoniously flopping off of Jules' lap and onto the pillow next to him, black spots swarming my vision.

Chapter Four
JUST MY LUCK
Jules

CLOSE TO YOU
Gracie Abrams

"Thea!"

At first I thought she was repositioning us, but now that I get a good look at her, she's pale and has a bead of sweat dripping down her temple. *Fuck.*

"Thea! Can you hear me?"

I think she's passed out, that thought hits me like a freight train, and now I'm freaking the fuck out. From my mandatory school trainings, I remember something about turning someone on their side if they are having a seizure. Is this even a seizure? I used to consider myself calm under pressure—put a beautiful, half-naked woman in front of me and that has apparently flown out the window.

Frantically, I start to roll Thea onto her side when she seems to come to. "Wha are youdoinn?" she mumbles.

"Oh my God, Thea. Are you awake? You are scaring the shit out of me." I lean my face down close to hers, and I can feel her breathing steadily which is a good sign.

"Wow, embarrassing," she says, making me laugh despite the bone crushing fear still coursing through my body. One wrong move and I might shatter right alongside her. "Crackers. Coat pocket," she continues, attempting to lift her hand and point in the general direction of her jacket on the floor.

Immediately I hop off the bed and find a package of peanut butter crackers in her coat pocket. I rip the bag open with my teeth—chuckling when I hear her mutter, "That was hot"—and hand her one, before grabbing one of the five-dollar hotel water bottles and twisting the cap. By the time I bring it to her, she's already munching on one of the crackers, and the color looks like it's coming back to her face.

I wait as she eats a few more crackers and takes a sip of water before I ask, "Thea... what just happened? Are you diabetic?"

She shakes her head, groaning as she pushes herself back into a seated position. She's still topless, which I am trying—and failing—not to let distract me.

"No, I'm not diabetic," she says and then pulls her knees up to her chest, dropping her head down on top of them. She looks so young in this moment which makes me realize I have no idea how old she is. At least old enough to bartend, but that's not very comforting. "I have low blood sugar and a bad habit of forgetting to eat," Thea confides.

"I thought you were joking about that earlier."

She stays silent so I scoot closer to her on the bed, running my hand through her silky waves. Selfishly, I kind of like that I'm getting to see another side of her. I have the overwhelming urge to get to know every part she'll let me see. "Hey," I whisper. "What kind of pizza do you like?"

She finally looks up at me, her brow furrowed and green eyes coated with unfallen tears. "Meat lover's. Why?"

"There's a bodega on the corner. I'm going to run down and grab some pizza. Stay here, okay? There's an extra T-shirt and boxers in my backpack over there, if you want to change."

She turns her face away from me, but I can feel when her

shoulders slightly shake. "Do you need me to stay?" I whisper, hand running soothingly up and down her back. "Are you okay on your own for a minute?"

"You're being too nice to me." She sniffs and my heart nearly breaks in two. *This* is too nice? Getting her a slice of pizza when she's just passed out from hunger?

"Thea, honey, this is the bare minimum. You obviously need something, so of course I'm going to get it for you. I don't know what kind of assholes you normally surround yourself with, but I am definitely not being too nice." I reach around and tip her chin toward me. "Got it?"

She sniffles again and gives me a forced smile. "Got it."

I'm halfway out of the door when I hear, "Thank you, Jules."

I haul ass down to the corner store, worried about leaving Thea alone for too long. I know next to nothing about this woman, but I grab a slice of meat lover's pizza, some Oreos, and a bottle of apple juice. At the register, I also impulsively buy two scratch-off lottery tickets hoping they'll lift her spirits a bit.

When I walk back into the hotel room, I feel a huge weight lifted off of my shoulders at the sight of Thea cuddled up in my Bardot Brothers Coffee T-shirt—one of the test shirts Gabe had printed—watching a sitcom rerun on TV. She's surrounded herself by fluffy hotel pillows, and the blankets are tucked up around her waist.

She looks like an angel, floating on a cloud of bedding. The sight makes me want to do some very *un*angelic things.

My chest tightens as it hits me just how fucked I already am.

"Hi," she mouths, a small smile tickling her lips.

"Hi," I reply. "I brought sustenance." I grab a towel from the bathroom and lay it out over Thea's lap and then take out her pizza, cookies, and juice.

"Jules, this is too much!" She looks at me like I just laid

diamonds in front of her, which makes my chest tighten with irrational anger.

"Say 'thank you' again, Thea, and see what happens," I warn.

"Like I said, this is bare minimum."

I pull the scratch-offs out of my back pocket, trying to lighten the mood. "I will let you thank me though, if you win big on one of these scratch-offs."

Her face lights up. "Oh my God, I love those things! Do you have a coin?"

Stuffing my hand in my pocket, I produce the penny I found outside of the venue earlier tonight and hand it to her. She carefully considers both of the tickets before handing one to me. "You'll thank me if you win big, right?" she jokes.

"I think I already won big tonight," I reply.

Thea takes me by surprise when she starts poking at my face. Her elegant finger stopping once on my forehead, once on my cheek, then down to my lips.

I quirk my eyebrow. "Care to explain what you're doing?"

"Just making sure you're real…" She bites back a smile and begins scratching.

Thea stuffs an Oreo in her mouth and after a moment of concentration, exclaims, "I won five bucks!"

"Nice!" I hold my hand up and she gives me a high-five.

She hands me the penny. "Your turn."

I scratch, and sure enough, I also win five dollars. "Feels like a sign that we both won the same amount." I pull her hand back toward me, pressing the penny into it, taking the time to fold each finger in until the coin disappears from view. "We'll have to go get coffee together with our winnings."

She scrunches her eyebrows in just slightly, eyes focused on where our hands connect, before shaking off the furrow and replying, "Yeah… maybe we can go to this shop." She points down at my shirt that she's wearing. "Is it in Boston?"

Huffing a laugh, I reply, "No, it's not."

I want to tell her about Sassafras.

I want to ask her for her number.

I want to find a way to make tonight last forever.

But, she looks exhausted, and it's almost four in the morning by this point. All of that can wait until morning.

"Somewhere else, then," she muses.

We spend the next twenty minutes snacking and talking, sharing small touches that send sparks flying all over my skin, and eventually Thea passes out curled up against my side. It's some of the best sleep I've ever gotten.

I wake up extremely disoriented with no idea what time it is or where I am. Fighting the all consuming grogginess, I stretch across the bed—and then freeze.

Because now I remember where I am and who should be in the bed next to me.

But Thea is gone.

Chapter Five
WELCOME TO SASSYASS!
Thea

SIGNS
Ethan Dufault

One week later

Moving with a four-year-old is its own special kind of hell. One that exists deep in the fiery pits, ruled by an inconsolable toddler who makes you walk around barefoot on a floor lined with legos.

Dramatic? Maybe.

True? Definitely.

We've been in the same apartment since before Chloe was born, and after this whole experience, we aren't leaving this new apartment any time soon.

Preferably never. Bury me here.

Over the last week, my dad, Hank, and I packed up our place in Boston, often repacking Chloe's coloring books and stuffed animals after she decided she *had* to have something and then promptly forgot about it.

It's been absolute chaos, and I'm sure it'll be weeks until I can shake the *Shit, I've forgotten something!* feeling.

Our rented U-Haul is loaded down with the few pieces of furniture we own, and I have sweat dripping down my back even though it's early February in Massachusetts. Lovely.

I am thankful that my dad is here to help, though. Hank Rose is a mountain of a man with a graying handlebar mustache and much more of a Texas twang than I have. His full name is Henry Redford Rose, Redford after Robert Redford, but he gets real pissed if anyone calls him anything other than Hank or Pop. He grew up in West Texas, like the many generations before him, and only moved up here with me when I joined the ballet.

It was time, he'd told me. My mom and his mom were gone by that point, and I think we both wanted to get away from all of the memories Texas held, both good and bad.

However, that did not stop him from flying down to Texas when he found out I was pregnant with Chloe so he could bring back some Texas dirt to put under my hospital bed. "No grandchild of mine will be born over anything other than Texas soil," he said. Soil sounding more like *sole*.

I had felt so ashamed that I was pregnant at nineteen with a devil of a man as the father that I didn't argue with Dad's crazy superstitions. Dad has never made me feel anything other than loved, so I let him get away with being a little kooky.

Chloe cannot stop talking about moving to a smaller town because it means we can afford a—very small—three bedroom apartment. She has decided the theme of her new room is going to be unicorns and rainbows, painted onto the wall by me, myself, and I, of course.

I am also thrilled to not be sharing a room with a snoring four-year-old anymore. Maybe I'll actually get some sleep for the first time in almost five years.

You slept pretty well with Jules the other night, my brain reminds me.

Stupid brain.

The truth is, I woke up freaking out that this man I had known less than twelve hours had already wormed his way into my very being. Quite literally, I was a snowglobe that hadn't been touched in ages until he shook me so hard, the little fake snow pieces would never quite return to their original places.

So I left. Before he could leave me.

I'll examine that later.

I pull the truck up to the parking spot in front of our new building, with Dad pulling the U-Haul in next to me. Hopping out of the car, I unbuckle Chloe from her carseat and throw her on my hip. She's getting so big, I know there will be a day I can't hold her like this anymore.

"What do you think, Chlo? Pretty cute little town, right?" I ask, squeezing her a bit closer.

"I like it, Mama," she replies, looking around as her ponytail whips me in the face. "But where are all the people?"

We've never taken Chloe down to my hometown in Texas, and now I'm realizing she's never really been out of Boston, a city always bustling with people.

"Well, baby, this is a smaller town so there aren't as many people as there are in Boston. I bet if we head over to the college campus there are more people wandering around."

Her little brow furrows as she looks around. "But who will be my friend in Sassyass?" she wails. Chloe is forever befriending literally anyone she meets, so I don't think that will be an issue here.

"Who is being a sassy ass?" Dad asks, getting out of the van.

"Language, Dad!"

He looks at me and then points to Chloe. "She said it first."

"I think she was trying to say 'Sassafras,' but it didn't come out quite right," I chide.

Dad takes a second to look down the main street too, heaving a big sigh. "It's not the south but it already feels more like home than Boston ever did."

"You and I both know we don't want to go back to the south

anytime soon," I remind him. "It's a little too... *Handmaid's Tale* down there."

We both shudder and then laugh at how similar we can be. He swings his arm around me, guiding me toward the nondescript door that supposedly leads up to our new place.

I open the door to reveal a set of stairs that leads up to the second floor. The building is only three stories with a cute little bar and some shops on the first floor that span about a block. The second and third floor are made up of four units each. I'm assuming most of the tenants are students at the nearby university which is walking distance from where we are.

The best part? The studio space is down the block, and when we drove by it looked like an adorable coffee shop is going in next door. I didn't get a good look, but I'm planning on walking the block after we get unloaded.

"Kathy said the apartment key would be under the mat, which doesn't seem super secure, but I guess that's small-town life for you." Sure enough, there's a welcome mat in front of apartment number 2B with a single silver key under the top right corner.

Chloe tries three times to unlock the door before Dad finally loses his patience and holds his hand out. She drops the key into it and says, "It's a little tough, Pop," making us both smile.

Dad pushes the door open and declares, "Home sweet home!"

Damn, I'm ready for a fresh start.

———

It takes less than five minutes for me to realize that there's only two bedrooms in this unit.

"Hold your horses," Dad warns. "This must be the wrong unit. Let me call Kathy."

"Do you see any other 2B's Dad?" I seethe. "I think this is the right apartment, but the listing is obviously wrong." I rub my temples, my hope of a good night's sleep becoming a fleeting dream.

"It's okay, Mama," Chloe says, tugging my arm down. "I like sharing a room with you."

And now I officially feel like shit.

I crouch down until I'm on her level, tucking the hair that's fallen out of her ponytail behind her ear. "I like sharing a room with you too, baby," I lie. "Mama was just looking forward to decorating your room with all of the rainbow, unicorn, sparkle magic I could find."

Now she tucks my hair behind my ears. "We can still decorate our room like that!" She smiles at me, a mouth full of crooked baby teeth, and I suddenly have a vision of her moving out on her own one day. It crashes into me so hard, I hear myself saying, "Of course we can, Chloe girl."

Dad walks back to us, his phone still in his hand.

"Kathy says many tenants use the living room as a third bedroom which is why they have that listed on the site. She was very adamant that a full bed fits quite nicely." He gives the room a wary onceover.

Groaning, I go ahead and fall back onto the floor, starfish style. "It probably did say that, but I signed this lease and the studio lease in the same afternoon, and I was running late to work so I didn't look as close as I probably should have."

My phone buzzes, and I look to see a text from Magnolia, my closest cousin and best friend.

MAGS

How's the new place?

There's only two bedrooms...

MAGS

What?! I thought you said there were three!!

Uncle Hank needs to find his own place

> You know how much I rely on him to watch Chloe

>> Move up here please??

> MAGS
> Hell no, it's too fucking cold

I stick my tongue out at my phone before closing it and rolling myself off the floor. Hyping myself up, I shake all of these negative thoughts off, knowing they won't get me anywhere. "Fine, we can do two bedrooms! No big deal, I'm totally fine with that. C'mon, let's start bringing stuff up."

I swing the front door open and stop dead because the man walking out of unit 2A looks a whole lot like…

"Jules?"

Chapter Six
OVERLY MASCULINE DICKHEADS
Thea

KEEP IT UP
Good Neighbors

The man, who I'm now realizing is definitely *not* Jules, raises his eyebrow and points to himself.

"I'm Ben," he says, slowly giving me a once over. But when he smiles, his dimples pop the exact same way Jules' did. "And you are...?"

I stare at him, dumbstruck, long enough that Dad comes around me, shoots a weird look my way, and puts his hand out to Ben. "Hank Rose," he says. "This is Thea." He points his thumb toward me. "And that's—"

"I'm Chloe!" my four-year-old shouts, cutting Dad off.

Ben holds his hand up for a high-five, and I realize his arms are empty of the tattoos that mesmerized me a week ago. Chloe jumps up and hits Ben's much larger hand right in the center.

"Nice to meet you guys," Ben says. "I just moved in across the hall with my brother, Gabe. We'll have to have you over sometime."

"Can we be best friends?" Chloe asks. "Mom says I'll be able to make lots of friends in Sassyass."

Ben chokes on his spit at that. "Damn, why have I never thought of calling it that?"

"Language," Chloe says—her stern voice makes me wonder if that's how I sound when I get mad at Dad for his language.

Ben surprises me by taking a deep bow. "My apologies, milady. Here's a penny for repentance." He holds his hand out with an invisible coin clutched between his fingers.

All three of us stare at him until Chloe bursts out laughing. "You're funny! You can call me Princess Chloe, and I really prefer real bills for pettance, whatever that is."

"Chloe!" I chide, finally getting my voice back.

But Ben just laughs and says, "Sure thing, Princess Chloe. Listen, my mom would probably kill me for not giving you all a proper Sassafras welcome, but I'm already late for a meeting. I'll stop by and check in later tonight, okay? It was nice to meet you, Princess Chloe, Hank—" He pauses giving me one more assessing look. "Thea."

And then he's off.

As soon as Ben is down the stairs and out of sight, Dad asks, "Who is Jules?"

"No one," I rush out. "I met him on my last night at The Dusty Barrel. Ben looks a lot like him. Just caught me off guard, that's all."

"Whatever you say," Dad replies. "C'mon, you," he directs at Chloe, and off they go to start unloading our things.

There's something about Ben that is so familiar, it's going to drive me nuts. I take one last look at the closed door to apartment 2A, kicking myself again for not leaving my number when I left that hotel room.

Too late now.

Several hours later, almost all of our things have been moved into our new space. Chloe quickly got bored with carrying small items from the car to the apartment and eventually found the box with her Barbie's. I set our old family iPad up on the floor of the living room and started streaming Bluey to help keep her occupied.

Even though I'm exhausted, I start to make a grocery list but quickly determine that will have to be a tomorrow activity. "Dad, you okay if I go down to the bar and see what food options they have? I also want to go peek in the studio really fast."

He's propped up in his old La-Z-Boy, with his "eyes closed" which is Hank speak for taking a quick nap even though he'll insist he wasn't asleep. He startles when I knock the back of his chair, quickly sitting up with an "I'm awake!"

"Great!" I reply, pretending like I'm not the reason for the end of his nap. "I'll be right back. Keep an eye on Chlo?"

He huffs in agreement as I ruffle Chloe's hair and tell her to stay with Pop until I get back.

Downstairs I pull the door open to Louie's—a local bar that looks adorably quaint.

There's an older man at the opposite end wiping down the bar top and a few students tucked into different tables. It's only five o'clock so it's still pretty early for the bar scene, but I know everyone is hungry after our long day.

I grab a seat at the bar and look around for a menu. All I see are sticky countertops, mismatched coasters, and a rogue ketchup packet.

"New in town?" the man behind the bar asks.

"Yes, sir," I respond. You can take the girl out of the south but you can't take the south out of the girl. Or so I'm told.

The man raises his brows at me. "That's very polite, young lady. How can I help you?"

"I'd love to order some food to-go if that's an option."

"Of course it is. Let me grab a menu real quick." He shuffles down to the other side of the bar right as the door blows open behind me.

"Louie!" someone yells. "Can you make Benoit here something fancy to drink?"

"Something fancy?" The older man who I now realize must own the place, calls back down the bar. "Ben, you were in Boston too long if you're requiring something fancy just to get drunk."

That catches my attention both because of the name and the fact that he apparently lived in Boston. I turn around in my chair and come face-to-face with my new neighbor and another man that looks around the same age but has slightly lighter hair.

"You're from Boston?" I ask by way of greeting.

"Hey, Thea," Ben replies. "No, just lived there for the last few years. Moved back a week or so ago. This is my brother, Gabe, that I was telling you about."

I lift my hand to wave at Gabe, but I'm still stuck on Ben being in Boston and looking so much like Jules. "We just moved from Boston."

"No shit!" Ben says. "What brought you to Sassyass—I love that by the way!"

By this point, Louie has rejoined us, and I suddenly feel like I have an audience. "I, uh… I'm opening up a dance studio. Down the street actually." I point toward the direction of the studio even though we can't actually see it from inside the building.

"That's great," Louie says. "We've needed someone to fill that space ever since Ms. Matilda retired a few years back."

"That woman was scary," Gabe adds, shuddering.

I picture Gabe in a dance class and smile. "Did she teach you?" I ask.

"Yeah," he replies. "Our mom made us all take classes when we were younger. She has always been very adamant that we not become 'overly masculine dickheads' I think are her exact words."

"She sounds like someone I'd like," I reply, a grin creeping up. I think I'm going to like having Ben and Gabe as neighbors. Hopefully I'll get a chance to meet their mom, too.

"Everyone likes Elaine," Louie chimes in. "She's a professor over at Hawthorne. Her 'Psychology of Sex' class is a big hit."

"Ew," Gabe and Ben say at the same time.

Everyone continues to chat while I take a look at the menu, smiling at the familiarity of the men around me. After placing a to-go order, I ask Louie if he minds if I swing back by to pick it up after I check on the studio.

Meandering down the block, I realize it's actually perfect to have the bar right below us. If we need some extra cash, I bet I can talk Louie into hiring me as a bartender.

There's an added skip in my step when I get up to the windows of the studio. I curve my hands around my eyes and take a look inside. You can tell it has been sitting unused for a while, but it's still perfect. I'm itching to paint the walls, scrub the dust off the floors, and re-hang the tilted barre. I'm physically bouncing on the tip of my toes, excitement pulsing through me—I can't wait to get the keys tomorrow.

I take out my phone, snapping a blurry picture through the window to send to Magnolia.

> Look!!!

MAGS
> Wow, what a shit hole

> Yeah, but it's my shit hole :)

MAGS
> All jokes aside, I'm really proud of you! I know you've worked your ass off for this.

I smile at my phone before pocketing it. After having Chloe, I thought I'd never dance again. But one of my former company instructors also worked at a local ballet studio and eventually hired me as a part-time teacher. I was so fucking lost back then.

Postpartum is a bitch, and I had no idea what was next for me, my plans completely up in the air. Finding joy in teaching dance classes saved me. It redeemed this thing that I thought was ruined forever.

I lay my head against the window and breathe. "I did it, Mom," I whisper.

Suddenly, the door to the shop next door swings open and an older woman walks out. I walk over to get a closer look at my new business neighbor. "Hi, I'm Thea!" I say as I approach. "I'm taking over the studio. Is this your coffee shop?"

"Just sold it, actually." The older woman beams up at me. "But don't worry, honey. Those Bardot brothers will take good care of it."

She closes the coffee shop door, locking it before heading on her way. There's a piece of paper taped in the window that says "Bardot Brothers Coffee Co. Coming Soon!" with a logo that looks almost identical to the T-shirt I stole from Jules.

My heart takes over and my feet are moving before I realize what's happening. I'm back at Louie's in a flash, throwing the door open until it crashes against the wall, scaring everyone in the bar.

Ben jumps up, looking concerned. "Thea, are you okay?" he asks.

"Do you know someone named Jules?" I rush out.

Gabe spits out his drink, and Ben just chuckles, looking slightly relieved.

"You could say that we know each other pretty well, actually."

Chapter Seven
SLOW DOWN, ROMEO
Jules

I FALL HARD
The Strike

"Oh, I love having all of my cabbages home!" Mom exclaims as Ben and Gabe walk in for Sunday night family dinner.

"Bex and Anders aren't here, Mom," I remind her.

She waves me off. "Bex said she would FaceTime us later so it's pretty much like she's here!"

I roll my eyes at that justification but continue seasoning the garlic bread that's about ready to go into the oven.

I am glad my twin, Ben, moved back home to Sassafras. It's been a while since so many of us lived here. I offered for him to move into my house, but when you have been essentially attached to someone since the womb, it's nice to have a little space from them. I was secretly relieved he decided to move into Gabe's place instead. Those two are more similar than Ben and I are—both kind of remind me of untrained puppies.

"Hi, JuJu!" Ben says, coming up behind me to squeeze my shoulders.

"Benoit," I reply. "How are you settling in?"

"Great! And Gabe and I signed the lease so you just need to run by Ethel's to add your signature."

My brothers and I are taking over the town's coffee shop, something that has been a dream of mine for longer than I'm willing to admit. Gabe is really just involved because he doesn't want to be left out, but Ben quit his corporate job in finance to come back here and make my dream a reality. It's all moved very fast—once Ben sets his mind on something, he's like a racehorse with blinders on.

"I'll run by tomorrow after school," I reply. I'm a music teacher at Sassafras High School, and I didn't feel right about leaving my students midyear. I'll finish out the semester and then start full time at the new Bardot Brothers Coffee Co. this summer.

Ben pats me on the shoulder once more before finding his way to the fridge for a drink. With his head blocked by the door he says, "Totally forgot—we have new neighbors."

Dad is the unofficial welcoming committee to new residents of Sassafras so he perks up at that. "Students?"

"Nope, a family. Looks like a grandad, his daughter, and granddaughter. The daughter is a real bombshell, probably early 20s. Right, Gabe?"

"Yeah, said her name was Thea. Know anyone named Thea, Jules?" Gabe asks at the exact same moment I open the oven to put the garlic bread in.

Instead, I momentarily lose consciousness apparently because the next thing I know the pan is clattering to the floor and slices of garlic bread are fanned out around me.

"I'm going to take that as a yes," Mom says, a knowing glint in her eye.

"You know her?" Dad asks.

"I—no. I mean, I know *a* Thea. Could be a different one. Pretty common name," I reply, even though I know on some cosmic level that this has to be *my* Thea. I've been googling random combinations of "Thea" and "Boston" for the last week like a fucking creep and haven't found anything.

"Does the Thea you know have long blonde hair, killer legs, and a cute-as-fuck kid?" Ben asks.

"Kid? I..." I think I'm about to pass out.

Ben's eyes go wide. "Fuck, you didn't know about the kid. Is it yours?!"

"For fuck's sake, Benoit—no it's not mine. If this is the same Thea, I just met her last week when I was in Boston." I sit down at the dining table, and Gabe brings me a glass of ice water.

"You just met her a week ago? And this is your reaction?" he asks, setting down the glass.

"Oh my god!" Bex chimes in—I hadn't even realized she had called. "This is the girl you were messaging about the other night!"

Mom sets her phone on the table, and Bex's face looks up at me, her daughter Elodie bouncing on her lap.

I rub my forehead, unable to truly comprehend that Thea—my Thea—might have just moved in across the hall from my brothers. With her dad. And her daughter.

Suddenly, I stand up, overwhelmed with a deep need to see her. See if everything I felt after one night together is real or if I've been blowing things out of proportion in my head.

"I have to go see her," I declare.

"Slow down, Romeo. Take a beat and decide what you want to say to her," Gabe suggests.

I sit back down. "You're right. I should wait."

"Why? Go get her!" Bex exclaims through the phone.

Elodie echoes, "Get her!"

"You"—I point at the phone—"have no room to talk." I rub my sweaty palms up and down my jeans. Bex and Anders took years to admit their feelings to each other. Though they're happy now, I agree with Gabe. I need to take a breath and figure out what I'm going to say to her. Thea acted like she never wanted to see me again, leaving without giving me any way to find her.

"What if she doesn't want to see me?" I ask out loud.

"That's not the impression I got," Ben replies.

That catches my attention. "Did she say something about me?" Desperation laces my words, and I don't even try to hide it.

"Damn, how are you already down bad?" Gabe asks, shit-eating grin plastered on his face. "She looked like she'd seen a ghost when she came bursting into Louie's the other night asking if we knew you."

"She called me Jules when we first met—that hasn't happened to me since before you got all those tattoos and grew your hair out," Ben adds.

"Why didn't you call me when this happened?" I ask, starting to get annoyed.

"The assholes wanted to see your reaction in person, I'm sure," Bex says.

"I had no idea it'd be this good, though." Gabe smirks. "Can we come with you when you see her again?"

"Fuck no," I reply, my tone stern. "Don't talk to her again until I can apologize for whatever you've already said to her."

"Chloe invited me over for a tea party, though!" Ben looks genuinely sad that I would prevent him from having tea with a child.

"Chloe is her daughter?" I ask.

Ben nods. "She's really fucking cute. She makes me call her Princess Chloe, and she can't get Sassafras right so she keeps calling it 'Sassyass.'"

Jealousy consumes me. I want to know every part of Thea's world, and I'm frustrated that Ben now knows more than I do. He can sense it too because he puts his hands up in surrender.

"I'll postpone tea," he concedes.

"Thank you. I think… maybe I'll go to Harriet's and pick up some flowers after I sign the lease documents tomorrow."

I take a deep breath, willing my body to calm down. It doesn't work, and I know the next eighteen hours will be torture until I can lay eyes on Thea myself.

I once told Bex that I'd never been in love, and that's still true. But after one fucking night with Thea, I'm starting to get all the hype.

Chapter Eight
FICKLE THINGS
Jules

ROSES
Matthew Parker

I might vibrate right out of my skin. That's what this feels like.

I've signed the lease with Ethel, picked up some white roses from Harriet—Thea seemed to like my rose tattoo—and now I'm headed to her apartment.

I almost turn around and leave three times before I convince myself to knock. Fear that seeing me might freak her out influences my actions, but the desire to make sure she's real wins out.

I knock on the door across from Gabe and Ben's before taking a step back. I have no idea if my brothers are home, and to be honest, I don't care.

The door swings open, and Thea looks oddly like a man in his late forties or early fifties. "Who the hell are you?" the man huffs.

Clearing my throat, I answer, "Jules, sir. Julien. Bardot."

He raises an eyebrow at me and his handlebar mustache

twitches, but he doesn't verbally reply so I continue talking. I would admire said mustache if I wasn't so nervous right now.

"I'm—is there someone named Thea here?" I ask.

Just then another voice chimes in. "Is it Ben for our tea party, Pop?" A little blonde head pokes out from behind the man's leg. "Woah," she says when she sees me.

I raise my hand in a wave and then remember I'm holding a dozen roses. The girl moves from behind her grandfather and takes the bouquet out of my hand. "Thank you, almost-Ben," she says.

"I think those were for your mama, darlin'," the man tells her.

"She won't mind sharing." And then she prances off back into the apartment with the roses I brought.

It all happens so fast, I haven't even had time to reply when the man says, "Well, thanks for stopping by." Clearly I've been dismissed.

He starts to close the door before I stick my hand out to stop it. "Wait! Is she here?"

Obviously, I look distraught because the man takes pity on me and shakes his head. "Nah, son, she's down at the studio." As if I know what that means.

"Right…" I take a step back. "Thank you."

He looks like the kind of man who would tell me I'm dumber than a sack of potatoes or some other old western saying. "The dance studio. Down the street." He makes a vague gesture and then slams the door shut.

The door opens behind me and Tweedledee and Tweedledum stick their heads out. "He's scary, right?" Ben says, rather unhelpfully.

"Are you going to go find her?" Gabe asks.

My only reply is a grunt in their general direction before I head down the stairs toward the abandoned dance studio right next door to the soon-to-be Bardot Brothers Coffee Co.

I try not to think about how awkward this will make things if she rejects me.

ENTIRELY YOURS

When I walk up to the studio window, there's one lamp turned on in the back corner.

And she's there.

And she's real.

I watch, mesmerized as Thea moves across the floor. Her motions so fluid, I can tell she was born to do this. Her long leg comes up in some sort of kick turn thing, and that's when she sees me. She freezes, her tentative stare taking me in.

The world stops spinning as we stare at each other. I smile and raise my hand to the window. For a moment she looks back and forth between my face and my hand pressed up against the glass. Finally, she takes a few steps forward and puts her hand up to meet mine.

"You found me," she says, her voice muffled by the window pane between us.

I'll always find you, I think.

"Can I come in?" I ask instead.

In answer, Thea removes her hand and my heart drops…until I realize she's unlocking the studio door to let me in.

"How did you know where I was?" she asks, slightly out of breath from dancing. Or maybe for the same reason I'm having trouble breathing.

I run my hands through my hair until they are resting on the back of my neck, noticing how Thea gives me an approving once over. Which may or may not make me flex just a little before I answer.

"I heard you met my brothers," I reply.

Her arms cross over her chest—her tights and leotard leaving very little to my imagination—and she sticks her hip out in defiance. "You didn't tell me you have a *twin* brother."

"You didn't tell me you have a daughter," I counter, dropping my hands.

She immediately deflates as if someone has told her that

having Chloe is a fatal flaw, some blemish on her reputation making her undateable, which makes *me* want to throttle whoever made her feel that way.

"She stole the roses I bought for you," I continue.

"Fickle things," she mutters, echoing the words she said that first night we met. "Look, if you came here to give me the whole speech about how we can put our night together in the past and move forward as neighborly citizens, I don't need to hear it. I know it was only supposed to be a one night thing and it's... inconvenient that I just happened to move here the very next week, but that doesn't have to mean anything—"

Interrupting her little rant I tell her, "I think it means everything."

"You—what?" This is obviously not the direction she thought I was going to take. "I assumed since I hadn't heard from you..."

Now it's my turn to be confused. "I got here as fast as I could. I would have come before school this morning—actually I would have come by last night but everyone told me to calm down."

"I put two and two together on Friday night when I came by the studio and saw the coffee shop logo. It looked suspiciously like the T-shirt you let me borrow—"

"The T-shirt you stole." I smirk.

"—I asked Ben if he knew you, and I figured he'd call you right after that to tell you I was in town. When I didn't hear from you Saturday or yesterday, I assumed that meant you didn't want to see me. Some people have been like that when they find out about Chloe..." She trails off.

"Chloe is fucking adorable, and anyone who thinks otherwise is an asshole."

I get a real grin at that. "She is adorable. Feisty, too."

"Reminds me of someone else I know." I eye her, knowingly, and then take a careful step toward her, dying to be as close to her as I can be.

She takes a step back, but the teasing glint in her eye tells me that I can keep going. I prowl toward her until her back hits the wall, the broken ballet barre tilting precariously behind her. Leaning in, I allow myself to get as close as I can without actually touching her.

"I didn't get to say goodbye," I whisper, barely brushing her lips. "You were gone when I woke up."

My hand comes up to her hip—because I can't fucking help myself—tracing the path where her jeans sat a week ago.

"I tend to get a little skittish," she breathes.

I take a sudden step back, immediately missing her warmth. "I can go slow."

My movement sends her off balance, and her hand shoots out to steady herself on the barre behind her. Instead of helping, however, the barre comes entirely off the wall, a rusted nail catching Thea in the palm of her hand. "Ow, fuck!" she wails.

And that's when I see the blood.

Chapter Nine
THE PITS OF HELL
Thea

FIRST NIGHT
elijah woods, JESSIA

Son of a bitch, that hurt.

I was planning to start fixing up the studio tonight—cleaning it at the very least—but I hadn't gotten around to it yet, and now Jules has derailed my whole night. He's thrown me literally and figuratively off kilter.

I had convinced myself that Ben told Jules about Chloe and he was immediately repulsed by my very being. That's how it usually goes. The really fun narrative running through my head was that Jules was planning to avoid me until one of us was forced to move to a new city. Obviously me—last in, first out and all that.

Chloe's dad didn't want me, or her for that matter, and the few guys I've tried to date find out about my spunky four-year-old and suddenly there's some excuse for ending things, the "it's not you, it's me" bullshit.

Men are trash. Some days I really wish I was a lesbian. Or at least bisexual. I'm living proof that sexuality is not a choice.

Unsurprisingly, I have taken great lengths to avoid men entirely until a week ago.

Also unsurprisingly, I don't do well with blood. And the blood leaking down my palm right now is going to make me pass out for the second fucking time in front of this man. I don't like blood and I don't like being vulnerable. The first is unavoidable at this precise moment.

Luckily, Jules seems to be more of a grown-ass adult than I am because he cradles my palm and guides me toward the door. "We can clean this up next door. Are you good to walk?"

"Uh huh," I say, unsure if that's true but unwilling to admit it's not. "I'm going to have to get another tetanus shot," I mumble before everything goes black.

———

My new pillow smells really good. It's slightly firmer than I'm used to but damn. I hope this isn't like new car smell where it eventually goes away.

I bury my nose into the pillow and take a deep inhale, trying to identify what exactly is so good about it. The answer is tickling my brain when all of a sudden, my new pillow moves.

And it's not a pillow at all.

It's a man.

With a very manly smelling chest.

And strong muscles that are carrying me bridal style.

I'm aware enough to realize that I shouldn't like this but not enough to actually do anything about it. I groan as the manly-chest-arm guy lays me down on a nearby couch. When I move to push myself up, pain shoots through my hand.

"Fuck!" I whine.

An authoritative voice filters from somewhere out of my line of sight. "Don't move, Thea."

I freeze, slightly concerned at how my body just reacted to Jules' command. Closing my eyes, I try to take inventory of what's going on, while also taking deep breaths in and out. I can feel him come to my side, even though I've decided to keep my eyelids firmly shut.

"May I?" he asks, lightly touching my hand to get a closer look. I nod in reply and he inspects my wound.

"Do we have to amputate?" I ask, trying to add some levity to the situation.

"Amputation isn't something to joke about," he replies firmly.

"Oh—Of... of course, I wouldn't—"

"I'm messing with you, Thea," he interrupts.

I'm messing with you.

My mind takes that phrase and runs with it.

I huff a laugh. "Obvious—OUCH! Ow, ow, ow!"

"Almost done," Jules soothes. "You're doing great. It's just a little water."

"From the pits of hell?" I whine.

I open my eyes and catch him smiling down at my hand, a wet rag dripping over the wound. "You're a fiery one." He chuckles. "You'll yell at me for cleaning up your mess but can't even keep your own head up right now. You don't like receiving help, do you?"

My head flops down. "No, I don't."

"Let me take care of you, Thea," he murmurs, and now I'm really unsure if he's talking about my hand or taking care of... other things.

Only the sound of our breathing fills the next few moments. I break the silence with, "I'm sorry I left the other morning."

He doesn't respond but I can sense him nodding.

"We could..." I clear my throat. "We could try again?"

Silence still. And I refuse to look at him and see pity, so I squeeze my eyes shut and continue. "Just one night, obviously. I'm not looking for anything serious."

This time I get a hum in response.

"I'm not really a one night kind of guy," he finally responds.

"You seemed fine with it the other night," I shoot back, admittedly feeling slightly defensive.

I'm still not looking at him, but I can hear the confusion in his voice. "We never said anything about it only being one night."

That catches my attention. I whip my head around to look him in the eyes. "What? Of course we did. I told you I was moving... I'm sure I said just one night."

"We were interrupted by several different things that night." He shakes his head and stands. "I never intended for it to only be one night."

I watch him walk away, stunned. He rustles around in a few cabinets before coming back over with a pack of gauze and some paper towels. Silently, he wipes up the mix of blood and water that fell to the floor and then takes a clean paper towel and pats my hand dry before wrapping it lightly in gauze.

"How are you feeling?" he asks, helping me to a seated position.

"Confused."

Jules smirks at that and helps me stand up. "Let's lock up and then I'll walk you home."

"I don't need to be walked home."

He lifts an eyebrow. "Well, then I'll walk a creepy ten feet behind you the entire way. Won't be weird at all."

Out of stubbornness, I lock up the studio and then let him walk behind me for about thirty seconds before I stop and turn around. "Fine, you can walk with me."

He digs his hands into his pockets, a smug smile on his lips. We walk the block, quietly taking in our surroundings. I try really hard not to break the silence, because it's not necessarily uncomfortable, just... confusing still.

When we are standing in front of my apartment door, Jules finally speaks. "You still owe me a coffee with your scratch-off winnings."

I don't think I could bring myself to trade in the scratch off for my five dollars. "I think actually, you owe me a coffee," I reply.

"Great. It's a date." He winks before turning and walking into his brothers' apartment, leaving me dazed in the hallway.

Chapter Ten
HEALTH CODE VIOLATIONS
Thea

BACK IN MY ARMS
Carlie Hanson

Twenty-four hours.

It takes twenty-four hours before I break down and knock on the door across the hall. Dad took Chloe to a children's program at the local library today, so when I picked them up, I got her a snack and then marched across the hall before I lost my nerve.

Ben opens the door. "Hey, Thea," he answers. "What's up?"

"Is your… is your brother here?" I ask.

He smirks. "Which one?"

I roll my eyes so hard I think I might have a migraine later. "Jules."

"Ah, but I'm the better looking one," he tsks.

"You are quite literally identical."

His phone dings and he pulls it out of his pocket, frowning. "Fucking red," he mutters, before remembering that I'm standing here, waiting on his answer to my original question. "Oh, sorry. No, Julien is not here."

Julien. I roll his full name around in my brain, loving the way it reverberates down to my toes.

"I would assume he's still at school and then will probably go to his house," Ben continues. "Want the address?"

"What? No. I—of course not." I'm feeling absolutely ridiculous for thinking Jules would just be hanging out here on a weekday afternoon, so I turn around and wave over my shoulder. "Thanks anyway!"

Instead of spending the rest of the evening dwelling on that interaction, I talk Chloe and Dad into going down to the studio with me. Chloe has gotten really into window washing lately—four-year-olds are weird—so I know I can get her to help clean the studio.

We spend a few hours daydreaming, sweeping, and dancing around the studio. Well, Chloe and I dance. Dad walks around and pulls all of the rusted nails out of the wall, telling me multiple times that I need to go get a tetanus shot for my hand.

When it's dinner time, we walk back home for a lovely meal of frozen pizza and apple juice. Later that night I tuck Chloe in, before returning to the studio with some paint samples. I'm hoping I can get the place up and running by spring break so I can offer trial dance camps to the local kids.

Daydreams carry me away as I think about possible camp themes, what class levels I should offer, and my never-ending to-do list. I'm lost in my head when I register a figure emerging from the shadows.

I'm so used to walking alone in Boston that my hand immediately reaches for my pepper spray before I realize that figure has a very familiar looking man bun.

I'd really like to tug that man bun out of its ponytail holder and run my hands through his thick, wavy—

"Hey," Jules says when he spots me walking toward him. "How's your hand?"

His eyes dart toward my still bandaged hand then up to my lips before meeting my eyes.

I hold my injured hand up. "Still here."

"Has a doctor looked at it?"

I groan. "I'll go, okay? Everyone needs to get off my back about the shots." I narrow my eyes. "Why are you here anyway? You've seen I'm alive, you can go now." I know I'm being snippy, but I don't know how to handle Jules. I don't know what to do with these... these *feelings*.

His only response to me is to rub his hand over his scruff. Always so calm, cool, and collected.

Avoiding this interaction is preferable, but he's blocking the door to the dance studio.

"Come have coffee with me."

I look at my wrist with its non-existent watch. "It's after eight o'clock."

"I can make tea," he continues, backtracking once he sees my nose scrunch up. "Or decaf coffee... Just come next door with me."

Although I know this is a terrible, horrible, no good, very bad idea, I find my feet moving toward the coffee shop door before I register what's happening.

I feel Jules' sigh of relief as his hand comes to the small of my back. From that one touch, my body explodes. Heat radiating through my jacket and shirt, warming me in too many places.

I must be ovulating.

Jules guides me past the couch I was passed out on last night, and I notice a blood stain on the fabric. "Oh shit, that's from me, isn't it?" I ask. "I can replace the couch." Though I have no idea where I'll get the money for that.

"No worries, I was arguing with Ben about whether or not to toss it, and it looks like I win."

"So... you own the coffee shop and you're a teacher? Seems like those would have conflicting schedules." I sit on the non-blood stained couch and watch as Jules grabs a few items from behind the counter and starts making a drink.

"How much has Ben told you?" he asks with—is that a hint of jealousy in his tone?

I narrow my eyes at Jules. "Ben hasn't told me anything. Notice how I'm sitting in here with you, not Ben."

Jules mutters something about a tea party before finally answering me. "I teach music up at the high school, but this will be my last year. My brothers and I just signed the lease on this place because Ethel, the previous owner, would only sell it if all three of us were in. That's why Ben moved back. He'll get it up and running while I finish out the school year. We've been up here testing recipes, I'd love to know what you think."

He finishes the drink and brings it over to me, sitting in a cozy looking chair nearby. We are close enough that our knees brush, but that really doesn't feel close *enough*. I take a sip of the iced coffee Jules hands me and—"Holy shit that's good. It's really decaf?"

He nods in reply. His leg stretches out between mine, and his foot hooks behind my ankle, guiding my leg closer to him. I watch as he props my foot onto his knee and begins to massage my calf. I can't help the groan I let loose.

As a dancer, I am always sore. I obviously do what I can to keep my muscles happy—I swear those massager guns are heaven sent—but more often than not, my body is aching. Which is why most professional dancers are young, retiring by the time they are thirty.

Jules hangs his head, kneading into my calf with his incredibly capable thumbs. I can't help the impulse this time. I reach over and yank the tie out of his hair, freeing his waves to cascade down to his shoulders.

He looks up at me through his now loose hair. "Better?" He smirks.

I set my coffee down and then reach out to run my good hand through his hair. It's his turn to groan now, and that has me up out of my seat and onto his lap in the blink of an eye.

Just like that, we are almost right back to where we were the night we met. Except there are too many layers between us now. I catch a glimpse of the gold chain around his neck and trace my finger lightly across where it lies delicately over his collar bone, enjoying his shuddering inhale that follows.

The lights in the coffee shop are off, and there are shockingly few people out and about tonight—something I had forgotten about small-town America—which emboldens me to take what I want from Jules. And what I want are his lips, his tongue, his hands. All of him, as soon as possible.

I grind down on his hardening erection, my yoga pants leaving little to the imagination. Jules immediately starts in on my neck. He nips and kisses and whispers sweet nothings before tugging my earlobe into his mouth.

Finally, his lips meet mine, and I am extremely pleased by the fact that I was not imagining the spark between us last time.

He kisses me and it's like a dream. He's somehow gentle and powerful at the same time. His entire personality seems to be communicated in this kiss. Understated but giving, commanding yet kind. He runs his hands up and down my thighs, behind to my ass, and then up to the back of my neck. I drop my head back as he pulls my coat off, savoring his attention.

Suddenly, I'm being lifted off his lap and carried over to the countertop. It would seem that Jules carries me through life now. Not that I mind.

"Is this okay?" he asks, pulling back to look at me.

"Feels like a bit of a health code violation, but other than that it's great."

His eyes crinkle at the corner. "We are closed for renovations for the next few weeks. Replacing the countertop is on the list."

"Excellent, you may proceed." I wave my hand toward our joined hips. Leaning over, I whisper in his ear, "Take my pants off, Julien."

Chapter Eleven
SCARS
Jules

VULNERABLE
Selena Gomez

I want to fucking devour this woman. I don't care that we are on the counter in The Coffee Shop. I don't care that anyone could walk by and see us.

Thea makes me feel feral. A feeling that has only intensified since I saw her again after thinking I'd lost her. I know she's skittish—she's told me as much—but I'm hoping my actions will show her that I want to try this with her. Try dating, try a relationship, and, yeah, right now I'd really like to try having sex. So I do what the woman requested, and I take her pants off.

And then I stay down on my knees.

I bite my way up her thigh. She moans but it cuts off suddenly when I get to the apex of her legs. "Wait!" she says, and I immediately pull my head back.

"I'm sor—"

"No," she interrupts. "Don't be sorry. I just want to say two things. One, I haven't had sex in a while, but last time I checked, no STIs. Two, I have a scar from my C-section with Chloe." She cringes and I wait for her to continue.

When she doesn't, I realize she's worried about my reaction to her scar. I nod but don't say anything, tapping her ass to get her to lift her hips. Once her underwear is sitting on the ground on top of her leggings, I brush my thumb over Thea's scar. It sits right in line with her hip bones, cutting part of the way across. As much as I want to taste her immediately, I need her to understand something.

So I lean down and kiss across that scar she's so worried about. Between kisses I look up and remind her, "You are brave. You are strong. You are a badass. You—" I pause for emphasis. "—are a great mom."

She exhales, whispering, "You don't know those things. You barely know me."

"I know enough," I reply. "Can I?" My finger trails lower, through her neatly trimmed curls, to the top of her slit.

"Please, Jules," she mumbles. "Please, please."

"I like it when you beg, Thea." And I reward her with a long lick around her clit as my finger slides in. She's dripping wet already, and she tastes so fucking good. It's going to take everything in me not to come in my pants. "I want you to make a mess of me."

I pump in and out, adding a second finger and then a third, curling them as she arches back. "You're doing so good." She is. I can feel her tightening, see her chest heaving. I would stay down here all night if she'd let me. Taste every inch of her sweet cunt.

I wonder if she'd let me…

A moment later, however, she explodes. Her legs clamp around my head, her hand pulling my hair back as she rocks her hips over and over again, chasing the waves of her orgasm. "That's it, fuck my fingers. Ride my fucking face," I encourage, the words falling from my lips without a second thought.

When she starts to come down, I stand, taking her mouth with mine. She groans when she tastes herself, and I love that sound. I would spend the rest of my life chasing the high that sound gives me.

Thea fumbles around, trying to use one hand to undo my jeans, the other still bandaged and unusable. I pull back, only so I can help her, and she haphazardly shoves my pants and briefs down. Her lust-filled gaze trails down to my cock, dripping pre-cum onto her thigh.

"Hot damn," she whispers, making an unexpected laugh burst out of me. She immediately covers her mouth and looks at me with wide eyes. "Did I say that out loud?"

"Yes," I laugh, planting another kiss on her full lips. "Two things. One, I've also been checked for STIs, and I'm clear but I'll use a condom."

"Okay, I'm on birth control too."

"Great. Number two, I have a scar on my stomach from when Ben pulled a sword on me in middle school."

Her eyebrows furrow. "Does it… affect your performance?" she asks.

I shake my head. "No, Thea. But you told me about yours, so I'm telling you about mine." Her lip curls up at that, and I reach into my back pocket, pulling the condom out of my wallet.

Thea helps me slide it on and then guides me to her, impatience radiating off of her. With one thrust, I'm in all the way to the hilt. We both gasp as we adjust to the sensation of each other. My forehead falls against hers, wanting to search her eyes. Wanting to see if she feels the same connection that I feel.

"Look at me." Her eyes pop open and I fall head first into their depths. I hike her knees up to slightly change the angle, pumping rhythmically into her tight cunt. "Good girl."

"Jules," she groans. "I'm going to come again." Her good hand threads into the hair at the base of my neck, pulling in a way that creates delicious pain.

"Wait for me," I reply, but she doesn't have to wait long because I've been dreaming of this exact moment for over a week now, and within moments, we're both tipping over the edge.

A blissful falling, waves of ecstasy crashing over us as together we pull every last drop of sensation out of each other.

Our heavy breathing is the only sound that fills the room. I can't take my eyes off of Thea. I study her face, mentally cataloging the freckles across her nose, the perfect cupid's bow of her lips, the long line of her neck.

I realize I've been staring when she clears her throat. "Sorry," I mumble, before pulling out. We both look down and realize at the same time: the condom broke.

"It's okay, I'm on birth control," she repeats, her voice breathless. "We should be fine."

In that case… I look between us again and see my cum dripping out of her. *Fuck it.* I use one of my fingers to slowly press it back in. Thea has apparently awoken a breeding kink in me.

She gasps, her head falling back and mouth gaping open. I pump my finger in and out a few times before pulling it out completely, raising it to her open lips.

"Suck." The raspiness in my voice undeniably communicates my desire, but I don't give a fuck. This woman drives me crazy.

Her mouth closes around my finger, and my dick twitches. I already can't wait to do this again.

She pulls back with a *pop* and licks her lips. "Thank you," she whispers, leaning in to place a kiss on my cheek. It feels so innocent and chaste compared to what we just did.

I watch as she hops off the counter and grabs her clothes from the floor. "Bathroom?" she asks, pointing toward the back. I nod like an idiot in response because I can't verbally process what's happening right now.

While I wait for her, I clean myself up and dispose of the useless condom.

I'm leaning against the counter when she walks back out. Her jacket is back on, and she looks like she's about to leave.

"You didn't finish your coffee," I say. A lame attempt at delaying her.

She gives me a wary smile. "Thanks again... for the coffee and the... other stuff."

"Wait. Are you really leaving right now?" I'm so taken aback by this turn of events. It feels so cold, so indifferent when I know she can't possibly feel that way.

She sighs, not meeting my eyes. "It was just supposed to be one night, Jules."

"Bullshit. I never wanted only one night with you, I told you that. Now you're going to what? Just ignore me even when we are inevitably going to cross paths? This is a small town, Thea, and you work right next door." I'm rarely ever angry, but I can feel Thea slipping away even though she's standing right in front of me. I'm desperate to do anything to prevent that from happening.

Her shoulders slump and, as angry as I am, I hate that I did that to her. "I should have been more clear, I'm sorry."

"Yeah," I reply. "Me too."

An arrow that hits its mark. She doesn't reply before turning and walking out the front door.

Chapter Twelve
MY FLOWERS ARE DEAD
Thea

INVISIBLE STRING
Taylor Swift

Two weeks later

I have been dutifully avoiding Julien Bardot for the last two weeks.

I still haven't quite figured out why I can't be with him—or at least try—but I'm sure it has something to do with the mommy issues. Or the deadbeat-baby-daddy issues. Or the shattered dreams issues.

One of those, for sure.

In those two weeks I've attempted to get the studio in working order, but I'm far from where I wanted to be. I painted the entire place in a light pink color and then decided that felt too on-the-nose. I wish I would have figured that out before the second coat was drying, but I can only do so much.

I'm painting the fourth sample of green on the wall when I hear a knock on the window. I don't even look over before yelling, "Come in!" Chloe and Dad have been popping by to help when they can, but most of the time it's easier to just do it on my own.

The door swings open, the little bell I installed tingling lightly. "Hi, my little chicken!" I call. "Come help me pick out a good color."

But it's not Chloe's voice that greets me. Instead, it's a voice that sends a mixture of dread and heat low into my belly. "I like the one on the left," Jules replies. His voice is rough, and I feel it like a tangible stroke down my spine.

I instantly jump to my feet which sends me stumbling sideways. The dizzy spells have gotten more frequent in the last few days, but I refuse to go see another doctor after I just had to go get that tetanus shot done. Jules looks like it physically pains him not to wrap me in bubble wrap and call it a day. He rushes over, taking hold of my elbow to steady me.

"I'm fine," I mutter, tasting the lie. "Just stood up too fast."

He pulls a pack of peanut butter crackers out of his pocket and holds them out to me. "Have you eaten recently?"

Obviously I hesitate for too long because he rips the package open, holding a cracker out to me. "I'm fine," I repeat, even as my traitorous hand grabs the food from Jules.

"Sure," he replies, already handing me another cracker. I shove it in my mouth and then turn my back to him.

Staring at the wall, I chew and pretend like I can't feel Jules standing behind me.

Dammit, he's right. The green on the left does look the best. Another cracker comes into my field of vision, and I snatch it out of his hand.

"Wha're you dofng heer?" I ask, mouth ridiculously full.

He huffs, clearly unimpressed by my avoidance tactics. "You can't keep ignoring me forever," he responds instead of answering my question.

Busying myself with opening the final sample, I paint a few strokes on the wall. "Who says I'm ignoring you?"

"You know, I remember thinking there was no way that Bex was *actually* clueless when it came to how much of a fool Anders was for her, but maybe it's just how you all are hardwired."

"Who the hell are Bex and Anders?" I ask right as the door opens, letting Chloe and my dad in.

"Ohhh, Mama! That's a bad word!" She skips right past Jules with a, "Hi, almost-Ben," before continuing over to the wall with assorted paint splotches. Silently she studies them for a moment, finally walking up to the one on the left and saying, "This is the best one, Mama."

"Good taste," Jules mutters, causing me to roll my eyes. The last thing I need is someone else on Chloe's side. She'd eat that right up.

"I think I'll do the one on the right," I state.

Dad decides it's his turn to chime in. "That one looks a bit like puke, darlin'."

Fuck, he's right.

"Why are y'all here?" I repeat, looking back and forth between my dad and Jules.

Dad holds up a bag of fast food that I didn't notice before. "Figured you were hungry."

Jules just raises his eyebrow at me.

Alright, I've had enough of this. "I'm a grown"—*stomp*—"ass"—*stomp*—"woman!" *Stomp.* "And I can take care of myself." My arms cross over my chest in defiance.

Dad saunters over and shoves a milkshake in my face. I narrow my eyes before taking a few sips. He narrows his eyes right back—I did learn from the best, after all—and asks, "Done with your little hissy fit?"

"Depends on what else you have in that bag."

His large mustache twitches as he finds a spot on the floor next to Chloe. "Sorry, Junior, didn't know you were gunna be here or I'd've brought you a milkshake," he says to Jules.

"It's Jules, sir." Jules clears his throat. "Julien," he clarifies.

"He has some peanut butter crackers if he's hungry." I take a seat next to Chloe, leaving room for Jules if he decides to join us.

"AB!" Chloe calls from her place on the floor. "My flowers are dead." She looks up at Jules with blatant skepticism, and I have to turn my head to hide my smile.

"AB?" Jules asks. He joins us on the ground, and it strikes me how much he just… fits here.

"Almost-Ben. Get it? Because it starts with A and B?" Chloe is clearly very proud of herself for coming up with this.

"What do I have to do to get you to call me Jules?"

I scoff. "Chlo is really big on nicknames so good luck with that."

My snarky daughter takes a bite of her chicken nuggets and says, "Maybe if you get me new flowers."

———

An hour later, I'm full of fast food and good conversation.

"Time to get this hooligan to bed." Dad tugs on Chloe's pigtail, urging her toward the door. When he gets right up next to me, he leans in and whispers, "Let Junior help."

I peek over his shoulder and lock eyes with Jules. His hands are shoved in his pockets, a loose hair falling out of his bun. He looks so fucking earnest, even after suffering through dinner on the floor of a broken-down dance studio with a broken-down family he's seemingly okay with inserting himself into.

I nod at Dad before scooping Chloe into my arms. "Goodnight, my chicken. I'll be home soon, okay?"

She grabs my face between her two hands and plants a kiss on the tip of my nose. "You're my favorite mommy," she says.

"You're my favorite Chloe," I echo. Then they're off.

It's silent for a few moments, only the sound of the space heater running fills the room. I take Jules in, and he seems to bask in the attention. He's so handsome, it hurts. And, not for the first time, I have the thought *Why does he care about me?*

I wince at my constant internal monologue, and he catches it. He takes a few tentative steps toward me, like he's worried I'll evaporate into thin air if he moves too quickly.

"Did I do something wrong?" Jules finally asks, coming to a stop a foot or so away.

"Jules..." My head falls forward. How do I explain something I don't really understand myself?

I feel his finger brush under my chin, guiding my eyes back to him. "Tell me about Chloe's dad."

Chapter Thirteen
TWENTY QUESTIONS
Jules

AUTOMATIC
Fly By Midnight, Jake Miller

Immediately it feels like the wrong thing to say. Thea rears back, a look of disgust on her face. But I can see through it. She's like a wild mustang—she's scared so she spooks easily, always ready to be on the defensive.

I want her to realize she doesn't have to defend herself against me.

"I'm sorry," I start. "I'm not trying to pry, just trying to understand."

"And you feel like one dinner together gives you the right to ask something so personal?" she retorts.

"No, it doesn't. But if I ever do earn that right, and trust me, I intend to, I want you to know that there's nothing that's going to scare me off. No choice you've made that I will ever have any right to judge, even if I do earn your confidence." I move slightly closer to her and make sure she's looking at me when I say, "I can tell you are one hell of a mom to that little girl. You love her fiercely and, God, she's fucking adorable. I'm sorry for asking something too personal—I just want to know you. Both of you."

I place a tentative kiss on the top of her forehead, holding still for a moment too long. Then I turn, take the paint sample that Chloe and I liked, and walk out the door. "See you tomorrow, Thea," I call, willing myself not to look back.

> I think I fucked up.

BB
Is this about the girl??

TWIN
She has a name, Bexy

Is this about Thea??

> Yes.

GABRIEL
She looked pissed when she got home last night so you probably did fuck up.

> I'm going to buy her some paint.

TWIN
Is this... a new mating ritual?

> Every time we text, I'm reminded why it's a bad idea.

BB
We love you! Go buy that paint! Have fun with it
;)

After school the next day, I run by Stan's hardware store to grab a few gallons of "Healing Green" before walking down to the studio. On impulse, I also pick up a single light pink rose from Harriet as a peace offering. It's a nice, almost spring-like day, and I feel a renewed sense of determination when it comes to Thea… Thea, whose last name I need to learn.

I come around the corner and peek into the studio. The long line of Thea's body immediately captures my attention, as it always does. She's on the wood floor, legs spread wide, toes pointing down toward the floor. She's bent over a notebook, scribbling furiously as she flexes and points her feet over and over again, in a slow, methodical manner.

Before I get caught staring, I tap gently on the window to get her attention. She looks over and surprise flits across her face. "I told you I'd be back," I call through the glass.

Thea stands up and unlocks the door for me. I hold up two gallons of paint and ask, "Shall we?"

She reluctantly nods, and her golden waves move ethereally around her face.

"I also got this for you," I say, handing her the rose. A gentle smile crosses her lips as she twirls the flower between her fingers. Taking a deep breath, I step into the studio and start prepping the paint trays. Thea helps by laying a drop cloth down on the floor and arranging it just so.

We work in silence until Thea blurts, "I think we should play twenty questions."

"Do you?" Anything to learn more about her.

"Mmhmm. I've been thinking about it," she continues. "We can pass if there's a question we don't want to answer, but we have to be honest if we do answer."

"Deal," I reply. "But if we don't get through all twenty today, can they roll over?"

She contemplates that. "Okay, I can agree to that. You first."

"What's your last name?" I ask.

A giggle bursts free, and I look over to see her face completely lit up. "Rose," she replies, casting a glance at the flower lying on the ground near her.

Several things click into place, and I can't help but laugh right alongside her. "Fickle things."

I want to kiss the smile that tugs at the corner of her lips. "Yeah…" she breathes. "We are."

We fall into comfortable silence, painting side by side. The green looks nice as the afternoon sun slants through the windows. "What's your last name?" she finally asks.

"That's what you've been contemplating?" I joke.

"Just answer the question, AB."

I roll my eyes at the ridiculous nickname. "Bardot. Hence the new coffee shop name."

A blush creeps up her neck. "I knew that. What a waste of a question."

"We won't count it."

She hums and continues to paint.

"What's your favorite snack?" Paint glides onto the walls as I wait for her answer.

"You already know the answer to that." I can hear the smile in her voice. "I'm a slut for some peanut butter crackers."

My mouth dries up. "What else are you a slut for, Thea Rose?" I look over and see her smirking. She knows exactly what she's doing to me.

She sets her paintbrush down, hips swaying as she moves closer to me. Popping up on her tiptoes, she gets so close to my ear I can feel her breathing. Goosebumps break out across my skin. I feel her smile as she says, "Pass."

I pinch the bridge of my nose, working hard to calm my racing heart. I hear the melody of Thea's giggle as she walks back to where she was painting.

But then she slips abruptly from confident woman into hesitant and insecure. "I'll tell you about Chloe's dad," she finally says, a slight shake in her voice.

"You don't have to do that."

"I know… I—It's hard, you know?" She stops painting and lays herself out on the floor.

Without saying anything, I find a spot on the floor next to her. I want Thea to feel safe sharing with me, however much she is willing to share. I don't want to pry or push, but I do want to offer her comfort in the only way I know how—sitting in the hard stuff together.

"Did you know I was a ballerina?" she asks.

Vaguely, I gesture around the room. "I sort of figured."

"No," she whispers. "A real ballerina. Obnoxiously large tutu, terrible looking feet, a season of performances in beautiful Boston theaters." A pause. "Dad and I moved up here when I was seventeen. I was recruited by Ballet Boston to join the school in hopes of eventually joining the company. It was... magical. Everything I had ever dreamed of. And living in a big city on top of all of that? I was in heaven."

She's quiet, and I let her process, deciding what she's comfortable confiding.

"Chloe's dad taught one of my classes. He... Well, he was larger than life." She pauses. "There's not a lot of straight male dancers in Texas, so this was really the first time I had come across a man in dance class that I could flirt with that... I don't know—he was ten years older. I basked under his attention. It remained pretty innocent until I turned eighteen. It's like he had a fucking radar or something.

"Without getting into too much detail, I joined the company a year after I moved to Boston. I danced a pas de deux with Guy— that's his name, it's so pretentious. Anyway, I danced this pas de deux with him for a donor show. We had a lot of alone time rehearsing, and one thing led to another... Dimples get me every time." She turns her head toward me, a weak smile gracing her lips.

Thea sighs heavily. I hate how sad she looks. "You don't have to tell me," I reassure. Even though I really want her to tell me.

Her eyes drift back to the ceiling. "It's okay. I found out I was pregnant shortly after. Guy immediately turned into someone I didn't recognize. He was... *mean*. He denied the baby was his.

Pushed me to end the pregnancy. Convinced me this would ruin both of us. I have nothing against women having a choice, but—and this is the worst part—I was actually kind of excited when I found out. I knew it would change things, but I had delusions of having the baby, continuing to dance, marrying Guy, and maybe even starting our own company or studio. I was nineteen when Chloe was born. Dad was there. I held out hope that Guy would change his mind once he met Chloe, but…"

I roll on my side to face Thea, maintaining a distance but letting her know that I'm still here. I'm not leaving. A single tear falls out of the corner of her closed eye and drops to the ground. On instinct, my hand finds hers, our fingers twining gently together.

"What an asshole." It's not an eloquent response, but damn, it's true.

A laugh bursts from Thea. And then she keeps laughing. And then we are both laughing so hard, different kinds of tears falling from our eyes. She rolls toward me, our legs mimicking the movement of our hands. A huge grin paints Thea's face, and I feel like I can release a pent-up breath.

Another round of laughter and then, "He—" she wheezes, "—really is."

Her face gets really serious then. Her eyes track mine, back and forth, back and forth. "No pity, though. Please, don't pity us," she whispers.

I untangle our hands, bringing my finger up so I can gently wipe the tears from under her eyes. "Thea…" I breathe. "I don't pity you. I fucking *admire* you. Every new thing I learn about you solidifies that, got it?"

A smile tugs at the corner of her lips.

"Got it," she replies. "Question number… I don't remember what question we are on."

"I was never going to stop you at twenty questions, anyway," I confess.

Another grin. "Question whatever: will you ask me on a date again?"

Fuck. I'm in so much trouble.

Chapter Fourteen
GRAY HAIR & TUMMY TROUBLES
Jules

OH SHIT... ARE WE IN LOVE?
Valley

A date.

She wants to go on a date. With me.

Not a one-night thing.

Well, she didn't clarify that it wasn't a one-night thing, but that's how I took it. Maybe I should clarify beforehand, just in case. I need her number so I can—

"Mr. Bardot, why am I failing your class?"

Report cards are going out next week, which means all of my high school students are suddenly realizing they should have done their classwork for the last few months. I will not miss this part of teaching.

"Mason, when was the last time you turned in an assignment?"

Mason Scott reminds me a lot of my brothers in high school —a future finance bro, captain of the basketball team, and kind of a dick. He looks at me like I've grown three heads. "I-I thought this was supposed to be a guaranteed A. I needed this class to boost my GPA. Coach won't let me play if I'm failing."

I lean forward, placing both elbows on my desk and folding my hands together. "Mr. Scott. What about Music Theory screamed 'guaranteed A' to you?"

Pinning him with a stare, I watch as Mason stumbles trying to come up with an answer. "You, uh... I mean you have tattoos. I thought you were cool." He makes his voice go up at the end, as if he's questioning how cool I actually am.

I don't reply, continuing to stare at him instead.

"That's not what I meant—of course you're cool. I'll, uh... finish my project and turn it in next week?"

My eyebrow raises.

"Tomorrow," Mason continues. "I'll turn it in tomorrow."

"Good man, Mr. Scott. I'm proud of you for investing in your education." I muster up a smile, my frustration slipping through.

At one point I think I liked teaching. I've always loved music, but what do you do with a music degree? I graduated, played some gigs, lived at home with Mom and Dad for a bit and quickly learned *that* was not going to work for me. I'm a good teacher, maybe even a great teacher. I've never felt passionate about it though, and teaching is a career where you have to be fueled by your passion. So here I was, back at my high school, teaching and thinking, "Is this it?" when Ben decided we were going to buy The Coffee Shop.

He is saving me from a lifelong feeling of needing to be practical, needing to make the responsible choice. I will never be able to thank him enough for that.

My phone buzzes, an unknown number popping up on the screen.

UNKNOWN

Hey Jules - I know we are supposed to go out tonight but I've been feeling terrible all day

> I promise I'm not trying to get out of it!
>
> This is Theo by the way
>
> Omg, Theo
>
> THEA! It's Thea

I bite my lip, keeping my smile back. She's so fucking cute, even through the phone screen.

> > Hi Thea. Thanks for letting me know.
>
> THEA
> I'm not making this up
>
> > I didn't say you were.
>
> THEA
> Oh no
>
> Are you one of those people that always texts in complete sentences?

Now I can't help but laugh. I know Thea is younger than me, but damn she knows how to make me feel old.

> > Maybe. I think punctuation is important. Is that a problem?
>
> THEA
> Do you ever use emojis?
>
> > No. :)
>
> THEA
> How old are you anyway...
>
> I'll go ask Ben

I type three different responses, trying and failing to come up with something witty to say in response.

> **THEA**
> THIRTY?!
> That means you were seven when I was born
> When you graduated high school, I was ELEVEN
> Do you have any gray hairs?

> I thought you weren't feeling well.

"Mr. B! Who got you smiling like that?" Honestly, I totally forgot my students were in here working on their project.

Quickly, I adopt a frown. "I'm not smiling."

Another student pipes up. "I don't think we've ever seen your real smile until now!"

Just then, my phone buzzes again, this time with an incoming picture. I cover my mouth to hide the obvious curl of my lips from my nosey students. I swipe the phone open to reveal a picture of Thea, her eyes peeking out over the top of a comforter, messy golden hair flowing across the pillow case. Her eyes look tired, sure, but she is a goddess.

> I'll drop by after school.

———

I ran by the pharmacy on the way to Thea's apartment and acquired several different kinds of medicine. I didn't even ask what was wrong earlier.

This woman fries my brain, in the best way.

My hand comes up to knock right as the door swings open. At first, my eyes meet empty air, but when my head tilts down I see a spunky four-year-old bouncing on her toes.

"Mommy's not feeling good," she states.

"I'm aware."

Chloe stares up at me, so I stare back at her.

"Let him in, Chlo!" Thea calls from somewhere in the apartment.

Chloe makes me wait another few seconds before waving me in with, "You may enter."

I duck my head in thanks, and she surprises me by curtseying in response. Feeling like that's my in, I get down on her level and whisper, "What's wrong with your mommy?"

"Her tummy hurts."

Great, Pepto Bismol it is. "And where's your grandpa?"

"Pop is at the dance studio with his hammer bag."

A chuckle bubbles up. "His hammer bag?"

She leans in. "Yeah, like for his hammer and tools," she says, eyeing me as though she's trying to figure out if I'm stupid for not knowing what a hammer bag is.

"Did you let him in, Chloe?" Thea calls again.

"I'm here. Can I come back there?" I ask.

Chloe's little hand grabs mine and guides me back to the bedroom. I pop my head in and am immediately greeted with a wall full of rainbow drawings hung up with painters tape. The queen bed has about twenty stuffed animals on one side and a sick Thea on the other side.

"Have you eaten?" The thought hits me. "I should have brought food. Let me call Ben."

"Hold your horses, I've eaten! Dad force-fed me some crackers because nothing sounded good," she mumbles.

I walk over and take a seat on the floor next to her bed. I should feel hesitant about taking care of this woman I barely know, but I don't. Reaching up, I brush a piece of hair off her forehead. It doesn't feel warm so that's a positive.

"Your medicine cabinet will be well stocked after this. I wasn't sure what you'd need." I hold up the pharmacy bag as proof. "Chloe says your stomach hurts. Have you taken anything?"

She shakes her head no, so I pull out a few Pepto chewables.

"Thank you," she whispers, a small smile gracing her lips. "The last time I felt like this I was—"

Her voice cuts off and her eyes go wide. Thea is staring at me as if she's seen a ghost.

"Is it the medicine?" I ask at the same time Chloe says, "You were what, Mommy?"

Thea looks back and forth between the two of us and then clears her throat. "I was… younger. I was younger the last time I felt like this…"

Her eyes meet mine and wince. It's like she's trying to communicate something without telling me, but as hard as I've tried, I'm not a mind reader. "How much younger?" I ask.

She looks from me to Chloe, back again. "Nineteen."

Chapter Fifteen
A WEIRD ASS PLACE
Thea

FALL INTO ME
Forrest Blakk

Fuck. Fuck.

FuckfuckFUCK.

"Language, Mommy!" Chloe chastises me. I guess I said that out loud.

I sit straight up in bed and push Chloe's hair back. "Sorry, my chicken. You can have ice cream if you don't tell Pop."

"ICE CREAM!" My fucks are quickly forgotten as Chloe runs to the kitchen. I can hear a chair scraping across the floor so she can reach the freezer.

Jules is still sitting on the floor next to my bed in stunned silence. I feel like I'm going to throw up.

"I need you to leave."

That wakes him up.

"Wha—okay, yeah. Should I... I can go pick up a test." He stands up, pulls the bun out of his hair, and then reties it.

A test. A test would make it real.

"No! No test," I reply. "Just, I need you to leave."

He really looks at me then, hurt flickering in his eyes.

"Thea… I'm not—"

"Jules," I interrupt. "I'm so fucking serious. I am freaking out right now," I whisper, trying to keep my voice down so Chloe doesn't hear.

"Which is exactly why I shouldn't—" he starts. I can feel him getting angry which just makes me more anxious for him to leave.

I stand up and walk around him, my shoulder bumping into his as I move by. He grabs for my hand and I quickly yank it away, stomping like a toddler to the front door. I swing it open and point into the hallway. "Get. Out," I grit.

Jules' hand runs furiously over his face, but I can tell he's resigned himself to leaving.

"Where you going, Juju?" Chloe pipes up when Jules passes the kitchen.

He looks at her and… shatters. The evident pain on his face almost makes me close the door.

Almost.

"I gotta go, Chloe," he finally replies. "I'll see you soon, okay?"

His steps slow when he gets to the door. "I don't want to leave," he says, his voice low enough that only I can hear.

I'm about to respond when the door across the hallway opens.

"What's up, guys?" Ben says, cheerful as always.

Despite myself, I want to smile when Jules murmurs, "Fucking awesome."

"Juju is going to take a test!" Chloe yells to her new best friend.

Ben raises a single eyebrow at his twin, who shakes his head in response.

"Princess Chloe, why don't you come hang out at my place for a bit? I can make tea!" Ben is trying to help, but I just want these stupid, handsome men to disappear so I can panic in peace.

"No, it's fine. Jules was just leaving," I reply.

"Okay…" Ben drawls. "Prince Julien." He opens his door and waves his hand with a flourish, welcoming Jules in.

Jules takes one more long look at me. I see the battle raging in his eyes, sorrow mixes with frustration and something else that I can't quite place. "We will need to talk about this," he insists. "I'll be here when you're ready."

And then he disappears into Ben's apartment.

I bury my face in my hands and slide down the door frame until I'm firmly planted on the floor.

The deep breaths are not helping with the nausea or the building anxiety. When I finally uncover my eyes, Ben is still standing in the hallway with me, texting furiously.

"Can you make sure he's okay?" I ask.

He nods, but he's still engrossed in whatever he's looking at on his phone. After another moment, he pockets it and takes a deep breath. "Alright so my—a girl I know, she's good people… don't tell her I said that. Anyway, she'll be here in a bit to… uh…" He shrugs. "Check on you."

"I can take care of myself."

Ben looks at me—really looks at me—and bends down like he does when he talks to Chloe. "I don't doubt that. You're a badass. But that's also not really how we do things around here, okay? You don't have to do it on your own anymore."

With that, he stands back up and walks into his apartment without another word.

Twenty minutes later there's a knock on the door. I had managed to drag myself to Dad's La-Z-Boy—he's still down at the studio, doing work that I should be doing—and turned on the TV in time to catch Fast Money on *Family Feud*.

Chloe loves to open the door to strangers so I hop up quickly and race her there, flinging the door open to a gorgeous red-headed woman, her arms full of paper grocery sacks. "Scoot over, these are heavy," she says, pushing her way past me into the apartment without introducing herself.

The bags are unceremoniously dumped on the counter before she reaches into one and pulls out a smaller paper bag. I still haven't moved from the open door, so she walks over and gives me a curious look. "Here." She hands me the bag.

I look down at it and then back up at her. "Sorry, who are you?"

"Are you fucking kidding me? Did Benjamin not tell you I was coming over?" She sends a scathing look across the hall.

"H-he did! He did not tell me who you were, though. Just that you were 'good people.'"

Surprise flickers across her face. "He said that?" Her perfectly sculpted auburn brow arches. She's making me feel very subconscious about the fact that I can't remember the last time I brushed my hair. "Whatever," she continues. "I'm Cole. Collette, but people call me Cole. Do you want to…" She eyes the package in my hand.

I peer in and see a pregnancy test. What a fucking jump scare. I shove it back in Cole's hands. "Nope."

"Okay." She shrugs. That's it? She's not going to push?

Right then, Chloe runs in. "I'm Chloe! I already have a best friend, but I like your hair so maybe you can replace him."

"Is it Jules? He's a pretty cool best friend." Cole jumps straight into Chloe's world without missing a beat.

"I like Jules… but Ben is my best friend."

Cole gets a wicked glint in her eye. "Oh, love bug, not for long if I have anything to say about it."

"Any mac and cheese in that bag? Chlo is pretty easily bought," I chime in.

Cole rubs her hands together, beginning to unpack the

grocery sacks. "Not only do I have mac and cheese… I have the best kind of mac and cheese—shapes!"

Chloe's jaw drops. "Mama never lets us get the shapes!" She drags a chair over to the counter to help Cole unpack.

I watch for a moment before I realize that this is actually an incredibly bizarre situation. I clear my throat. "Cole, um… Sorry this has just been a very overwhelming day. You really don't have to do this." But she's already found a pot and started boiling water.

"Listen," she starts. "Sassafras is a weird-ass place—"

"Language!" Chloe calls.

"Right… a weird 'bleep' place, and the Bardots tend to be fairly persistent, but they are also some of the best people in the world. Benjamin excluded, of course." She pauses. "Chloe and I are going to make our *Frozen*-shaped, cheesy-pasta deliciousness. You go… do whatever you need to do." She looks meaningfully at the test on the counter.

I chew on my lip. If I take it, it's real. But maybe I'm wrong? I'm probably overreacting anyway. No way am I… That doesn't accidentally happen to people twice, right? God, I should just take it.

It'll be negative.

"Fine." I grab the bag and walk into my bedroom to meet whatever fate awaits me.

Chapter Sixteen
I DON'T OWN A CAT
Jules

NOTHING SEEMS TO MATTER NOW
VICTORS

I wake up the next morning, after getting a shitty night's sleep, to a mewing coming from somewhere in my house.

At least, I think it's in my house. My head is pounding thanks to the aforementioned shitty sleep, so I have to physically drag myself out of bed to investigate. I pull on sweats and wander into the living room. I feel like I'm playing that hot or cold game you play as a kid.

Living room... colder.

Back into the bedroom... warm.

Over to the window... on fire.

Pulling the curtain open, sure enough there's a cat sitting on the outside sill. It's completely black and incredibly fluffy.

Feels like a bad omen.

Its yellow eyes stare at me, unblinking, waiting for something.

This is not my cat.

I don't own a cat.

I close the curtains, walk away, immediately feel like an asshole, turn around, and pop open the window. "Shoo. Go back to your home."

The cat tilts its head at me. "Go on," I try again, attempting to spook it without actually touching it. The fluff ball jumps off the sill and down onto the ground, slowly slinking away with one last scowl toward me.

Shutting the window, I wander into the kitchen to start my coffee. As I go through the motions, I replay the events of yesterday for the millionth time. It's taking everything in me not to go back over to Thea's apartment now to check on her. The possibility of her being pregnant makes me simultaneously terrified and... fucking elated.

The desire to be a dad has been ingrained in me for as long as I can remember. I was always the one taking care of my siblings when we were younger—the stable constant. And I liked it that way. I want to be useful. I want to fall in love. I want a family of my own.

It's so easy to see all of that with Thea and Chloe. If that's what she wants, too. Which feels unlikely since she kicked me out of the apartment yesterday.

I have no idea how I'm going to focus on work today.

Meow.

My head snaps up. What the fuck?

The fluff ball is now sitting on the kitchen window sill, staring into my soul.

As long as I can remember, we have never had an issue with stray cats in Sassafras. The larger wildlife that have found their way to our town usually take care of that. No, this guy—or girl—must have a home.

Since I'm feeling incredibly useless this morning, the cat has arrived at the perfect time, giving me something to do. Something to focus on.

I pop this window open and resign myself to stopping by the

shelter on the way to school this morning. The owner will be located by the end of the day, and that will be that.

Fluffy slinks through the window as soon as I open it. I hold my hand out for it to sniff, smiling as it nudges my fingers a few times with its wet nose. Upon further inspection, and now that the coffee is brewing, the cat is pretty cute.

It walks along the counter, pushing its head against my hand and purring loudly. There's no collar that I can see, but it definitely seems good with people. I give it a few scratches under its chin and then watch it as I walk away to pour myself a cup of coffee.

The cat continues to prowl across the countertop, paying me no mind as I watch and drink. Fluff ball nudges the cabinet door open, batting at a box of pasta until it tips over.

"Good thing that box was closed, or else I'd be very annoyed with you," I murmur. The cat simply stares at me while it bats another box over. I think I've entered into a cat staring competition, but we both lose when there's a loud knock at the door. The sound is loud enough to spook the cat, who goes running toward my bedroom. I'm about to follow it when another knock sounds.

"Coming!" I call, assuming it's my impatient mother who often likes to drop off "a little treat" on her way to work. A peek through the peephole leaves me breathless, however, and I don't think twice before swinging the door open.

"Thea," I pant.

She takes a long look at my chest, and I feel like I'm back in the kitchen doing the staring contest with the cat. Except Thea is very much not looking at my eyes. "Muscles," she whispers.

I give her a minute to compose herself, though, I definitely don't mind being admired. "Eyes up here, *ma chou*."

That gets her attention. "What does that mean?"

I ignore her question because she's putting me through the wringer, and I need some semblance of control here. "Why don't you come in? I'll make you some coffee."

Her internal debate is obvious, and I see when she eventually gives in, passing me to walk into the house.

"Nice place," she states, attempting small talk. And it is a nice place. I bought it two years ago after saving up overtime money and extra from random gigs. Sassafras had fairly reasonable home prices at the time, and though it didn't make much sense for a twenty-eight year-old single man to buy a four-bedroom house, I did it anyway.

I observe Thea as *she* observes the living room that gives way to the kitchen. I watch as she takes in the violin propped up against the wall, the assorted sheet music scattered across the coffee table, the thriving snake plant in the corner. I wish I could read her mind in this moment—hear what judgments, good or bad, she's making about the space. "Can I get—"

The sound of shattering ceramic interrupts me. "Fucking cat," I mutter, back tracking into the kitchen where, sure enough, my favorite coffee mug is in pieces on the tile floor, surrounded by most of my first cup of coffee for the day. The cat is lying on the counter, licking its paw. The asshole doesn't even bother to look up as I walk in.

"You have a cat?" Thea's voice is right behind me now, and I can sense her peeking over my shoulder.

"No."

"You guys kind of look alike."

I turn and raise my brow at her. "Do we?"

"Yeah, he just needs a bun. What's his name?"

"He's not my cat," I reply, bending over to start cleaning up the mess it made.

"We had barn cats back in Texas, but I always wanted one of my own," she muses.

I look over at her, and she's still several feet away from the cat, staring longingly toward it.

"It let me pet it earlier."

Tentatively, she reaches her hand out, quickly pulling it back before the cat even has a chance to decide whether he likes her or not.

"You scared, Thea?"

Her whole body slumps in response. "Yes," she whispers, and I know she's not talking about the cat anymore.

"Go sit down, I'll be there in a minute."

She does what I ask while I finish cleaning up the broken mug. I get down two new cups and pour fresh coffee for both of us. I don't ask, just add some cream and sugar into hers. Coffee is placed on the table in front of her, then we sit in silence for several moments. I want to give her time to process what she wants to say, but I need to know for sure why she is here.

"I support you no matter what. If... if the results of your... test. Or if you didn't take it, I can help. But it's your body. It's your decision. And I will be with you—I mean, I'll be here to—"

"It was positive." She finally takes pity on me and cuts in.

I rub my hands down my face, hiding my smile. "That's... that's great." I grin.

Thea looks at me like I just spoke a foreign language.

"I mean—fuck. I'm messing this up."

"No, I'm surprised by that reaction. That's all." She's wringing her hands in her lap, and that's when it hits me. Of course she's surprised. From what she's told me, Chloe's dad was a bastard who did not take the news of Thea being pregnant well at all. I stand up and move around to sit on the coffee table directly in front of Thea.

"May I?" I ask, holding my hands out for hers. She untangles her fingers and places them in mine. I give her a reassuring squeeze. "Thea... I have always wanted to be a father. This might not be the way I would have gone about it, but I am not upset or disappointed. I also respect *you*, very much. And I respect whatever choice you want to make. Take some time and think about it. I know you haven't met them yet but my mom and sister are great people and would make good, non-judgmental, sounding boards."

A tear slips free from the corner of Thea's eye, and I make a decision.

"I'm going to call in to work real quick, and then I'm yours for the day, alright?"

She frantically begins wiping at her face. "You don't have to do that."

"I know that, Thea. I want to. You don't even have to talk to me. I'll put on a record or a TV show and sit silently."

She huffs a laugh. "You do always have that creepily silent, brooding way about you."

"I resent that, I just used a lot of words for you," I joke.

I walk into the bedroom to call my principal and tell her I won't be in today. By the time I make it back to the living room, Thea has passed out on the couch, and my heart aches a bit as I watch the cat curl up next to her.

Chapter Seventeen
STRESS MUFFINS
Thea

TILL WE BOTH SAY
Nicotine Dolls

I wake up on a strange couch with a crick in my neck, to the smell of... is that butter?

My eyes pop open, reorienting to this new environment. I sit up and stretch as reality punches me in the gut.

Pregnant. Again.

I can't believe I have royally fucked up for the second time. Not that Chloe is a fuck up—she's the best thing that ever happened to me. And I feel immediate guilt at the thought of classifying her as a mistake. Tears pop into my eyes—*I am the fuck up, not her.* I'm barely managing one kid, the thought of doing it all over again is terrifying.

Jules says he supports me no matter what, but I don't really know the man. I thought I knew Guy and look how he reacted.

No, men cannot be trusted no matter how hot they look when they answer the door without a shirt on.

"You're up," Jules states, walking out of the kitchen. He has an apron on that somehow makes him even more attractive, which instantly irritates me even more.

"Are you baking?" I ask, noting the flour spots splattered across him.

He pulls his hair from his bun and then reties it—something I'm starting to suspect he does when he's nervous. "Yeah. I got a little antsy while you were napping. I was going to take the cat to the shelter, but it hissed at me when I tried to pick it up off of you."

That's when I notice the black cat curled up at my feet. I had forgotten about it. "You can't take it to the shelter," I reply. Though I am slightly terrified of small mammals, I don't want it to die either.

"It's a no-kill shelter," Jules replies, reading my thoughts.

"We should make signs. You can keep him here, right?"

Jules smirks at me, his brow furrowing. "Sure."

A timer dings in the kitchen, and Jules turns without saying another word. I carefully slide my feet out from under the cat and follow him.

"Holy shit." The counter is covered in—"Muffins?"

He lets out a nervous chuckle. "Yeah… I got really into *The Great British Bake Off* a few years ago and muffins seemed like the easiest place to start." He points around the kitchen. "Chocolate chip, blueberry, coffee cake, and in here"—he opens the oven—"is the lemon raspberry."

Wide-eyed, I stare around the space. "I wasn't sure which kind you like," he continues. "Or if you hate muffins, I'll take them to the teachers lounge on Monday."

"Who hates muffins?" I ask, picking up one of the coffee cake ones and taking a huge bite. "Fuck, that's so good," I say around a mouthful of food. "You really missed out on a great 'bun in the oven' joke, though."

I look up to see Jules watching my mouth which causes a furious blush to creep up my neck. No idea why I'm blushing at the man who has already impregnated me, but here we are.

"Sorry, I didn't even ask if I could have one."

He meets my eyes. Shrugs. "I made them for you."

At that very moment, his phone starts ringing, saving me from responding to his sweet admission. He looks down at the screen, and whatever is on there pulls a genuine smile out of him. "It's my sister, Bex, do you mind if I answer?"

"Oh, of course not. I'll just..." I point awkwardly toward the other room. Jules answers the phone, grabbing my hand at the same time to keep me in place.

"Hi, BB," he says.

"JuJu!" A feminine voice comes through the line, but Jules is facing toward me so I can't see the screen. "Mom said you called in today, everything okay?"

He laughs. "Mom is nosey. Yes, I'm fine."

"I have a hard time believing that. I can see all the muffins on the counter behind you. Is it that girl you've been trying to date?"

Jules locks eyes with me, a soft smile gracing his lips. "You could say that," he replies.

"What are you looking at? Oh my God, is she there?! Is that why you aren't at work?" His sister's voice keeps getting higher with each question.

The cat decides it's the perfect time to join us. He—or she—rubs up against my legs and lets out a loud meow.

"Was that a cat?" the voice asks. "I feel so out of the loop!" she whines.

Another voice comes over the phone. "Who are you talking to, Baby Bardot?"

"Hi, Anders, it's Jules." He rolls his eyes and mouths "sorry" to me, his fingers still tangled with mine. I should pull my hand free.

I don't want to.

"JuJu has a girl there!" Bex whisper-shouts to Anders.

Jules groans. "Enough about that. How are you feeling, Bex?"

I hear a loud sigh through the speaker. "Like a fucking whale."

My eyebrows shoot up, which Jules catches. "How many more weeks?" he asks her.

"Too many," she says at the same time Anders says, "Four."

"I just want to get this baby out of me! I don't know how Mom did this four times."

And now I get it—she's pregnant too. *Too.* Ugh, I want to vomit.

I think Jules can tell because he puts an end to the conversation pretty quickly. "I'll call you back later, okay?"

"Need to go make out with your giiiiirrrrllfriend?" Bex drags the word out for emphasis, but Jules just shoots her a disapproving look. "Use protection!" she adds, and then she's gone.

"If only she knew," I reply.

"She'd be fucking elated," he says. "She'd probably make Anders pack up their entire apartment and move back here tomorrow."

"Is it her first?" I ask.

"Second. Elodie is two and they're having another girl. They won't tell us the name, and I think it's because they can't decide."

"Where do they live?"

Jules hands me another muffin. "New York City. Anders is an actor. He's also Gabe's best friend—that's how he and Bex met."

"So you're an uncle. That's why kids don't scare you?"

He ponders that for a moment. "I wouldn't say they don't scare me. But the excitement outweighs the terror."

"Newborns are hard. They just scream at you all the time."

"I believe that," he says. "You also didn't have anyone to help you last time."

I'm immediately defensive. "I had my dad."

He nods. "You're right. And I love the relationship he and Chloe have, from what I've seen of it. You know he'd be there for you this time, as well. You'd also have my parents, Ben, Gabe, Bex and her family if they do eventually move back... and you'd have me, Thea."

Hesitantly, he brushes my hair off my face, tracing down my cheek until his finger rests under my chin. "This time could be different."

"Maybe," I breathe, willing myself to pull away.

"I'll take 'maybe,'" he whispers before kissing my forehead in one of the most tender gestures I've ever received. "Now, let's go make some posters, shall we?"

And that's exactly how we spend the rest of the afternoon. Making posters, hanging them around town, and keeping my mind occupied. I shouldn't be surprised that Jules knows the perfect way to help me process everything, but I am. By the end of the day, when it's time to head back to the apartment for dinner, I've made my decision.

As we are walking down the sidewalk, I turn to Jules, butterflies erupting in my stomach. "I'm going to keep it. If that's okay with you."

He ducks his head and smiles, tucking his hands into his pockets. "Yeah," he replies. "That's definitely okay with me."

Chapter Eighteen
WE'LL BE OKAY
Jules

WE'LL FIGURE IT OUT
Smithfield

I tentatively approach my family home, unsure of how tonight's dinner is going to go. I fire off a quick text to Thea to make sure she's still okay with our plan.

> It's still fine if I tell everyone tonight?

THEA
I mean, Ben and Gabe already suspect…

> And we can leave them suspecting if that's what you're comfortable with.

THEA
Just… rip off the bandaid I guess

Hesitation consumes me. I want to call her, but I need to trust that she was being honest when she said I could tell my family about the baby.

> Would you like me to be there when you tell Hank?

THEA
> No
>
> I'm a big girl

> We can do this. *high five emoji*

THEA
> ......
>
> Wow that was weird
>
> But thank you Jules
>
> Call me later?

> Yeah, I'll call you.

Pocketing my phone as I walk in, the usual Bardot family chaos greets me like an old friend. Gabe and Ben are arguing about the best cut of meat for a steak. Ben, the more practical of the two... barely, has chosen the crowd favorite: filet mignon. Which makes a hell of a lot more sense than Gabe's choice of—

"Tomahawk, Gabriel? That's really what you're going with?" I interject.

"C'mon! You have to admit it's the coolest cut of meat. You can use it like a meat sword!"

Ben pipes up then. "Mom, did you drop Gabe on his head a lot when he was a baby?"

Unbothered, she answers, "I think that was your father's doing, my cabbage." She's sitting in her favorite plush armchair, drinking a glass of red wine—pinot noir if I had to guess. Bending over, I place a quick kiss on the top of her head. She responds by patting my cheek and saying, "How are you feeling, darling?"

When I answer her with a confused look she continues. "You took a sick day on Friday, no?"

Oh. I see what she's doing.

"You know I wasn't sick, Mother."

"Don't 'Mother' me! I'm doing my duty—it's my job to make sure my children are taken care of."

Heaving a sigh, I fall back onto the couch across from her and cross my ankle over my knee. "You and I both know if you were actually concerned about my wellbeing, you would have come to check on me before family dinner tonight."

Mom takes a sip of her wine, eyeing me over the rim. "People might have seen you and a certain young woman out and about and let me know that you didn't look sick at all."

I look over at Ben and Gabe, but they both shrug, holding their hands up to convey innocence. Innocence I'm not entirely convinced is genuine.

"Looks like everything is going well with… what was her name again?"

"Thea," Gabe answers.

"She knows her name, Gabriel. Mom is trying to get me to talk, which I was actually planning on doing anyway if you would stop being so weird about it." I aim the last part at Mom who looks completely nonplussed.

Again, I'm doubting the authenticity of this reaction.

"Where's Dad?" I redirect.

"In here!" he calls from the kitchen. "Dinner is ready—everyone come sit down."

It's only my brothers here this week, as it has been most Sunday nights since Bex moved. I know Mom and Dad would love for the dining table to be busting at the seams, we just… aren't there yet.

We eat dinner and make the usual small talk. Dad asks about progress with the coffee shop—non-existent as we wait for quotes from contractors—and Mom tells us all about her current group of students, updating us on some of the grad students she's grown attached to. The entire time I feel like a ticking time bomb. At any moment I might explode, yelling, "Thea's pregnant!" at the top of my lungs.

When we reach the end of the meal, Ben suggests we give Bex a call to check in on her family. Which means I need to find a way to calm myself down so I can reveal my life-changing news. Bex picks up on the third ring, a bowl resting on her belly and Elodie climbing across the couch pillows behind her. I rub my sweaty palms up and down my jeans as everyone waves to Bex and El.

"I'm still pregnant," is the first thing she says when she answers.

"And you're doing great, mon chou," Mom calls.

Ben, who is sitting directly next to Mom, winces and covers his ear. "You don't have to yell, Mom. She can hear you."

Even though it's hard to see Bex on the tiny screen, I know her well enough to know that there's a wicked glint in her eye. "Acutally, can you speak louder? It is pretty hard to hear you."

"Of course, darling!" Mom continues, her voice a notch louder than it was before. "Where's my favorite son?"

"Rude," Gabe mutters at the same time Anders' voice comes through with, "I'm right here, Elaine!"

Anders' face pops onto the screen. "Don't be jealous, Gabey Wabey!"

I reach back, untying my hair and running my fingers through it a few times trying to figure out the best time to interject.

"Hey!" Bex cuts in over Anders and Gabe bickering. "What's wrong with you?"

"Me?" Gabe replies. "I didn't—"

"Not you!" she replies. "JuJu. Why are you messing with your hair? What's wrong?"

Tying my hair back up as quickly as possible, I reply, "I'm fine. What are you talking about?"

Her eyes narrow, seeing straight into my soul even through the phone screen. "Bullshit."

A sigh rushes out. Of course Bex knows my tells. I scrub my hands down my face, leaving them there so I don't have to see anyone's reaction. "Thea's pregnant."

Anders is the first to respond. "Oh shit."

Bex follows right behind him with, "I'm sorry, what did you just say?"

"Thea is pregnant," I repeat.

"Didn't you two just meet?" she asks, disbelief in her voice.

Mom chimes in with, "It only takes once—you should know that, Rebecca!"

I peek between my fingers and see Ben holding his hand out to Gabe who is pulling his wallet out of his back pocket.

"What the fuck is that?" I point between them.

Ben shrugs. "I was right."

Looking over at Mom, she's beaming. "And what is *that*?" I wave a hand in her general direction. She clasps her hands together under her chin, her eyes shining in the overhead light. "Are you… crying?"

"This is so exciting, Julien!" Mom wails. "I get to be a grandma!"

"You are a grandma!" Bex scolds, making the smallest smile appear on my face.

Dad looks like he's trying to contain himself, after all, he is the more levelheaded of my two parents. "How are you feeling about everything?"

His voice cuts through the chaos, soothing me so that I feel like I can give him an honest answer.

"I'm terrified," I reply. "But… I'm also really fucking happy."

"Good man," Dad says, his grin matching mine now.

In fact, when I look around the table I see that everyone looks as excited as I feel. And that's when I know that we—me, Thea, Chloe, and this baby—are going to be perfectly fine.

Later that night, I call Thea to check in. She sounds groggy when she answers.

"Did I wake you?" I ask. I'm sitting in my back garden, the damn cat curled up on my lap, looking up at the sky. I've always been in awe of the vastness of the universe, the stars that connect everyone in this huge, but also incredibly small, world.

"I dozed off on the couch," she replies. "How did it go? Did you tell your family?"

"Yeah." I scratch behind the cat's ears—the feel of its purring body grounding me. "They were thrilled."

"Thrilled?" Thea's surprise makes me laugh.

"Yes, Thea. My family... as chaotic as they may be, they love hard. I've never seen them hesitate when it comes to whether or not to accept someone new into the fold."

"But they don't even know me," she whispers. "What if they realize I'm some wicked witch of the west?"

"They know me, Thea. They trust me and I trust you," I confess. "How did Hank take the news?"

She's quiet for a while, so I wait. I can hear her breathing, so I match my breath with hers. She'll talk when she's ready, so I don't push.

"It was weird," she finally starts. "With Chloe's pregnancy, I think he went into fix-it mode. He never liked Chloe's dad... plus the whole ending of my career thing—it was a shock. This time he nodded and said, 'I like Jules.' And that was it. The entire time we ate dinner, I kept staring at him, waiting for him to say something else about it. Eventually he told me to cut it out, so I did."

"We're going to be okay, Thea."

"I might need you to tell me that a few more times before the baby gets here," she replies.

"I can remind you every day, if that's what you need."

"That would be nice," she sighs. "November, I think. If I'm doing the math correctly."

"November seems like a good month."

"Yeah," she says around a yawn. "It does, doesn't it?"

"Go to bed, Thea. I'll check on you tomorrow, okay? Remind you that we'll be okay."

We say our goodbyes and hang up. I spend a few more minutes outside, enjoying the cold night air. November seems so far away, but I vow right then and there to continue to show up for Thea. Not to rush her, to give her the space she needs, to show her that this can work. That we can build a family.

Before I head inside, I take one last look at the midnight-black sky full of stars winking in encouragement.

"We're going to be okay," I whisper to those stars.

They seem to reply with, *Yes, you are.*

Chapter Nineteen
ELEPHANT GESTATION
Thea

SAFETY NET
Ariana Grande

> I have some news...

MAGS
What kind of news? fun news? Did you sleep with Tattoo McHottie??

> Yes and...

MAGS
Omg was it soooo good???

> It was and...

MAGS
And what Thea? Spit it out!

> What can happen when you have sex with someone Magnolia?

Incoming call from Mags

ENTIRELY YOURS

The next several weeks fly by. I still feel the occasional morning sickness, which actually comes at any point in the day, but for the most part I'm just exhausted.

Jules gets an OBGYN suggestion from his mom, and Cole—who seems like she's forcing her way into my life more and more—confirms that Elaine Bardot is a reliable source. I haven't met Jules' parents yet which seems odd because I see his brothers all the time.

Maybe Jules is ashamed of me? Of *us*? He doesn't really act like that is the case, but I'm too nervous to find out the truth, so I just haven't brought it up.

I know that Guy's reaction to my pregnancy with Chloe did a number on me, but it's become even more evident now that I feel like I'm reliving that entire reality four years later. Logically, I know that Jules and Guy are as different as they possibly could be, like comparing apples and oranges, but my body is having trouble remembering that truth.

I tense up every time I get a text or call from Jules, or even when he's quiet for too long, which is also a distinct possibility with him—that man is the definition of the strong, silent type. I'm learning he prefers to listen and process rather than interject his every thought. It feels as though he's giving me the space to make my own decisions about everything, which is great, but also… different than what I'm used to.

There was so much I had to prove to Guy. He was my superior in the ballet company, and though he obviously developed a liking toward me, he was always so hot and cold.

If I questioned him in class, he wouldn't return my calls for a week.

If I was five minutes late to rehearsal, he'd move me to the back row for a number.

If I didn't pick up on choreography fast enough, he'd make

me practice with him at his home studio until he was satisfied I wouldn't forget it.

But, damn. When I did get it right?

He'd take me out to dinner and spend the rest of the night lavishing me with praise. Or a new pair of pointe shoes would show up at my apartment. One time, he even had me demonstrate a lift to the rest of the company. I had never felt so important.

Then I would make some minuscule mistake and the cycle would start over again. This continued until I found out I was pregnant with Chloe, which was apparently the ultimate betrayal.

Fuck him.

My phone dings, dragging me out of my spiral.

JULES

Did you get an appointment?

> Yeah, it's next Thursday. I'll be about 8 weeks along.

The three little dots pop up and then go away and then pop up again. I hate that I stare so intensely at the screen while I wait. Finally, he responds.

JULES

Would it be okay if I came to the appointment?

Oh. I honestly hadn't thought about that. I scrunch my face up and repeat the mantra I've had running through my head lately: *Give him a chance.*

> Ok.

The day of the appointment, I'm a nervous wreck. I haven't seen Jules in over a week, though we've texted back and forth—he makes sure to remind me daily that we'll be okay. He also left some nausea remedies in a bag on my doorstep last weekend but didn't knock to let me know he'd dropped by.

When Ben and Gabe are home, they usually prop their door open so Chloe can run back and forth between the two apartments. She loves her newfound freedom now that I don't feel like I have to watch her like a hawk.

She's over there now, and Dad is dozing in his La-Z-Boy. I think he appreciates other adults being around, too, but would never say that outright. I walk over and lightly shake his shoulder.

"Dad, wake up."

His eyes pop open. "Huh? What? I was awake. What're you on about?"

He always claims he was actually awake and not taking a nap. "Right, well I'm about to leave. You still good with Chloe?"

He nods the affirmative, so I head over to get her from her new best friends' house.

Walking into the hallway, I almost run smack into baby daddy himself. He's holding a single stem rose—this one is peach.

"Holy shit, you scared me! How are your steps so quiet?" I demand.

His usual smirk appears beneath his trimmed facial hair, and I can't help but ask, "Have you ever considered a mustache?"

Jules raises an eyebrow, holding the rose out for me. "Hello to you too, Thea."

I take it, thanking him, and respond with, "I think we've moved past that, though, it's been so long since I've seen you, maybe formal greetings are in order."

He opens his mouth to speak when a little blonde streak runs into the hallway, pausing long enough to take the rose from me. "Hi, JuJu! Bye, JuJu!" And then she's gone, but I immediately clock the flinch that crosses Jules' face.

"I can tell her not to call you that if you don't like it."

"No!" he rushes out. "I-I like that she calls me that. My sister does, too. I…" He shoves his hands in his pockets which draws my eye to his tanned and tattooed forearms. "I always want to make sure I'm respecting your boundaries with Chloe."

My eyes snap back up to his because that is oddly refreshing to hear from a man. I take a deep breath. "Listen, we are going to be co-parenting, which will obviously be new for all of us. I really cannot see you crossing any lines that you shouldn't, but I'll let you know if you do. Deal?" And for some reason it feels like a good idea to hold my hand out for him to shake.

He stares down at it for a beat before sliding his hand into mine. It's rough and warm and—dammit! This is the reason we are here in the first place.

I snatch my hand back and brush past him toward the stairs. "Right. Let's go," I call over my shoulder.

Jules doesn't respond but I can feel him behind me.

In fact, he's silent all the way to the doctor's office. He insisted on driving, opening the door for me, and even helping me into the car, though, that felt like an excuse for us to touch again.

I didn't mind.

What I do mind, however, is the silence.

My palms are sweating, and I really should get an award for the amount of times I hold back from blurting out a random statement. After we park, Jules reaches over and stops my hands from rubbing up and down my thighs for the zillionth time.

"I'm nervous, too," he says.

"I'm not nervous! I was just thinking about how an elephant has, like, an abnormally long gestation period and how terrible that must be. Chloe was early. Did I tell you that? Not like crazy early but still totally caught me off guard. Though, I think I also would have been caught off guard if she had been born on time. But, yeah. Elephants. Longest gestation."

"I always thought it was the sperm whale."

"You might be right... that would be ironic. We'll need to google it. Can you google it?"

I can feel him smiling. "I'll google it when we get inside. How about that?"

Nodding vigorously, I unbuckle my seatbelt and hop out of the car.

Per usual, I can feel Jules' presence behind me.

We walk into the office, and I check in while Jules finds a seat. When I sit down next to him he says, "You were right. Elephants have the longest gestation period. They weigh up to 300 pounds at birth."

"Fucking hell. Chloe was five pounds and I thought I'd never recover."

Jules eyes me warily. "I'm kidding. Obviously I knew I'd recover." I didn't. I was nineteen and terrified.

Ten minutes or an hour passes by before a nurse comes out and calls my name. Jules and I both stand, but he immediately grabs my elbow. "I can wait here or I can come with you, either way."

The thought of being alone right now does not sound appealing. "Come with me, please," I whisper.

The nurse, an older woman who looks like she's seen thousands of pregnant women in her lifetime, takes my vitals, and then we are ushered into a room where I'm instructed to undress before the nurse leaves.

"I'll just..." Jules turns around.

I stand there awkwardly as the last time I was undressed with Jules flashes into my mind. Quickly I remove all my clothes. I'm about to put on the ultra-flattering medical gown when the nurse knocks twice and pops the door open before I have a chance to say "Wait!"

Her eyes are covered but she does have a plastic cup in her

hand. "Forgot to give you this!" Jules is closest so he takes the cup from her, turning to hand it to me. He obviously didn't realize I wasn't dressed because the full frontal view he gets causes him to drop the pee cup he's holding.

"Shit." He immediately covers his eyes, dropping down to the floor to feel around for the cup. I wrap the gown around me as fast as I can—a terrible attempt at covering what he's already seen—and tell him he can open his eyes. Instead, he slots his fingers slightly open but keeps his hand up just in case. I watch as he looks around, finds the cup, and murmurs, "I'll get a new one," before leaving me alone in the room.

Chapter Twenty
ORAL SEX LECTURES
Jules

PASTA
New Rules

The first thought that flashes through my mind is, *Fuck, she's beautiful.* Even standing in the fluorescent office lighting, I know the sight of her bare chest will be flashing through my mind for months to come. Unfortunately, my body doesn't recognize that this is not the time nor the place, and I can feel my dick hardening. I close my eyes and start humming the birthday song in an attempt to distract myself.

"Everything okay, Daddy?" *Well, that will do it.* The older nurse pops out of nowhere to check in, effectively scaring the shit out of me and providing the distraction I was looking for.

"Uh, I dropped this," I say, holding up the cup. "Can we get a new one?"

"Sure, honey! Just a sec."

She quickly returns with a new sterile cup, and I knock on the exam room door, waiting for confirmation before entering. I keep my eyes averted as I shuffle in.

"Jules, I'm covered. You can look at me." Thea sounds

annoyed by my modesty so I meet her eyes, holding contact until she's the one who looks away.

"Is that for me?"

I hold the cup up, examining it. "No, they want me to pee in it."

The look on her face is pure confusion, so I wink and hand her the cup. That earns me a huge grin as she guffaws at my attempt at humor. It's enough to break the ice, and I can feel the tension floating out of the room.

"I can't believe you just made a *joke*, Julien Bardot." She laughs, hopping off the table. "Be right back."

She is back a few minutes later, and I definitely do not spend the entire time thinking about her naked breasts. The cup is still in her hand and still empty. I raise my brow in question. "The nurse said she didn't realize the doctor wanted to do a sonogram so she told me to wait," she answers. I nod, and we sit in comfortable silence until the doctor knocks on the door. "Come in," Thea calls.

Dr. Mitchell has been friends with my mom for years, both strong women working in the medical field.

"I see the oral sex didn't work," Dr. Mitchell starts. Another thing she and Mom have in common—neither one of them have a filter. She winks at me as Thea splutters, her face reddening.

"Good to see you, too, Dr. Mitchell," I reply. "This is Thea Rose, my—" I have no idea how to finish that sentence.

Thankfully, the women in the room ignore me and shake hands. "Hi, Thea! I'm guessing Elaine didn't give you her oral sex lecture based on that reaction," Dr. Mitchell jokes. Instead of answering, Thea looks at me, wide-eyed.

"I'll explain later," I mutter.

Dr. Mitchell claps her hands together. "Well, let's get into it! We'll do a sonogram first, just to confirm everything looks good. I saw on your intake paperwork that this isn't your first pregnancy. Want to tell me a bit about your first pregnancy and birth?"

Thea sighs. "I was very young, and it was a pretty uncomplicated but stressful pregnancy. I ended up going into labor at thirty-four weeks." My head snaps up at that because this is the first time I'm hearing this. I know Thea said Chloe was early, but I thought that meant maybe a week or two, at most. "My previous doctor thinks it was due to stress. Chloe was five pounds two ounces when she was born and spent seven days in the NICU."

"How is she now?" Dr. Mitchell asks.

A small smile graces Thea's lips. "Perfect."

Dr. Mitchell places a comforting hand on Thea's shoulder. "I'm so glad to hear that. Let's take a look at this new baby, shall we?"

She gets the sonogram machine ready, maneuvering us so that I'm up near Thea's head and we can both see the monitor. "I usually have the sonographer do this, but as soon as I heard it was a Bardot baby, I knew I wanted to be the one to do it. A little pressure," she says to Thea.

"I can leave if this is too intimate," I whisper to Thea.

"I'm fine. Look."

Tearing my eyes away from Thea, I look at the monitor and—"Oh my God."

The blob on the screen looks nothing like a baby but after a few taps on Dr. Mitchell's machine, we can hear the heartbeat. It's the most magnificent sound I've ever heard. Looking back at Thea, her smile is shaky but present. I feel an immense relief knowing she's not disappointed in the confirmation we're seeing on the screen.

Dr. Mitchell's voice draws me back to the sonogram. "Baby looks good! Measuring eight weeks three days. We'll do a blood draw and urine analysis before you leave, and I'll see you in four weeks!"

"Wait, that's it?" I ask. I want to keep watching the blob—my blob—on the screen.

Dr. Mitchell laughs, grabbing the printouts and passing them to Thea. "You can look at the pictures in the meantime. See you both soon. Thea, if you need anything between now and then, don't hesitate to call the office!" And with that, she's gone.

Thea sits up, handing me the photos. I run my fingers over the image, in complete awe that I helped make that.

"You didn't tell me Chloe was born that early," I say, looking up at Thea.

"You didn't tell me your mom gives oral sex lectures," she diverts.

I scrub my beard. "My family can be... a lot."

Thea chuckles at that. "I've met your brothers." She sighs. "I wasn't trying to keep Chloe's prematurity from you. I still have a lot to process about the entire situation. Lingering trauma, I guess. The doctor seemed pretty confident it wouldn't happen again as long as I can keep my stress levels down."

"I'll help however I can with that," I promise.

"I know you will."

I bob my head, so much more to say, but I have no idea how to say it. After a moment, I start with, "Thank you again for letting me come today. That was... the coolest thing I've ever seen."

"Just wait until it actually looks like a baby," she replies. "Well, more like a little alien but it's still pretty cool."

I can't wait, but I don't tell her that. "I'll step out while you get dressed," I say instead.

When she comes out of the room, I have the undeniable urge to hug her. She's so strong, and it's hitting me even more now that I know how much she had to go through alone during her pregnancy and birth with Chloe. "Can I—I'd like to hug you, if that's okay."

"Yeah, Jules. That's okay." I catch the smallest of smirks before she steps into my arms. I feel her take a deep breath and sink further into me.

"I support you, Chloe, and this baby no matter what, okay?" I ask. I feel her nod in response. "Let me support you, yeah?"

This time there's a moment's hesitation, but finally she nods again—a huge weight lifting off my shoulders as she does.

Pressing my lips to the top of her head, I murmur a quiet, "Thank you."

She takes one more deep breath before pulling back and subtly wiping at her eyes. "Alright, enough of that. Let's go," she sing-songs, a false cheeriness in her voice. A mask I'm beginning to recognize.

She takes off before I have a chance to say anything else, and I follow her. Something I find myself more and more willing to do.

Chapter Twenty-One
SLEEPOVER AT JUJU'S
Thea

JOLENE
Dolly Parton

Between Chloe's preferred sleeping position—feet planted firmly on my lower back—and the amount of time it's taken to finish painting the studio—I still need to come up with a proper name—I am exhausted. And maybe a little bit snippy.

"Thea?" my Dad bellows from the kitchen.

"What?!" I snap. Nothing drives me crazier than when someone yells across the house for you instead of just walking to find you.

Okay, maybe I'm a lot bit snippy.

Dad gets the idea, though, and within a few moments he's poked his head into my room. "Everything alright, darlin'?" he asks.

"You mean aside from being accidentally impregnated again?" I flop down onto the bed, abandoning the laundry I was folding.

Dad's head swivels around to check for Chloe. I still haven't told her that she's getting a little brother or sister. She's entirely too inquisitive right now, and I'm not ready to answer those questions. "She's 'doing her makeup'"—I add the air quotes—"and listening to Dolly with her headphones on."

"I thought I heard her singing the chorus of *Jolene* a moment ago."

"Her favorite," we say simultaneously, because yes, my four-year-old is obsessed with a song about a woman trying to steal another woman's man.

"In Dolly we trust," he adds before we both cross ourselves like we are offering a prayer up to Dolly Parton herself.

"Anyway, did you need something?" I ask.

He reaches up and twists his mustache. "Yeah, I was thinkin' about enchiladas for dinner. That sound good to you?"

The newest pregnancy symptom this week is food aversions. Dad was cooking ground beef last week and I had to go over to Ben and Gabe's to escape the smell. "That's fine, just no beef." I want to throw up just thinking about it.

"Chicken enchiladas, aye aye, Captain." He salutes and then turns on his cowboy booted heel and walks out of the room.

One thing about Hank Rose is he'll always be wearing cowboy boots. It doesn't matter that we've lived in Massachusetts for almost eight years at this point. He also cooks Tex-Mex any chance he gets because he has yet to find one restaurant that is up to his standards. One time he even went as far as to leave cash on the table and walk out when a waiter brought over queso that looked alarmingly neon.

I'm about to get back to the laundry task at hand when I hear a blood curdling, "MAMA!" A sound that cuts to the soul of any parent within hearing distance.

Sprinting to the bathroom, Dad, Chloe, and I all converge outside the door. Immediately, I bend down and check for injuries. "What's wrong, baby? What happened?" I don't wear any sort of smart watch but if I did it would probably be telling me to go to the hospital for an abnormal heart rate.

"I didn't do it!" she wails, one eye covered in blue eyeshadow and blush across the entirety of her forehead.

"Didn't do what, Chlo?" Dad asks, also bending down to her level.

"It"—*sob*—"just"—*sob*—"did"—*sob*—"it!" And another sob for good measure.

I push Chloe's hair back and place her hand on my chest, a strategy we use to help regulate when we feel big emotions. "Honey, you have to breathe so you can tell us what you're talking about. Did you break something? It's okay if you made a mess, we can clean it up."

"Water!" she wails again.

"I can get you some water, will that help?" I ask.

"Shit, Thea, look." Dad pushes the door open and, sure enough, there's water everywhere.

"Fuck!" I yell.

"Language!" Chloe sobs.

"Get some towels," Dad grumbles.

All three of us scramble to throw towels onto the ground to soak up the water. It doesn't take long to find the busted pipe under the sink, spewing water faster than we can sop it up.

"How do we get it off?" I'm panicking as the water starts to make its way into the hall.

"Call the landlord," Dad instructs. "I can't do much while the water is still on."

I quickly find my phone and dial our landlord, Kathy, who does not answer even after three back to back calls.

"Go ask Louie!" Dad suggests, still attempting to manage the water flow.

Chloe's little hand finds mine, and I run out our front door, across the hall, and pound on the Bardot brothers' door.

Gabe answers. "Woah, Thea everything okay?" His eyes flash down to my stomach.

"Can you watch Chloe for a second? One of our pipes burst,

and I need to go find Louie because Kathy isn't answering her damn phone!"

He doesn't even hesitate before saying, "Go, go! I've got Chloe."

As I'm racing down the stairs I hear Chloe say, "I'd rather have Ben." The cheek on that one. I wonder where she gets it.

Thankfully, Louie knows just what to do, and we finally get the water off, but not before it floods both bedrooms and part of the living room.

Once we've cleared as much as we can out of the path of water, I go back down to Louie's to check and see if he had any damage. He confirms he's fine, shooing me back upstairs.

Instead, I take a moment to breathe, the cool night air a shock to my system. I am *this close* to breaking down in tears when I spot a tall, brooding, and dark man running down the street toward me. TBD to the rescue, again.

"Thea! Is everything okay? Gabe called."

This fucking man isn't even out of breath.

I open my mouth to answer him but all that comes out is a weird half-hiccup, half-whimper.

He wraps me in another one of his hugs that I like way too much. He's so solid and warm and I really want to play with his hair.

That thought makes me laugh, and all of a sudden I'm laugh-crying into the shirt of the man who put a baby in me.

He gives me one last squeeze before he says, "C'mon. Let's get some bags packed for you guys. You'll stay at my house tonight."

And I really don't feel like arguing.

―――

Obviously I've been to Jules' house before. What I didn't realize last time was that its got four fucking bedrooms. FOUR. I've never lived in a place with four bedrooms. What does he do with all of the space? When I asked him why all four of his bedrooms had actual beds in them, he rubbed the back of his neck and said something about not knowing what else to do with them.

The room he put me in does have several instruments and a whole computer set up that looks like it's built specifically for musicians. Little slidey knobs on a board and a mic that looks like it cost more than a month's rent.

Chloe, of course, flipped her shit when she realized she would get her own room. "Just for tonight," I reminded her several times.

Jules and Dad both responded to that line with, "We'll see about that," before eyeing each other warily. It was pretty cute, actually.

Jules is going to be a great dad. It's confusing because he exudes protective-dad energy but also *daddy* energy at the same time. The whole situation is messing with my head.

Chloe was also thrilled when we arrived last night because Jules still hasn't found the owner of the cat we made posters for. She decided on a very original name of Mayor Cattington the Third or "Cat" for short. Dad snorted and asked what happened to Mayor Cattington the First and Second—"They died, obviously," Chloe informed him—I rolled my eyes, and I'm pretty sure I saw Jules quickly order an entire cat mansion to make Chloe happy.

Now the morning has rolled around, and I'm refusing to get out of the bed that gave me the best night's sleep I've had in years.

I'm refusing, but—is that bacon I smell?

Slowly, I peel the covers off and trudge into the kitchen. Not only is there bacon, but there's also fancy coffee because apparently Jules has no flaws.

"Mama! Look! JuJu made me coffee, too!" Chloe chirps.

"It's hot chocolate," he whispers as he passes me a mug.

I walk over and sit down next to Chloe at the breakfast table, ruffling her hair. "That's fun, my little chicken. How'd you sleep?"

"So good! But I missed you, Mama. I know you sleep better with me."

I'll let her believe that's true, for now.

"Well, hopefully we'll be back in our bed together tonight," I say, mustering as much false enthusiasm as I can before drinking any coffee.

"You won't," Dad chimes in. He's scowling down at his own coffee, and I can't tell if that's because it's not his usual tar or because of the words that just came out of his mouth. "Talked to Kathy before you woke up, and she said it'll be a few weeks before we can get back in. We can go by today and get whatever is salvageable, but we definitely won't be sleeping there tonight."

"We—I—*what?*" I know our rooms were partially flooded, but it didn't seem several-weeks bad.

"A plumber went by to check things out and found some additional leaking. Kathy apologized profusely for not answering your calls, by the way. Said she was in the middle of a rousing game of cribbage."

I snort. "Is that a euphemism?"

"What's a u-mism?" Chloe asks.

All of the adults in the room look at each other. "Uhm, it's a game," I finally come up with.

"I love games," she replies, taking a big sip of her hot cocoa and leaving a chocolate mustache in its wake.

I turn back to Dad. "I'll look around today for other apartments. Surely there's somewhere we can stay temporarily."

"You'll stay here." Jules is standing at the kitchen counter, arms crossed, and a look of finality on his face.

My mouth pops open.

"Close your mouth, darlin'. You look like fresh caught catfish." Thanks for that analogy, Dad.

"But—we can't—"

"You heard the man. We're staying here." Dad sips his coffee, unbothered. "I like the cat."

Kathy did indeed give us time to go by the apartment and pack up our things. Jules decided to come with us too, but what he didn't tell me is that he's recruited the entire Bardot family, minus his sister and her family, to help. They're all lined up outside of Louie's waiting for us.

The man doesn't even have the audacity to look ashamed at this. In fact, he's got one of the biggest smiles I've seen on him yet. Which is to say, he's smirking with a twinkle in his eye.

He walks up to the curly headed woman that must be his mother. I can immediately tell that her personality is much more akin to Ben and Gabe's. She squeezes Jules' cheeks and shouts, "Good morning, my cabbage!"

"Morning, Mom." He leans down and gives her a kiss on the cheek before turning to his dad and giving him a hug.

Mr. Bardot is... *hot*. He looks just like Jules will in twenty to thirty years, and it has me questioning my decision to keep Jules at arms length.

"Mom, Dad, this is Thea, her daughter, Chloe, and her dad, Hank. Rose family, this is Elaine and Hugo Bardot. You can blame them for those two." He gestures to his brothers who both pretend to be deeply offended.

Elaine looks like she's about to burst. "It's so nice to meet you. God, you're gorgeous—good job, Julien." This last part is aimed toward her son. "Can I give you a hug?"

I barely nod before she's rushing over, practically tackling me in an embrace. "I've always wanted a daughter."

"Don't you—"

"I'm telling Bex you said that," Gabe calls.

Elaine lets go of me and scolds, "Gabriel. You will say

nothing unless you want me to dethrone you as my favorite son."

"Everyone knows Anders is your favorite son," Jules chimes in.

"I think Benoit is my favorite son right now, actually."

"Benoit? Your name isn't Benjamin?" I ask.

"No, but that's a very common assumption," Ben replies.

"It's not an assumption, that's what Cole calls you."

Ben's head immediately snaps to me at that. "Cole talks about me?" He sounds like a puppy who is finally getting attention from his owner.

All of us stop and stare at him. He seems to realize what he just said and backtracks with, "I mean, ha! Yeah, that Cole. She always calls me the wrong name. Silly really…"

Even Chloe can see through Ben's bullshit. She tilts her head, inspecting him before she says, "You kind of look like Kristoff when he realizes Anna went on an adventure without him."

"Enough of that, Princess Chloe!" Ben picks her up and carries her over to the apartment building entrance. "Let's get your things, shall we? I heard you get to stay at JuJu's house." He looks over his shoulder and winks at me.

"News travels fast around here." I scowl.

"Yes, it does, dear." Elaine pats me on the arm. "We can talk about any other news at Sunday dinner tonight."

Great.

Chapter Twenty-Two
BOSSY
Jules

PLAYING HOUSE
phem

I underestimated how chaotic it would be to live with a four-year-old. I also underestimated how much I would love it. People assume I like the quiet because *I* am quiet. But really I much prefer to be around people, as long as they understand that I'll likely be an observer to the goings-on.

That, and this house needed living in. That's partially why I haven't looked too hard for Mayor Cattington's owners. The vet said he wasn't chipped and was probably a stray. After Chloe's reaction to him, he's no longer a stray.

It didn't take long for the seven of us to pack up Thea's apartment, even with Chloe's lack of help and everyone scolding Thea every time she tried to lift something. I could tell she was frustrated because she kept mumbling, "I'm pregnant, not dead."

Most everything was salvageable, except for a few pieces of furniture and most of the stuff in the bathroom, but the apartment was definitely a sopping mess. I could see some of the water stains on the walls and parts of the ceiling beginning to bubble. I'm glad we got them out before something worse happened.

Chloe was a bit sad when she realized she wouldn't be across the hall from Ben for the time being, but he promised to visit often. Plus, I think all thoughts of Ben left her mind when Cat greeted us upon our return.

Thea laid down for a nap as soon as we got back. She emerges now, sleepy-eyed and glowing—I guess it's true what they say about pregnancy. Or maybe I'm just in way too deep already.

"Your mom said something about Sunday dinner?" she asks, plopping down beside me on the couch.

I hum. "It's kind of a recurring thing we do."

"Y'all eat dinner together every Sunday night?"

"Mhmm."

"That's adorable. I don't want to intrude though, we can make something here. I'll just need to run to the grocery store," she rambles.

I laugh because having the Roses at Sunday dinner would be the furthest thing from an intrusion. It's always been *the more the merrier* at the Bardot house. I think that's why I crave a little more chaos in my own home. "You'll come to Sunday dinner, Thea. No need to cook anything here."

"Bossy," she mutters.

"I can be..." I let the innuendo linger.

She hesitates. "Tempting, but I think that's how we got into this situation in the first place." She rubs her belly, which is not even showing yet, and it does something... *primal* to me.

"What time is dinner? We typically eat early because toddler bedtime is a delicate dance. But I can get Chlo a snack to hold her over."

The aforementioned toddler is currently drawing her twelfth picture of Cat using all of my printer paper and a sharpie because I don't own any washable markers. She hears the word snack and abandons her pursuits. "Mama, I am *starving*."

Thea raises her eyebrow at me as if to say, *the drama!*

"Have you ever had ants on a log?"

Chloe scrunches up her nose. "Gross! I would never eat ants or logs, JuJu!"

Smiling, I say, "Come with me."

Dinner that night is a little earlier than usual out of respect for Chloe and her bedtime. Everyone is there aside from Bex, Anders, and Elodie. They'll sometimes take the train up if Anders is off, but Bex is due any day now so their visits have slowed. I wouldn't be surprised if a FaceTime call happened before we left, though.

Shockingly, Hugo and Hank have become fast friends. Hank's no-nonsense southern drawl can be heard from the back deck where turkey and veggie burgers are on the grill. When I told Thea earlier that we were doing burgers tonight, her face turned green and she ran out of the room. I immediately called Dad and asked him to pick up an alternative.

Another reason I'm glad to have Thea living at my house—I had no idea her food aversions were so bad.

"It's not right to turn vegetables into a burger," Hank bemoans as I slide the back door open. "I might have to run out and grab some real dinner after Thea goes to bed—no offense," he says to Dad.

"None taken. I remember when Bex was pregnant with Elodie, she was craving fried pickles specifically from Louie's. Anders drove up here on several occasions just to get them for her. There's no way they were any good by the time he made it back to the city, but what are we supposed to say to a woman who is carrying our baby? No?" Dad laughs, as if that idea is unfathomable. I think about Thea rubbing her belly earlier, and I realize it *is* unfathomable.

"Thea's mom loved sushi. It's all she wanted when she was pregnant. I'd make her different variations of 'sushi' with ingredients she was allowed to have." He pauses, reminiscing on a memory that it seems like he hasn't thought of in a while. "She hated every last version I made," he laughs. "We lived out in west Texas at the time and there aren't a lot of reputable sushi options—at least not back then. We had to drive to the big city as soon as we left the hospital so Shirley could get her some sushi."

Hank flips a burger over and says, "I'd do it all over again in a heartbeat."

Silence descends upon the three of us. More reverent than uncomfortable, though. A mutual understanding of the role we play. I feel honored that I get to be a part of this hallowed tradition, men taking care of their women, as primitive as that sounds. I suppose that's evolution—the innate desire within us to care for the young and the vulnerable.

That thought causes me to chuckle though, because I think if Thea heard me call her vulnerable, she'd pack up all of her things and move her ass out of my house.

Bex told me once that I needed someone to take care of me instead of me having to do the caring all the time. But I think deep down she knows how much I love it. How fulfilling it is for me. It's why I went into teaching in the first place, even though that has definitely become too draining.

I can't envision taking care of Thea ever becoming draining.

I look inside and see Thea teaching Ben how to braid Chloe's hair, and I think, *This is it. This is exactly what I've always wanted.*

Let's just hope Thea will actually let me have it.

She looks up just then and catches my eye. Her soft smile makes me think I might have a chance. I wink at her, enjoying the hell out of the blush that creeps up her cheeks.

Chapter Twenty-Three
THE BIRDS AND THE BEES
Thea

STUCK ON YOU
Meiko

Sunday night dinner at the Bardot house feels like being wrapped in a fluffy blanket on a cold winter day. Like the feeling of sitting by the fireplace with a new book. Or like that one time Guy took me to a nice hotel, and when I got out of the shower, the floors were warm. Damn, my feet were so toasty.

"Do you have heated tile in your bathrooms?" I ask Jules when he finishes up cleaning and comes to sit on the ground in front of me.

"I can if you want me to," he says, voice low. It's like now that he has me under his roof he's decided to turn up the sex appeal to a level twelve.

Tucking my feet up under me, I say, "That's a no."

"Unfortunately, that's a no. But I have been wanting to redo my bathrooms…" He trails off, tapping my leg in a manner that tells me he wants me to put my feet back down next to him.

"My feet are gross. They're so beat up and deformed after years and years in pointe shoes."

He nods but doesn't stop pulling at my leg. When I finally give in, he takes one of my feet and presses his thumb into the sole.

An ungodly sound leaves my body.

I've gotten used to pain over the years. As a professional dancer, something always hurts. If you stopped to attend to every ache and pain, you'd never get back up.

That and the fact that no one has ever so willingly offered to rub my feet.

This is what heaven feels like.

Jules continues his work while asking me questions. "How's the studio coming along? Think you'll be ready for summer classes?"

"I actually, ahh—" Jules' hand immediately stops to my utter dismay. "No! Don't stop."

He spears me with a wicked look and mumbles, "Yes, ma'am."

Clearing my throat, I continue. "I roped some college students into coming in for a few master classes next weekend. Between that and the fliers I've been passing out at all the local schools, I think I'll have some interest for the summer. I wanted to be open for spring break, but with everything going on, I don't think that will happen."

"I think you'll have a lot of interest for the summer," Jules confirms. "I heard some of my students talking about the new studio the other day. Apparently for the last few years, people have been commuting to the next town over for classes."

I can't help the excitement that bubbles up. And also the strange, warm feeling I get in the center of my chest knowing that Jules supports me in this dream.

I sigh. "When I had Chloe, I thought my life was over. All I had known for my entire life was ballet. I knew my career would look vastly different after having a baby, but I could only dream I would be able to continue dancing in some capacity. This studio is… it's an opportunity for me to take a chance on myself. It's completely terrifying. I think that's why I haven't been able to come up with a name for it yet."

Jules listens intently, his fingers are magic in the way they massage, and I'm sad when he switches feet. After a few minutes of silence, he says, "I get that. I feel the same way about the coffee shop. Maybe when we open, we can do some sort of promo—sign your kid up for dance class, get a free cup of coffee."

"That is… maybe the sweetest thing you've ever said to me." Truly, I might cry. Which is probably the hormones. "When are y'all planning to open by the way?"

"The million dollar question." He shrugs his shoulders. "We signed papers right around the time you moved here. I need to finish out the school year, and Gabe has a full-time job too, so it's really Ben that's managing everything right now. Once I'm off for the summer, I can help him more, and we can get the renovations done before opening."

"It's kind of convenient that we'll be next door to each other," I say.

He furrows his brows and quirks his lips. "Convenient is one word for it. How do your feet feel?"

A contented breath leaves me. "I'll let you do that anytime you want."

"Deal."

"Thea, dear! Come join me in the kitchen!" Elaine calls from the nearby room.

My eyes widen in Jules' direction. "I'm being summoned."

He smiles at me, knowingly. "Don't worry, she doesn't bite. She also doesn't have any boundaries so just signal if you need rescuing."

"Signal how?" I panic-whisper as Elaine pokes her head around the corner to make sure I'm coming.

"Can you whistle?" he asks, deadass serious.

"No, oh my God! I'm doomed."

"How about I come and check on you in about ten minutes." He squeezes my calf in an effort to calm me. It helps—sort of. I haven't had a mother figure since Grandmother passed when I was fifteen, and I desperately want to make a good impression on Elaine.

I hope she doesn't think I tricked her son into impregnating me. I walk into the kitchen with that wild thought running through my mind.

"Hi, Mrs. Bardot, thank you again for a lovely dinner. Sorry about the burgers," I add.

"Call me Elaine. And don't even worry about it, I quite prefer a veggie burger anyway." She smiles, and I can picture her raising four kids. Always with a comforting glance at the ready. I relax just a bit as she pulls out a kitchen chair for me and slides over a plate of cookies.

Seems a bit like bribery, but it's working.

"Everything went well with Dr. Mitchell?" Elaine asks.

I'm mid-bite of cookie already, so I finish chewing before answering. "Yes, she was very… blunt. But kind. Thank you for recommending her."

She waves me off. "Of course, we go way back. She was actually in one of my courses years ago, and I'm glad she ended up back in Sassafras after med school."

"Oh yeah, Jules mentioned you were a professor."

She hums. "Have been for a while now, yes. I still practice part time but most of my focus is on my work at our local university, Hawthorne."

"Practice? Are you also a gynecologist?" I must have missed that memo.

Elaine's boisterous laugh fills the room. "No, dear. I'm a sex therapist. My courses at Hawthorne focus on gender and sexuality."

Oh. Duh. "That makes the whole oral sex lecture thing make sense," I mumble.

"I was hoping to get to know you better before giving you that lecture, however, it seems I would have been too late anyway." She glances pointedly down at my stomach.

My face blazes. "I was never very good at the birds and the bees."

"Seems like you're plenty good at them, actually," she chuckles.

Mortified, I bury my face in my hands. "Oh my God. Signal! Signal!" I cry, hoping Jules hears me.

Elaine's hands find mine and peel them from my face. "Relax, my cabbage, I'm only joking. We speak very openly about sex around here. Well, I do, at least. Any one of my children would kill me if they heard this conversation." She winks and gives me a reassuring squeeze. "Hugo and I—we worry about our kids. You and Bex understand that better than any of the boys. Jules is learning, it seems. He's going to be a good father, and I can see after one day with you that you, dear, are an excellent mother. This baby is very lucky."

Tears well up almost instantly. It's been so long since someone mothered *me* instead of the other way around. "Thank you." It comes out gurgled.

After one last squeeze, she lets go of my hand. "Anything you need, you let me know, okay? I know you have your dad, but we also love babysitting and don't get to see our granddaughter Elodie often enough! Chloe is welcome here anytime."

I nod because if I open my mouth, the well of tears will start streaming and may never stop. I realize in this moment just how tired I am and how good it feels to be seen. Chloe has Dad and me, but to think about this baby having all of the Bardots? It's a life I never could have hoped for.

Just then, Jules finally wanders into the kitchen. "She signaled for you, darling," Elaine coos.

His concerned eyes meet mine and seem to silently ask if everything is okay.

I'm fine, I mouth.

"Julien, you make sure to take good care of her, yes?" his mom asks.

"I will," he promises, looking me directly in the eye.

And I think I'm starting to believe him.

Chapter Twenty-Four
CAN I HAVE A SNACK?
Jules

BIG PLANS
Why Don't We

It only took me a week to realize I never wanted Thea to move back to her apartment. Honestly, it took less than twenty-four hours, but I tried to get myself to chill the fuck out.

It took me two more weeks, however, to work up the nerve to attempt to tell Thea that I think she should just stay here.

We had our second appointment with Dr. Mitchell yesterday, and everything looked great. Apparently there's a blood test you can do to find out the sex of the baby, so we should know that soon. I want to do something special for Thea, but I have no clue what. I keep opening my mouth to say something to her and then quickly closing it. She's definitely noticed, but has been kind enough not to say anything about it.

Fuck, I want her. But it's more important to me that she feels safe with me—that she wants me to be a part of the baby's life.

She told me from day one that she'd be skittish, and I will never forgive myself if I scare her away.

So instead, I think I've run my hand through my hair about a thousand times a day for the last few weeks.

I'm doing just that when there's a knock on my bedroom door.

"Come in."

The door creaks open and Thea pokes her head in. "Hi."

She hasn't done this before so I'm instantly worried something is wrong. I sit up and ask, "Is everything okay? Are you—"

"No, no, I'm fine! I'm sorry, didn't mean to freak you out. Can I—?" She gestures into the room.

I pat the bed next to me, inviting her to come sit. But as soon as she sits down I realize she's here. In my bed.

"Uh, need water? I can go get some." I start to get up but am stopped by a soft hand on my arm.

"I'm fine, Jules. I just came to talk. It should be time to tell Chloe soon"—she gestures down toward her belly which looks like she's eaten one too many enchiladas—"and I wanted to run that by you before I told her."

"Of course you can tell Chloe. How do you think she's going to take the news?" I ask. With Chloe's larger than life personality, I could see it going either way.

Unlike Thea, who I have lost the ability to communicate with, Chloe and I have become fast friends over the past few weeks. Though I suspect that's mostly to do with Chloe wanting to replace Ben, and I just happen to be here. She helps me make dinner and in return I've sat through about a dozen tea parties. Typically the menu involves no tea, because Chloe says tea is disgusting. I don't think she's ever actually had it before.

I look back over at Thea. She's clad in one of her typical dance outfits, a tight workout top and even tighter leggings. I have the hardest time resisting the urge to touch.

"Great question," she chuckles. "She's around so many adults, I don't think she's ever really thought about having a sibling." Her head falls back against the pillow as she contemplates. "Do you—what's it like having such a large family?"

I mirror her position, crossing my hands over my stomach. Out of the corner of my eye, I see Thea gazing at my forearms. I might flex slightly for her benefit.

"Most of the time I loved growing up as one of the Bardot siblings. We're all very close in age, so it really did feel like having built in best friends. I think Mom and Dad did a great job of feeding into our individuality—I never felt like I had to be the same as my siblings. The toughest part about it was being a twin, I think."

Thea hums in acknowledgment. I like that she's listening to me. Usually I'm the one listening. I run my hand over my beard and continue.

"Ben and I are… different. There was a time where I felt like that was a bad thing. He and Gabe are so…"

"Loud?" Thea suggests.

"Yeah," I huff. "Larger than life, for sure. I typically didn't require as much attention as they did so I kind of got lost in the shuffle. Everyone always just assumed I was fine because I didn't say otherwise."

"But you weren't fine?"

I sigh because that answer is complicated. "I—Yes, in the sense that my parents didn't have to worry about me going off and doing anything crazy."

"The tattoos weren't considered crazy?" She smirks.

That makes me smile. "No, I think Mom was glad I was finally doing something a little rebellious. I don't know that I would call myself a rule follower, but I didn't like to rock the boat. There was enough going on at our house, simply because of how many of us there were."

"I always wanted a tattoo, but I think I would have been blacklisted from any ballet company," she laughs. "And honestly, I think my dad would be much more upset about that than the pregnancies out of wedlock."

"Well, we'll have to take you to go get one once you're able to," I say.

Her head falls to my shoulder. "I think I'd like that. Can I?" Her fingers linger on my wrist, and I have to hold back a shudder.

"Mhmm."

I hold my breath as her fingers begin to trace over the rose at my wrist, up to the staff of swirling music notes, and over the other florals interspersed.

"Is it notes for a song?" she asks.

My tongue feels stuck. "Yeah."

"Which one?" Her green eyes flash up to me, and we are so fucking close. Her thick eyelashes fan out in a perfect frame of her light irises, and she has a faint pattern of freckles across her pale skin. I can't help but wander down to her mouth—a perfect cupid's bow atop full lips. Her tongue darts out, and I want to feel it run across *my* lips.

"Jules," she breathes. I lean in so our noses barely brush. "Jules," she says again, and I want to record the sound and use it in every song I ever write.

"Thea, I—"

"JuJu!"

Thea shoots off the bed and attempts a casual lean against the wall which does not look even remotely casual.

"In here," I call. Chloe rounds the corner with Cat on her heels.

"Oh hi, Mama! Did you want to play with JuJu too?"

I cover my laugh as Thea chokes on her words. "Something like that," she finally gets out.

"Well we were going to go plant seeds in the garden, wanna come?" Chloe asks. I don't remember planning to work in the garden today, but I guess that's what is happening.

"Sure, baby, let me change and we can go out there."

"C'mon, JuJu!" Chloe calls over her shoulder as she turns to leave.

I take a moment to collect myself before following her out there. My garden is a nice haven in the Spring. Mom helped me get it going when I first moved into the house. She brought clippings from her rose bush and reminded me of the best plants for our climate, when to plant them, and how to take care of the fickle ones. It's another hobby I took on out of loneliness, but also because it is good, grounding work—literally.

By the time I'm outside, Chloe has decided she needs to build a fairy house in the garden and begins collecting twigs and fallen buds. A few minutes later, Thea joins us. She's changed into a flowy white dress and tied her hair back with a bandana.

The thought crosses my mind that I'd marry her right here, right now, and that's when I know I've actually gone insane.

Thea walks over to help Chloe on her mission, looking at me the entire time as if she's trying to communicate something to me that I'm obviously not picking up on.

"Hey, Chlo," she starts. "Have you ever wanted a baby brother or sister?" Thea winces slightly at her wording.

Chloe pauses and seems to really think about her answer. Finally she shrugs. "Not really."

"Right..." Thea continues. "But what if you got a baby brother or sister?"

Bent down in the dirt, Chloe begins to put sticks together in an attempt to make a tiny shelter. "Would it live with us?" she asks.

I can tell Thea is struggling by the pleading glance she sends my way. Sitting in the dirt next to Chloe, I say, "Most babies live with their grown-ups. I had a lot of fun with my siblings, I'm glad I have them."

"What's a sibling?" Chloe asks.

"You know how Ben is my brother?"

"Yeah, he's your twin." Chloe looks up, dirt smeared across her cheek. "I think I'd like a twin. Can I have a twin, Mama?"

I love four-year-old logic. "A twin would have to be born at the same time as you. But..." I look up at Thea, who nods.

Kneeling down next to the two of us, she says, "Chlo, Mama has another baby in her belly. You get to be a big sister."
　　"Cool!" Chloe says in quite the about face.
　　"It is… cool. Do you have any questions?" Thea prompts.
　　Chloe stands up and puts her hands on her hips. "Yes, I do."
　　We both look at her expectantly.
　　"Can I have a snack?"

Chapter Twenty-Five
PLAY ME SOMETHING?
Thea

SURRENDER
WALK THE MOON

"Thanks for stopping by on your day off—really just finishing touches at this point."

Cole has become somewhat of a friend since Ben introduced us. She can be incredibly hard to read, but I'm taking her presence here as a positive sign.

"Does the place have a name yet?" she asks.

The million-dollar question.

"I've had such a hard time deciding. It feels like naming a baby, you know?"

Cole laughs. "I do not know, but you do. I'm sure you'll come up with something."

"Whirlwind Dance Studio is what has been sticking out to me lately... I feel like it encapsulates this whole experience really well," I confess.

"Oh, yes. I like it," Cole encourages. "The place really does look great. Not going to lie, it was giving a little more crack den than ballet studio before you took over."

She's not wrong. The studio was falling apart when I got the keys. Between that and early pregnancy disdain for doing anything other than sleep, it's been slow to open. Today Cole is helping me apply a film to the windows that will let light in but prevent my dancers from getting distracted by people walking by. A surprisingly difficult task due to the size of the front windows.

Dad is watching Chloe and Jules is at work. I can tell he's at the point in the school year where he's ready to be done. There's still a lot to do next door at the coffee shop, and from what it sounds like, his seniors checked out a while ago.

I don't often feel the age gap between Jules and I—having a baby will force you to grow up quickly, and seven years doesn't really feel like *that* big of a gap—but when I think about the fact that Jules could have been *my* teacher, I get a little... okay so maybe it turns me on just a bit.

And I'm pretty sure I've officially entered the horny stage of pregnancy. A wet rag could probably turn me on right about now.

"Earth to Thea," Cole interrupts me.

"Hmm? Oh! Sorry, what's up?"

Her eyebrow raises, and her fiery red ponytail swishes from side to side as she eyes me. "You were thinking about sex, weren't you?"

"What?! No! Sex? What's that? I—"

"Mhmm, very convincing. So are you and Jules...?"

I stare at her. "Are me and Jules what?"

Her eye roll could move mountains. "Fucking, Thea. Are you and Jules fucking?"

I know my face is on fire so I turn around and pretend to be very busy doing... only there's nothing for me to do except help Cole. I whip back around, ready to get us back on track.

Cole is standing there, hip cocked, finger tapping her chin. "So, that's a no. But you want to be."

"I-I-I can't. We can't! I'm pregnant."

Cole's exasperation is palpable. "Which means obviously you can."

"It was just supposed to be a one time thing!" I cover my face and slump down to the ground.

"They say all it takes is once." The sarcasm in her voice eases some of my tension.

I drop my hands and stare up at the ceiling. "Jules is almost too perfect. He cooks, he gardens, he plays an instrument. He and Chloe get along great. He bought Cat an entire scratch-post village. He wants to go to doctors appointments and be involved in the pregnancy. It's driving me crazy."

I'm met with silence after this little rant. When I finally look over at Cole, her eyes are narrowed into slits. "Did you hear all of the words that just came out of your mouth? You are saying the man is *too* perfect?"

"Have you seen his tattoos? The man bun? No one single person should be that hot and kind and talented. It's not fair!"

"So, let me get this straight, you aren't sleeping with Jules because he's the perfect male specimen?" She asks the question with the silent *Are you an idiot?* left off the end.

"Correct."

"I mean, it's not the choice I would make, but…"

Groaning, I go full starfish on the floor. "What if I'm not perfect and all I do is fuck up relationships and maybe I don't want to do that with someone who is going to be in my life, well… forever!"

Cole takes pity on me, crossing over and taking a seat. "Just because Chloe's sperm donor is a douche canoe that wouldn't own up to his part in her creation, doesn't mean all guys are like that. I've known Jules since high school, and he's always been a good one. Yes—" She holds up her hand to stop me from interrupting. "It is annoying. The man should have at least *one* flaw. But as far as I can tell, he doesn't. And even if it didn't work out romantically between the two of you, he would never let that affect his relationship with his child."

She's right. I know she's right. And I do want Jules, I just don't know how to go about that.

Cole pats my leg, effectively ending our heart to heart. "I've got to go, I have a date tonight."

"With Ben?"

She makes a face as if to convey that she'd rather have a date with the piece of gum stuck on the sidewalk out front.

"Ew. No. Why would you ask that?"

Smiling, I say, "He seems to seek your approval like a puppy dog looking for scratches."

"He can scratch his own ass," she mutters.

"This feels like a 'you're not fucking but you want to be' type of situation," I challenge.

The eye roll is back. "Bye, Thea! Off to go get ready for my date with Garrett—not Benjamin. See if I come back to help again after that sass." She waggles a finger in my face for good measure.

"Bye, *Collette*! Good luck!"

She's gone less than a minute before the door swings open again. "What did you forget?"

"How good you look when you're a little sweaty," comes the answer in what is definitely not Cole's voice.

I sit bolt upright. Speak of the devil... well, one of them, at least. The more handsome one, in my opinion.

Jules saunters in, his violin case in one hand and a single lavender rose in the other.

"What are you doing here?" I ask.

"I got off work and went to check on the shop." He nods next door. "I was about to head home to see you when I ran into Cole out front, and she said you'd be here."

"Here I am," I say, stupidly.

"Here you are." He smiles.

"Is that for me?" I ask, nodding toward the rose. It's a pretty color I've never seen before.

He holds it up to his nose, taking a deep inhale. "This? No, this is for Chloe."

Oh.

"I'm joking, Thea," he chuckles. "Of course it's for you."

"Very funny," I scold, taking the flower from his outstretched hand. "It's beautiful, thank you."

"It is," he replies, but when I look up his eyes are on me, not the rose in my hand.

Something shifted with Jules the other night. It seemed like he was about to kiss me when we were lying in his bed. At the time, I was glad for Chloe's interruption, but ever since then it's been all I can think about.

He looks around the studio. "You know... I've never seen you dance before."

With a start, I realize he's right. Something that's so ingrained in who I am as a person and he's never seen it. That feels wrong.

I nod toward his violin as I stand. "Play me something?"

Jules sits on the bench by the window and unpacks his violin. Within a few minutes he's begun playing, and another shock runs through me because I've never heard this part of him, either. I close my eyes and listen to the unfamiliar tune.

It doesn't take long before I've caught on to the rhythm, slow and methodical.

And I dance.

And it feels so fucking *freeing*.

I can feel Jules' eyes follow me as I move across the floor. His playing speeds up and so do I. The intricate footwork is a part of me, deeply personal and natural. Each flex and bend of my body releases pent up stress that I've been holding onto for weeks.

The music pulls me in and I *chaînés* turn until it suddenly stops, and I'm in his arms.

He gives me a searching look—waiting, asking.

I barely nod before his lips are on mine.

It feels like sweet surrender.

Chapter Twenty-Six
HUGE DADDY ENERGY
Jules

BIG ENERGY
Latto

Thea's body molds to mine, and it's complete bliss.

Earth shattering, wave breaking, bliss.

She tastes like mine—at least that's what I keep telling myself. I've felt protective over her, drawn to her, since the night we met, and I'm overwhelmed again by how lucky I am that she's carrying *my* baby.

Mine.

My hands graze down her spandex clad body. Over her small baby bump, around to her ass. I can't get enough, and yet it's somehow too much.

I break away, breathing heavily. The sound of our mingled inhales and exhales fills the room. I take in the look on her face, smiling when I see that her dazed expression matches exactly how I'm feeling.

My forehead meets hers. "Dance with me, Thea."

By no means am I a dancer—or have any idea what I'm doing—but I do have a sense of rhythm, so I spin her out and back in again to an invisible beat. We sway as her hips roll into mine. She groans when she feels exactly what she does to me, and that sound makes something in me snap.

I lift her up into my arms and press her against the nearby wall. She gasps, and I take that as my opportunity to get another taste. I grind into her sweet warmth, careful not to squish her too much.

"Jules…" Her head rolls to the side, and I kiss my way down her neck.

Thea. *My Thea.*

She looks so pretty when she's surrendering to me.

"I want you," she moans. "Please."

"You have me." The truest words I've ever spoken.

I turn around and sit down on the hardwood, guiding her to straddle my lap. Thea grinds down on my already rock-hard cock.

She undoes me.

We're frantically nipping, licking, kissing—I don't want it to stop. But it has to. "Thea, wait."

"Mmm, no thank you," she responds.

Gently, I pull her away. She opens her eyes, and I see they are full of confusion.

"I gotta say"—she grinds down again—"you're really sending mixed messages here."

Her face tilts down, doubt creeping into her expression. My thumb comes under her chin, urging her to look at me. "This is… this is more than one time for me, always has been."

Our chests rise and fall, meeting each other and then pulling away, as she contemplates what I'm saying.

"I'm scared, Jules. It feels easier to hold you at arms length," she admits on a hushed exhale.

The fact that she's admitting that makes me feel hopeful.

"I know, it is scary. But, look at me." I wait until she does. "It's us." My hand travels down to the swell of her stomach. "Look at what we've already created."

"What if I fuck it up?"

"Impossible."

Her snort is derisive. "I'm serious. I couldn't even do a good job of telling Chloe about this." She gestures downward.

"Does Chloe feel loved?" I ask.

Thea looks away and shrugs.

"Let me rephrase—Chloe feels so loved." I squeeze her hips in emphasis. "She trusts you to love her and keep her safe. That's why she didn't have questions. I'm sure some will come up, and she'll feel comfortable asking you when they do. But for now, she looks at her beautiful mom and trusts that you will always do what's best for her."

When she falls forward into my chest, I catch her. My arms work soothingly up and down her back. "Try this with me? Give *us* a chance."

Ever so slightly, she nods and mumbles something into my chest.

"What was that?" I ask.

She pulls back, a renewed determination in her gaze. "I said 'Okay,'" she states, as if it's the most obvious choice in the world.

"Okay?" I double check.

"Okay," she sighs. "Now, will you fuck me already?"

She's not going to like this, but, "Not yet. But I will make you come." I wink.

Her hand smacks me lightly across the chest. Her indignation is endearing. "Julien! Why not?"

"Call me Julien again," I command, nipping her bottom lip.

Thea's mouth comes to my ear, sending a tingle down my spine. "Only if you fuck me," she whispers. "I might even call you Daddy if you do it right."

"Fuck, Thea," I grit. "Why does that fucking turn me on?"

"Oh, you have huge *Daddy* energy. Everyone thinks so."

I pepper kisses across her chest. "Only care what you think."

"I think… I want you to fuck me, Daddy."

"I've changed my mind. I am going to fuck that pretty little cunt until you can't walk straight. Stand up." I help her off my lap and watch as she rises above me, both of us practically vibrating with anticipation. "Go lock the door. Then come take your clothes off."

She listens like I knew she would. When she's back in front of me, I pull down my sweats, just enough to allow my cock to spring free. Thea watches as I run my hand slowly up and down my shaft. She takes a deep breath, then pulls off the cropped sweater she has on. Underneath is a workout tank top and leggings that hug every single curve of her body.

Thea maintains direct eye contact with me as she steps out of her leggings. I glance down and see that this woman is not wearing underwear. I immediately stop touching myself because it is highly likely that I would come early if I kept at it.

Next, she reaches down and pulls her top over her head. Her tits bounce free, leaving me no choice but to close my eyes and collect myself for a moment.

"Your turn," Thea prompts.

I take a deep breath and then stand to do as she says. Once I'm up, though, I can't resist pulling her into me—feeling her naked body against my fully clothed one. She's simultaneously soft, smooth skin, and lean, toned muscle from years of honing her body. It's been weeks of torture as I've been allowed to look but not touch, all the while knowing exactly what touching feels like.

I indulge my senses for one more kiss and then tug my shirt up over my head. Thea decides she can't wait any longer, tugging the sweatpants from my waist until they fall to the floor.

"I—" She stops to kiss up my stomach before finishing that thought. "I can't lie flat on my back. I mean, I probably can since I'm not super pregnant yet, but it always makes me nervous."

"I know, I've been reading articles."

She looks surprised. "You have?"

I feel like that is the bare minimum of what I should be doing, and her surprise makes me angry. I thread my hands up through her hair, pulling it free of her bun. "Of course I have, Thea. I told you, I'm in this. For you. For the baby. Hell, I'm in this for Chloe too. Just because you've had a terrible experience before doesn't mean I'm going to follow in that asshole's footsteps."

She looks sufficiently chastised so I give her a quick peck on the nose to soothe my harsh words. Quickly, I turn and arrange our clothes into a bit of padding for us before guiding her back down to straddle me.

When she fully sits, I can feel how wet she already is. "Eager, are we?" She lifts a brow at that, moving her hips until my dick is coated in *her*. My finger finds her clit, rubbing melodic circles to work her higher and higher. She leans over, tits on full display, and positions me at her entrance. I slide in with my eyes squeezed shut. If I look at her while this happens, I will absolutely blow my load. "Thea, fuck you feel so good."

I keep my finger working while she slowly starts bouncing up and down on my cock. Her tight cunt wraps around me like a vice, and it's like nothing I've ever felt before—because it's her.

It's us.

We continue like that for a moment, my eyes trained on her, noting every breath and moan as she gets closer and closer to release. When it looks like she's almost there, I pull my finger away and lift her off of me, turning her around so she's on all fours.

After making sure our clothes are still padding her knees, I slide in from behind. I miss her body, though, so I pull her up and sit back on my knees so she's still able to bounce a bit on top of me.

"Look." I hardly recognize my voice, but I'm captivated by the picture we paint in the studio mirror across the room. Thea's lean body, flushed from her chest up to the roots of her hair. The contrast of my dark, tattooed arms wrapping around her pale, delicate form.

It's delicious.

It's erotic.

It's beautiful.

My hand snakes down to return to my ministrations. Thea's mouth pops open as her head falls back onto my shoulder.

"No." I shake my head. "Watch yourself come."

Her eyes meet mine in the mirror, gifting me with being able to watch *and* feel her shatter. I'm not far behind, and I try my damndest to keep my eyes open so I can continue witnessing her undoing.

It takes a bit for our breathing to even out, but once we've both come down, I turn us back to our original position, relishing in how Thea immediately curls into my chest. We sit there naked and sweaty for several minutes until Thea finally pulls herself off to run to the bathroom.

I pick our clothes up and follow her, waiting as she cleans up and gets dressed. Everything gets packed up and put away for the night, but before we leave, I stop Thea and turn us both toward the mirror again.

Wrapping my arms around her from behind, I whisper, "You're beautiful." I punctuate it with a kiss on her exposed neck. "And talented." Kiss. "And funny." Kiss. "And an amazing mother." I look into her reflection for this last one. "Thank you for allowing me to be a part of this."

She turns, kissing me back now. A reply that doesn't require any talking.

———

I'm debating sneaking Thea into my room for the night when my phone rings. It's Mom calling which is unusual for this time of night.

I answer with, "Everything okay?"

"Yes, yes, my cabbage! Everything is great—you're about to be an uncle, again!"

"Holy shit, Bex is in labor?" I ask.

Mom's screech of excitement causes me to pull the phone from my ear. "Yes! I'm headed to the city first thing in the morning. She wants you to come, but I told her I wasn't sure if you'd want to leave Thea."

As if being summoned, Thea appears in my bedroom door. "I'll talk to her and call you back, yeah?"

"Sounds good, dear. I love you!"

"Love you, too, Mom."

I hang up and turn toward Thea.

"Bex is having the baby," I say, patting the bed next to me.

Thea jumps up and down a few times before settling down on top of the comforter. "Oh! That's so exciting! Go—you have to go."

"Well, that's what I wanted to talk to you about. Are you alright with me being gone for a few days?"

She gives me a *Seriously?* look. "Yes, Jules. We'll be fine. And hopefully the apartment will be done soon, and we'll be out of your hair."

I can feel my automatic grimace at those words. I don't want the Rose family out of my hair. I want them *more* in my hair. Or home. Whatever.

Leaning over, I plant a kiss on Thea's forehead. "We'll talk about that when I'm back."

She smiles sweetly up at me. "Okay."

We lay next to each other in bed talking about nothing until we both fall asleep. I wake up when I feel the bed dip.

"Where're you going?" I mumble.

"Sorry, I didn't mean to wake you," she whispers. "Go back to sleep. I have to go to my room in case Chloe tries to find me in the middle of the night."

I pull her into me for one last sleepy kiss before she tiptoes out.

I spend way too long plotting how to make her a permanent resident, not only of this house, but of this bed.

Of my life.

Chapter Twenty-Seven
I MISS HIS COFFEE
Thea

SHOWER
Becky G

Jules left early this morning to go with his mom to New York City to see the new baby.

I think I miss him?

He's only supposed to be gone a few days, but after last night, I know things have changed between us. Changed in the best way. The scariest way.

Dad walks in while I'm staring out the kitchen window, absentmindedly petting Cat. "Everything okay? You look like you're fixin' to rub that cat raw."

"Oh!" I pull my hand off Cat, and he bats at my leg in protest. "I'm fine. Feels weird around here with Jules gone…"

Dad eyes me. "He's only been gone a few hours."

"Right! Of course. I just miss…" I look around the kitchen trying to figure out how to finish that sentence. "I miss how he makes coffee, is all."

Dad looks like he doesn't believe one word that is coming out of my mouth, but he's not going to ask me about it. That's one of the things I love about my relationship with him—he's never going to try to force more information out of me than I'm ready to give.

He leans in and whispers, conspiratorially, "I like the way he makes coffee too."

I clap my hands together. "OK, enough of that. We need to go in today to get Chloe signed up for kindergarten."

Chloe will turn five next month. She's never been to school before, so I'm a little bit nervous about how she's going to handle being in kindergarten next year. Dad says it'll be good for her to be around kids her age, and I have to agree with him. The other day she asked me why all her friends were old. By old, I think she means the Bardot brothers who have adopted her as one of their own. I didn't have a good answer for her.

Chloe seems excited about going to school next year. I've cried about it at least a dozen times.

Dad knows how I feel about the whole kindergarten situation, so he doesn't push any further. Instead, he makes a pot of his typical tar coffee, and we eat our breakfast in comfortable silence.

"I noticed the studio is almost done," he comments as we're cleaning up. One thing about Hank Rose is that he's always supported me in whatever I set my stubborn mind to. He knew nothing about dance, but he insisted on being hands on when it came to raising me after my mom died. He learned how to do a perfect ballet bun, he honed his stage makeup skills with the help of my grandmother, and even stitched ribbons onto my shoes when I started en pointe.

"Yup. Signage is in the mail, and the website has started taking summer sign ups. It's happening whether I'm ready or not." I did finally decide on the name Whirlwind Dance Studio after confiding in Cole. Something about saying it out loud, the studio having an actual name, made this whole thing feel that much more real.

"You're ready." His confidence makes me smile.

"We'll see," I sigh. "I'll admit, it was pretty cool signing Chloe up for a class at *my* studio. I even met with a Hawthorne student the other day about helping me with classes. I think she can co-teach with me for a bit before taking over a few of the pre-school and beginner groups."

"That's great, hon. I'm really proud of you."

I don't feel like I've done a lot in my life to make my Dad proud, but I think he would scoff if I told him that.

Of course he can tell I feel some type of way because he changes the subject. "The coffee shop is looking good, too. It'll be nice once the baby is here to have Jules so close. That baby is going to grow up sippin' espresso while they pirouette."

"I love that you know what a pirouette is."

He looks mildly offended. "I only spent years practicin' every flippin' dance with you. 'Course I know what a pirouette is."

"Thank you, Dad. For everything you've given me, never judging any decision I've made. I couldn't do this without you."

Again, his confidence in me is astounding. "You could. But it wouldn't be as fun now, would it?" He winks, patting my shoulder as he leaves the kitchen.

I go back to staring out the window, only looking away when my phone buzzes.

JULES

Baby is here! Meet Molly Louise Bardot-Olsson.

A picture is attached and ho-ly fuck. If I wasn't already pregnant with his baby, I think my ovaries would explode. Jules has his hair pulled back in one of his signature man buns, his facial scruff is broken up by a huge, toothy grin, and his tattooed arms are wrapped around a tiny bundle of blankets. Sleeping Molly looks perfectly content in her uncle's arms, and I don't blame her one bit.

> She's beautiful! Congratulate the family for me.

Another picture comes through, this time of Bex, Anders, and baby Molly. Mom and dad are beaming at each other, and without ever having met them in person, I can tell their love is different. Seems like it runs in the Bardot family after seeing the way Elaine and Hugo interacted, as well.

Dad never got over Mom's passing—never moved on to another partner. I don't blame him at all. From the stories he tells occasionally, they were soulmates. One doesn't move on from that easily. The result, unintended or not, was that I never got to see what a healthy partnership looked like, first hand.

> Do they always look at each other like that?

JULES
> Yes. I think I'm supposed to say it's sickening, but I've always admired their relationship.

Jules isn't afraid to have his own opinions about things. He may be quiet, but I'm learning he likes to vocalize things that are important to him.

> I think I miss you.

JULES
> I know I miss you.

I bite my lip and smile down at my phone, debating what to say next. Cat butts his head up against me, so I decide to send Jules a picture of the two of us.

> Cattington also misses you, but he'd never admit it

JULES

Nah, Cat only has eyes for Chloe now. I'm old news.

> Well, you are old...

JULES

I'm 30, Thea. Not dead.

> Does it ever bother you how young I am?

JULES

No.

I huff a laugh at his directness. Well that answers that.

> You were driving before I could even sit in the front seat of the car
>
> I bet you haven't even seen some of my favorite TV shows because you were too old for them by the time I started watching

JULES

We can watch them together.

> I'll watch your old people shows with you, too. I feel like you are the kind of person who would watch a nature documentary

JULES

What if I am? Are you bothered by how old I am?

I think about his question and watch as the three dots appear and disappear several times before Jules' next text comes through.

It's a grandpa emoji.

> Idk, that took you a while to find

JULES
Spell the words out, Rosie girl. Your old man needs it.

Rosie?! I've never had a nickname before. Thea is kind of hard to shorten. I stare at my phone, blushing furiously.

> Yes, sir.

JULES
I like that too much.

I need to run. Can I call you later?

> Now we have to talk on the phone? Ugh

JULES
I'm taking that as a yes. Talk to you soon.

"Your face is so red, Mama."

My phone nearly flies out of my hand. "Holy shhhandwiches. Holy sandwiches. You scared the—"

"The turkey out of you?" Chloe finishes.

I laugh. "Yes, my little chicken. You scared the turkey out of me. Ready to go register for kindergarten?"

"WOO kingergarten," she yells, mispronouncing the word.

Seems like my chicken is ready to fly the coop.

Chapter Twenty-Eight
SOUL STIRRING
Jules

YOU'VE GOT A FRIEND
James Taylor

Molly is just as cute as her sister, and I'm glad that I could be here for Bex and Anders to help with their transition to a family of four, but, damn—I miss my own little family.

A picture comes through my phone of Chloe manhandling Cat. My cheeks hurt from how much I've been smiling lately. Thea has been sending me updates of their whereabouts throughout the day, and I'll admit, it's helping a bit.

Today is Bex and Molly's last day at the hospital before they are discharged tomorrow. Mom is going to stay with them a bit longer, but I'll head back once the family is reunited at their apartment.

Bex and Molly are both sleeping—at least I thought they were until I hear Bex ask, "Why are you smiling at your phone?"

"Why aren't you asleep?" I respond.

"Your happiness woke me up."

"I actually don't think that's possible."

I can tell I've irritated a woman already deprived of rest. "Just answer the question, JuJu," she snaps.

"Thea sent me a picture," I respond.

That immediately gets a reaction out of Bex. Wiggling her eyebrows, she asks, "Ohhh a sexy picture? How bold of her."

My head falls back onto the uncomfortable hospital couch. "God, no." I cover my eyes. "A picture of her child with our cat."

"*Our*, is it?" Bex muses.

Out of anyone, the cat probably belongs to Chloe most, but I don't correct my sister.

Bex plows on. "So how are things—having them at your house? Is it weird going from living alone to living with three and a half other people? I'm counting the new baby as half."

"Don't forget the cat."

She rolls her eyes. "This is starting to feel very sitcom-y. Very… *loud*, for someone who is used to solitude."

I can tell she's concerned for me but doesn't want to say it outright.

"What's it like living in a tiny New York apartment with your extremely boisterous husband and toddler daughter?" I ask, turning it around on her.

"Mass chaos." She pauses for a beat. "And I love it. I can't wait to bring her home to it." She nods toward a still dozing Molly.

I lean forward, running my hands over the top of my hair. "Well, there's your answer," I reply.

"Oh my God," Bex whispers. "She stirs your soul."

I huff, secretly loving that Bex remembers that conversation.

"Yeah, BB. She does."

―――

The train ride home feels never-ending. I'm ready to see my girls again. I'm ready to ask Thea to make the move into my house permanent. I'm ready to *really* be with her.

When I get home, the house is quiet apart from the low melody of James Taylor coming from the record player. Walking into the living room, I see Thea asleep on the couch with Cat curled up behind her knees. She's wearing a crop top, revealing a baby bump that has definitely popped in the last few days. She looks peaceful, and I'm glad she's getting some rest.

I set my stuff down in my room and then begin to make some coffee, wondering if Thea needs me to make a snack for when she wakes up. Deciding she's probably eaten terribly over the last few days, I start making hard boiled eggs—her newest pregnancy craving.

The eggs are just about ready when I hear her padding into the kitchen. "You're home early." Her smile is lazy. Indulgent, even.

Because I can't help it, I walk over and plant a kiss on that sleepy smile. "I am. And I made you some eggs."

"Mmm, thank you," she drawls. Foraging through the refrigerator, she drops a metaphorical bomb. "Dr. Mitchell's nurse called and said the results from my blood test are uploaded to the portal… if we want to find out the sex of the baby."

Do we want to find out the sex of the baby? That seems like something I should defer to her. She turns around holding a bottle of hot sauce in her hands, which doesn't even phase me at this point. "Like I've said, I'm always going to do what you feel most comfortable with. We can find out the sex or we can wait. It's totally up to you."

"I—" She grabs a hard boiled egg, douses it in hot sauce, and pops it in her mouth. Before she's finished chewing she says, "I wanna find out."

Thank God.

"Me too." My words echo the relief I feel. I would have waited, but I really want to know.

My hand finds her belly. She pushes her crop top up further, giving me permission to touch. "I've been feeling it move."

"Really?" My hand flattens against the side of her stomach.

"You won't be able to yet, but there's definitely been some flutters in the last few days."

I'm instantly disappointed and my face must show it.

Thea's hand reaches up to cradle my face. I nuzzle into it, enjoying every second that she allows me to be near her.

"I missed you," she whispers. "I'm not supposed to miss you."

Kissing her palm, I ask, "Would you feel better if I said I missed you too?"

She nods, pulling me down until we are forehead to forehead. "How on earth have you so quickly wriggled your way into my life, Julien Bardot?"

"It's been several months, Rosie girl."

I feel more than see her smile. "I like that I get a nickname."

Pulling back, I tuck a rogue piece of hair behind her ear. "That first night we met, you told me roses were fickle. Do you remember?"

"I do." She grins. "I was right, wasn't I?"

"More than I could have imagined. But I think you think fickle is a bad thing." My brow furrows. "Thea, you're loyal, careful, strong. You may be slow to trust, which makes sense given everything you've been through, but you are quick to defend those who have earned that trust. Rosie fits you—maybe a bit prickly at first, but always worthy of admiration."

"I think you have on rose-colored glasses," she counters.

"Maybe I do. I hope they never come off."

She shakes her head. "Being with your new niece made your baby fever even worse, didn't it?"

It's a deflection, I know. She's never had someone want her for exactly who she is.

"I would feel this exact same way, even if you weren't carrying my baby. I need you to understand that." My tone is serious and she instantly sobers.

"It's… harder than I thought it would be."

"I know, but trust me, okay? Try with *me*," I beg.

"Okay," she whispers. "I'm trying. I want to try."

Our kiss is deep, full of unspoken promises. She wraps her arms around my neck, and I lift her up onto the counter. My hands explore every inch that I can reach. Our breaths quicken, tongues meeting in an insatiable dance. I'm about to carry her to my bedroom, or honestly bend her over the counter when she pushes me back.

"Wait! I still want to find out what we're having."

"For dinner?" I've completely forgotten what we were talking about before we started making out.

She laughs, smacking me across the chest. "No! The baby! Let me grab my phone."

Right, the baby. Now I remember. My stomach feels like it might fall out of my ass.

Thea comes back, typing something out on her phone. Once she's done, she looks up at me. "Ready?"

Yes. No. "Yes," I answer.

She turns around, leaning into my chest so I can peer over her shoulder and read what's on the screen. A lab report pops up, and we both scan, trying to figure out what it's saying.

"There." She points. "'Fetal Sex: Male.' Holy shit."

It's a boy.

"What am I supposed to do with a boy?" Thea asks, laughing in disbelief.

"I'm no expert, but I would assume when they're babies, it's pretty similar," I joke. "How do you feel?"

"Surprised…" she admits. "But also excited. I'll have to see if Elaine can give me some advice."

I have no doubt my mom would be overjoyed if Thea asked her for advice. Kissing the top of Thea's head, I soak her presence in. I almost ask her to move in, it's on the tip of my tongue, but I don't want to ruin this moment.

Before I work up the courage to do it anyway, Chloe runs in, shouting "JuJu!" when she sees me. The opportunity passes, and I promise myself to find a way to ask her soon. Maybe not today, but soon.

Chapter Twenty-Nine
DADURDAY
Jules

SUGAR, YOU
Oh Honey

"There's a Bardot family tradition that my dad did with us as kids, that I would really like to do with Chloe."

"You have my attention." Thea smirks. Chloe has already gone to bed, and Thea's head is resting in my lap. I braid and rebraid her hair as she watches reruns of *Jeopardy!* I'm nervous for this conversation because I never want to assume anything about what Thea might be comfortable with or what my role is in Chloe's life.

"Dad always took us kids out of the house for a few hours on Saturday mornings so Mom could sleep in. We'd get donuts, go to a park or indoor playground depending on the weather. Sometimes it was just the Sassafras rec center so we could get our energy out by running circles around the gym. It became known as Dadurday, and it's one of my favorite childhood memories. I'd love to do it with Chloe. I-I know I'm not her dad, but…" I trail off unsure how to finish that sentence.

I'd like to be, feels like I'm coming on too strong.

She turns to fully face me then, her green eyes sparkling in the glow of the lamp. "Dadurday, huh? I like the sound of that," she whispers. "You'd want to hang out with a four-year-old on a Saturday morning?"

"Chloe is important to me. I may not be as fun as Ben and Gabe, but I want to get to know her, and I want her to get to know me. Spending Saturday mornings together is a good start."

"Saturday mornings? Plural?" she questions, a single eyebrow raised.

Busying myself with the braiding again, I say, "Yeah, it's a recurring thing. Every Saturday morning. And when the baby gets here, he can join too."

Thea hesitates before responding. "Once we're back in the apartment it'll be kind of a pain to come get them, won't it?"

"About that…" I muse, feigning nonchalance. "What if you didn't go back to the apartment?"

Her hand reaches up, running along the stubble coating my jawline. "You are a good man, Julien Bardot," she mutters.

I finally work up the courage to make eye contact, just in time to catch a single tear roll down her cheek and disappear into her hair. My hand shakes slightly when I wipe the tear away. "Is that a yes?"

Thea's eyes dart back and forth between mine, as if she's trying to figure out if this is something I actually want. I do. I hope she sees that.

"Let me think about it, okay?" she eventually replies.

I nod in agreement. I can let her think about it. I decided a long time ago I would wait as long as it takes Thea to be ready, I'm not going back on that now.

Saturday morning rolls around and at 6:01 on the dot, there's a knock on my bedroom door.

"JuJu!" Chloe whisper-shouts. "JuJu! Can we go now?!"

Thea ran the idea of Dadurday past Chloe the day after I asked her about it. We aren't calling it Dadurday... just "hang out time with Jules" which is not as catchy, I have to admit. All Chloe had to hear was the word donuts and she was in.

I know Chloe tends to wake up early, so I'm not surprised to see her dressed and ready to go when I open the door.

"Go get your shoes and jacket on. I'll meet you in the kitchen," I tell her, watching as she scurries off to do just that. I quickly change clothes, cracking the door to Thea's room to make sure she's still asleep before I head to the kitchen.

Chloe is bouncing on her toes in excitement while Cat watches from her resting spot on the counter. "How long have you been up, Chlo?"

"My clock said five four one! Mama said not to wake you up until it was six zero zero, so I played in my room until the clock changed."

She's got an adorable bedhead situation going on, so I ask, "Do you want me to braid your hair before we go?"

Chloe looks at me in surprise, her movements halting. "You can braid? I love braids! Can you do two?"

"Of course I can, I used to braid my sister's hair when we were little, and I was practicing on your mom the other night." I say that out loud and realize it sounds weird. "Braiding... I was practicing braiding," I clarify.

"Obviously..." Chloe sasses. "Let me get my hair bucket!"

She runs out of the room and comes back with an actual bucket full of hair ties, bows, headbands, and a brush. Handing me the brush, she picks out one pink hair tie and one yellow one, as well as two mismatched unicorn bows. I try to be gentle as I brush her hair, parting it down the middle and starting the first braid.

"Can you teach me to play music like you?" Chloe asks when I'm midway through her second braid. "That's your job, right?"

"For now, yes. But I would teach you even if it wasn't my job. Done," I reply, adding her chosen bows to the end of each braid.

"Thanks, JuJu! Let's go! Bring the lio-lin," she instructs.

"The what?"

"The lio-lin, JuJu! Your music!"

Oh, *violin*. Got it. I oblige because I can't help myself with the Rose women, and while we sit in the corner of the donut shop that morning, I teach Chloe how to hold my violin. It's entirely too big for her, but she gets a kick out of it anyway. I don't give her the bow yet, but let her pluck a few strings so she can hear the music.

When she's ready to move on, we go to a local park. Chloe immediately heads toward the swingset, screaming "higher!" every time I push her. She requests my help across the monkey bars and insists that I slide down the slide with her. We play tag, hopscotch, and a game Chloe made up that pretty much only consists of finding different rocks that meet her specifications.

I'm still unclear what those specifications actually are, however.

Once we've been playing for about an hour, I find a shady spot for us to sit down. Chloe takes long drinks of water as I enjoy the late spring breeze. "Hey, Chlo?"

"Yeah?"

"How would you feel if I took your mom out on a date?"

One of her braids has fallen out, the bow stuck haphazardly into her undone hair. She looks at me quizzically. "What's a date?"

Right. Should have expected that question.

"Well, it's when someone likes someone else and wants to spend more time together." That's the best I can come up with off the top of my head.

"Kind of like us right now. You want to take Mama to the donut shop and park?" she asks.

Laughing, I reply, "I guess it does kind of seem like what we're doing right now, but it's more than just wanting to be friends with someone. It's like…" How do I explain this?

"Like you want to marry Mama?" Chloe supplies.

"I—" I mean, she's not wrong. "I think a date is a way to decide if you want to marry someone. People usually go on lots of dates before they get married, though."

She flops back into the grass. "You can do a date with Mama. Tell me if you marry her, okay?"

Smiling at that, I say, "Okay, Chlo."

When we get home a little while later, Thea is sitting at the breakfast table eating one of the muffins I baked for her this week—coffee cake this time. Chloe pushes past me, hopping up on the chair next to her mom. "JuJu is going out on a date!" she exclaims.

Thea drops the piece of muffin halfway to her mouth, looking at me horror-struck. "Chloe," I scold. "You were supposed to let me ask her."

"Oops!" She giggles and then gives me a *go on* gesture. Thea looks back and forth between us, realization dawning.

"You, Rosie girl," I cut in. "I'd like to go on a date with *you*. We never did get our chance."

Chloe stands up on the chair, putting her face right next to Thea's. "You should say yes," she whispers, loud enough for me to hear.

Thea turns to me. "Yes." She smiles as Chloe squeals.

"Yay! He's going to take you to get donuts, then you'll go to the park and play games…" Chloe's voice drones on as she details all of the things she thinks Thea and I should do on our date.

I watch as Thea smirks, taking another bite of her muffin.

"Tonight," I interrupt. "Are you free?"

Thea stands, bringing her plate over to the sink. "I'll have to check my calendar…" she teases, her hand brushing mine as she walks past.

"I'll pick you up at six." I wink, not waiting for her answer as I walk out of the kitchen.

"Wait!" she calls. "Where are we going? I need a dress code!"

"Anything you wear will be perfect, Rosie girl." My laugh echoes down the hall when I hear her dramatic "Ugh!" in reply.

Good. I'm ready for her to be a little flustered around me.

Chapter Thirty
EVERYONE HATES VEGETABLES
Thea

THIS WILL BE
Natalie Cole

Jules never did tell me what I should wear tonight. I landed on a floral sundress that leaves room for my growing baby bump and a light yellow cardigan.

It's almost six, and I'm still in the bathroom finishing up my hair. I check the time on my phone again, hoping Jules didn't have something planned where we have to be exactly on time. Just then, it lights up with a text from Maggie.

MAGS

What are you up to? Can we FaceTime with Chloe before she goes to bed?

Can't tonight... I have a date

MAGS

If this is with someone other than Jules, I stg Thea *knife emoji*

> Calm your tits woman, of course it's with Jules

MAGS
> Good. I've seen the pictures, that man is fiiiiiiiine

A loud knock sounds from the front door. Dad and Chloe went to the Bardot's house for dinner tonight so I wait for Jules to answer the door. A few moments later, another knock comes. I poke my head out of the bathroom. "Jules, can you get that?"

Silence.

Where the hell did Jules go?

I stomp my way over to the door, a clip holding up the hair I haven't had a chance to curl yet. A third knock happens right when I get there, so I fling the door open wondering who the heck is so impatient.

"Who is it—" Any other words die on my lips as I stare at arguably the most gorgeous man to ever walk the planet.

Julien *mother fucking* Bardot is standing in front of me wearing a button-down shirt rolled up to expose his thirst-trap forearms and a pair of jeans that hug him in all the right places. In one hand, he holds a bouquet of red roses—his own rose tattoo peeking out behind the real flowers.

"You look beautiful," he breathes.

"I'm not ready yet."

"Doesn't matter." He scrubs his hand over his trimmed beard as his eyes rove over my body. He steps over the threshold, invading every inch of my space. "I think I'm supposed to wait until the end of the date, but I'd really like to kiss you now, if that's okay with you."

I barely nod before his lips are on mine. I have only a moment to enjoy it before he's pulled back. Stepping toward him, I attempt to get back to his lips, but I'm met with a chuckle. "Later, Rosie girl. Go finish getting ready."

I sulk back to the bathroom and am greeted with a string of unread texts from Maggie.

> **MAGS**
>
> Have fun! but not too much fun!
>
> Actually, I guess *that* doesn't matter much at this point
>
> Are y'all already having fun?? *wink emoji*
>
> Never mind don't answer that

> Gracious Magnolia, what are you on tonight?!
>
> He just showed up at the door of his own house to pick me up with a bouquet of red roses

> **MAGS**
>
> SWOON

Swoon is right. I put my phone down and quickly finish my hair, also taking the time to touch up my lipstick. Jules greets me when I walk into the living room. He's already put the bouquet in a vase, and I watch as he unties his hair and ties it back up again.

"Don't be nervous, it's just me," I say, alerting him to my presence.

He sighs, a little smile curving across his lips. "There's no 'just' about it, Thea. It's you."

Are those…? Yup, pretty sure an entire flutter of butterflies just took flight in my stomach. Jules holds out his hand for me, and I take it, excited to see where the night will lead.

As it turns out, the night leads to a cozy little Italian restaurant, dimly lit with candles on every table. Jules and I split the best spaghetti and meatballs of my life—thank God I can eat beef again—and it all feels very *Lady and the Tramp*. He called ahead to make sure they could make a mocktail for me and even let me order two desserts because I couldn't decide between the chocolate cake or the cannolis.

He's perfect.

After I've cleaned both dessert plates, Jules leans back in his seat and asks, "Ready for our next stop?"

"There's more?" I blurt.

His eyes crinkle with his smile. "Of course. Let's go or we're going to be late."

The aforementioned next stop is the park, I realize as Jules brings the car to a stop. "I thought Chloe was kidding when she said you would take me to the park," I joke.

"Well, we aren't going to play tag… unless that's something you're into."

An image of Jules chasing me—catching me in his beautiful, muscular arms and spinning me around with ease—flashes through my mind. I can feel my face flush, giving my thoughts away.

Jules turns to me with a raised eyebrow, his finger traces the blush as it climbs up my neck. "Noted," he whispers before leaning into my ear. "I love that I can see exactly what turns you on, Rosie girl."

"I will mount you right here in this car, like two teenagers with raging hormones and nowhere to go," I tease.

I feel Jules' chuckle against my skin. "Don't tempt me." He plants a single kiss under my earlobe before pulling away. "Another time."

Jules climbs out of the car, leaving me hot and bothered in the passenger seat. I hear him open the trunk and then close it again. By the time he makes it around to my side, I'm still recovering. "You coming?" he asks, opening the door.

"I wish." When I look up at him, he has one of his rare grins plastered across his face and a large blanket under his arm.

He holds out his free hand to me and I take it, letting him guide me into the park and over a small hill. On the other side is —"An outdoor movie?" There are several blankets spread out across the lawn, a big projector standing on the opposite side playing the beginning scenes of *The Parent Trap*. "I love this movie!"

Jules just smirks as he lays out the blanket he brought toward the back of the crowd. Wrapped in the blanket were two sweatshirts and a pack of peanut butter crackers, perfect for the chilly night air and my perpetually hungry belly.

We sit down, watching the movie quietly for a little while, our fingers lightly intertwined between us. Eventually my head makes it down into Jules' lap, and I enjoy the way he immediately starts playing with my hair. As Hallie and Annie leave camp to swap lives, I turn to face Jules and ask, "Do you have any flaws, Julien Bardot?"

He looks down at me with a sheepish smile. "Of course I do, Thea Rose."

"Name one," I reply.

"I snore."

I wrinkle my nose. "I don't remember that."

"You're right, I don't snore." He shrugs.

"See! No flaws!" I exclaim, and I'm immediately shushed by the people in front of us. "Sorry!" I mouth, giving them a little wave.

"I hate vegetables," he tries.

"Everyone hates vegetables."

"I'm terrified that I'm going to scare you off," he admits.

Oh.

"That's why you won't tell me your flaws?" I whisper.

"Maybe..." he replies. "Or maybe I am flawless." A joke. A deflection.

"The night we first met, I called you TBD in my head."

Jules looks confused. "To be determined?"

"That, and you were tall, brooding, and dark in what I've come to learn is your signature black ensemble." I gesture to his current outfit as proof. "You initially put on this tough guy air, but you're secretly a softie."

"I've never been in love," he confesses.

I hum. "Not necessarily a bad thing."

"For a long time," he continues, "I thought maybe I wasn't capable of it."

"What changed?" I breathe, wanting to know. No, needing to know.

Jules looks me in the eye and gives me a partial answer. "A few things."

It's not a declaration—I think he knows I'm not ready for that—but it does reach deep down into my soul and soothe some of the more frayed bits of me. It's another way for him to reassure me.

"We're going to be okay?" I ask.

Jules pushes away a hair that's fallen across my face. "Yeah, Rosie girl. We're going to be okay."

Chapter Thirty-One
FAMILY DINNERS
Thea

GOOD ENOUGH
Carlie Hanson

Life has been hectic over the past month. Jules finally finished his last semester of teaching and has been up at the coffee shop most days in preparation for their grand opening this weekend. He continues to do little things to reassure me—there was a definite shift with us after our date—but I'm still struggling to really commit. Still afraid that I'm missing something.

On the flip side, I am now firmly in my second trimester and have been feeling amazing physically. My summer dance classes started a week ago, and to my complete and utter shock, people actually showed up.

I love teaching the little kids, but I think my favorite class has been my advanced group. They are blowing me out of the water with their talent—I can't wait to watch how they improve now that they have a studio in their own town. Ben mentioned something about a Labor Day festival that Sassafras puts on every year, so I'm hoping they'll allow some of my classes to perform.

Oh, and the apartment should be ready to move back into any day now.

I'm not as thrilled about that as I should be.

Jules gets a new wrinkle every time I bring it up, but he also insists that he wants me to do what's best for me. I'm more concerned about the fact that we have come in and completely destroyed this man's life and, no matter what he says, that has got to be taking a toll on him.

I'm glad I have a little more time before I have to make any decisions.

We also had our anatomy scan with Dr. Mitchell. Baby boy is looking great, and is *definitely* a boy. I still don't know what the fuck I'm supposed to do with a son—it does put Jules and I on a little bit more of an even playing field, though. This particular experience will be brand new for both of us.

I arrive at Bardot Brothers Coffee Co. and am greeted by three shirtless men. "I didn't realize the coffee shop was *that* kind of establishment," I tease.

Jules greets me with a kiss. "The A/C went out. You two," he calls to his brothers, "put your shirts back on."

"And take away all my fun? No, thank you." The more I let Jules into my life, the more brooding and overprotective he gets. It's as if he was holding it all back while I figured out how I felt, and now that I've shown a modicum of interest, he's letting it all run free.

He scowls, throwing T-shirts at Gabe and Ben.

"Boo! I'm rating this place one star on Yelp."

Ben laughs but puts his shirt on anyway. No one wants to mess with grumpy Jules. "Hey, Thea! How's my favorite nephew?"

Everyone is excited about the bouncing baby boy that's on the way. Well, everyone except Chloe who asked if I was able to fix that before he was born. For the girl who didn't have any questions when we first told her about my pregnancy, she now has a new question every hour.

How did the baby get in there?
How does the baby get out?
Does the baby have a daddy?
Is JuJu going to be my daddy too?

That last one really threw me for a loop. Chloe doesn't ask about her dad much, and when she does, I try to be as honest as possible, telling her some people aren't ready to be parents and have a hard time taking care of themselves as it is. What I want to say is, "Your sperm donor is an asshole, and you're better off without him."

But I don't. Guess I'm maturing.

Thankfully, I was able to avoid answering that last question when Cattington brought in a dead bird. Chloe wouldn't look at him for a week, she was so mad that he would disrespect another creature like that.

"Your *only* nephew is great, just like he was yesterday," I say, coming back to Ben's question.

Gabe chimes in. "I can't wait to take him to go throw the football around. Babies kind of freak me out, but I like the idea of hanging out with him in about six years."

After getting to know Gabe, that checks out.

"How are y'all feeling about the grand opening?" Looking around, it seems like there's still a lot of work that needs to be done.

All three of the boys eye each other. "It'll get done," Ben finally answers, ever the optimist.

"Well, if I can be of any help—"

"No," Jules interrupts. "Unless by 'help' you mean sitting over there and telling me how hot I look." He smirks.

Gabe elbows Ben, whispering in a volume that's clearly meant to be heard, "I've never seen him like this. Have you?"

"Nope," Ben replies, making sure to pop the "P," then adds, "And I've been with him since the womb."

A blush climbs up my neck. "Alright, I can see that I'm a

distraction. I'm going to get some work done next door. See you at home?"

The word falls so easily out of my mouth. Jules definitely notices because he gives me a raised eyebrow. "See you at *home*, Rosie girl." And the bastard winks.

The entire Bardot family, including the Bardot-Olssons, are having dinner at Elaine and Hugo's tonight. Bex, Anders, and their kids are in town for the opening of the coffee shop—"Memories," Anders muttered when he walked in and saw the updated space. When I first met Bex, she kept giving me weird looks and then muttering in her husband's ear. Jules finally told her to knock it off, to which she responded with an eye roll and a chuckle. It felt like I was missing something, but I'm terrified to find out what exactly that would be.

Dad and I are about to load Chloe into the car when my phone rings.

"Jules? What's up? We are about to head to your parents' house."

Over the line, I hear him sigh. "Change of plans. We are moving dinner to the coffee shop. There are too many finishing touches, we can't afford to take the night off. Everyone can come here and eat, and then we can get back to work."

"Let us help you, Jules."

I can picture the furrow in his brow as he contemplates this. "Maybe. Come eat, and then we can talk about it."

When I sit down next to him at dinner—tables pushed together to fit all of us—he pulls me closer and ghosts his hand down my thigh. I'm learning that Jules is a feeler in every sense of the word. It's almost as if he's subconsciously checking to make sure I'm still there. I lean into him and give him a quick peck on his cheek.

Bex immediately breaks into a fit of giggles.

"Is your sister okay?" I whisper into Jules' ear, eliciting a shiver. "I feel like I'm missing some secret you two are in on."

He turns toward me, nose brushing mine. "I'll explain later, promise."

Just then the door bangs open and Cole walks in. "Sorry I'm late!"

Ben rises from his seat. "We aren't open, Collette. What are you doing here?"

"I invited her," Elaine responds.

Oh damn, she is good. Bex seems to think so, too. Her attention is firmly on the new drama unfolding before us, and she has a feline smile unfolding across her face. I think I hear Anders say, "Down, girl," but it's too soft for me to make out.

"Cole! Come sit by me!" Chloe can't resist a budding friendship. Ben looks at Chloe with heartbreak in his eyes.

"Really, Princess Chloe? I thought we were closer than that." Ben's shoulders slump.

"Don't be mean to Princess Cole and maybe we can be friends again." Kids are brutal.

"Hear that *princess*, we can't be mean to each other." Ben holds eye contact with Cole for longer than strictly necessary—long enough for Bex's smile to turn maniacal.

"What's happening with them now?" I whisper to Jules, vaguely gesturing toward the two grown-ass adults locked in a staring contest.

Jules takes a big bite of pizza, shrugging. "No idea. They're always like that. Thought maybe it was getting better, but someone probably said something that pissed the other person off. Thus, back to complete loathing."

"My guess is that it's some weird form of foreplay," I muse.

Bex pops out of nowhere, forcing her way between the two of us. "I've always thought the same thing. Here, can you hold Molly for a sec. I want to try and get a picture of this."

Before I have a chance to take the baby, Anders swoops in. "So sorry about her," he says, reaching for his youngest daughter. "Bex does not do well on maternity leave. Listens to too many true crime podcasts and watches entirely too much Bravo. Something about the postpartum hormones makes her addicted to the theatrics of it all. After Elodie, she spent six full weeks convinced that I was having an affair with my eighty-year-old vocal coach." He shudders. "That was a dark time."

"You two were made for each other," Jules comments.

Anders' free hand comes down on Jules' shoulder. "Thank you, Jules. That means a lot."

"Are you—are you tearing up?" I ask.

Anders wipes under his eye. "Fatherhood, man. It's softened me."

"You were pretty soft before," Gabe joins.

"Not around me," Bex teases.

All three of the Bardot brothers grimace as Bex and Anders high five.

Cole plops down next to me, as if she didn't just spend several minutes staring daggers into Ben. I open my mouth to ask what the hell just happened, but her hand comes up to silence me before I have the chance. "We'll talk about it later."

Noted.

After we've all had a sufficient amount of pizza, the men continue working on finishing up the shop. Jules does let Hugo, Anders, and Dad help, and even gives Chloe and Elodie a few manageable tasks. Which leaves me alone at the table with Elaine, Bex, and Cole. As soon as everyone else is out of earshot, three sets of eyes turn to me.

"Sooooo…" Bex starts.

I look down to see what I spilled on my shirt. That's the only explanation my brain can come up with for why they're all looking at me. Not seeing anything, I ask, "Soooo what?"

Cole heaves an exasperated sigh. "Are you guys fucking yet or what?"

My eyes shoot to Elaine because I cannot believe those words came out of Cole's mouth in front of *his mother*.

"Not to worry, dear. It's important to have a healthy sex life and can be even more pleasurable in pregnancy." Elaine's smile is placating.

Bex leans back and crosses her arms over her chest. "I'm so glad this conversation is pointed at someone else now."

"I—we—" I stammer. Words have suddenly become incredibly difficult.

"Aha!" Cole shouts, drawing the attention of the rest of the room. "I knew it."

"Shhh," I plead. "He wants me to move in with him." Hopefully that tidbit of information will keep them from asking any more questions about our sex life.

Cole's face scrunches up. "You already did that part... This whole relationship has been entirely out of order."

"No, no. I'm *supposed* to move back into the apartment once the damage from the pipes has been fixed."

Bex scoffs. "I bet Jules does not like that idea."

"He decidedly does not," I reply. My eyes meet Elaine's, and I see the silent question there. A question mirrored in the eyes of all three women staring at me. *What's holding you back?* They seem to say.

My hands come to rest on my stomach. "It's... it's complicated."

Elaine nods. "Such is life, my cabbage."

"It's not that I don't want to. My ex was... well I'm beginning to realize that he was an emotionally abusive asshole. It still makes me nauseous when I think about his complete and total rejection of Chloe and me." I take a deep breath before continuing, everyone content to give me the time I need to collect my thoughts. "Right after Chloe was born, I remember thinking there was no way he could say no to her adorable little face. Surely now that she was here, he'd take one look at her and fall as madly in love with her as I had.

"I called him from the hospital to update him. Tell him he had a daughter and I was willing to let him be a part of her life."

This next part hurts, a dull ache that has never quite faded. I turn my head and see Jules has stopped working and is watching me intently. His attention soothes that never-ending ache, little by little.

"Anyway, when I tried to call, I couldn't get through. He knew I had kept the baby… I can only assume he knew I'd call when she was born so he preemptively blocked my number." I shrug, attempting to convey a nonchalance that I do not feel.

"Bastard," Bex whispers, a tear trailing down her cheek. She pulls Molly close, gazing adoringly down at her sleeping baby. "I can't imagine anyone not wanting to know their child."

"But you have to know Jules isn't like that, right?" Cole asks.

Elaine looks my way, giving me a knowing smirk. "She has to figure that out on her own now, doesn't she?"

"C'mon, the man is head over heels in love with her, dammit. It makes even my shriveled up ovaries hurt," Cole challenges.

Love. No, that's way too much. Too fast.

"He's not—no, we aren't—"

The three knowing stares are back, and I have no idea what the fuck to do with that.

Abruptly, I stand up, eager to get away from this—this ambush, or whatever it is. "Well, it's been… fun isn't the right word. I've got to take Chloe home. Bedtime. You know how it goes. See you later, bye."

Finding Chloe, I haul ass out of the coffee shop like a complete coward.

Chapter Thirty-Two
FATHER FIGURES
Jules

ARE WE A THING
Leidi

As Thea hightails it out of the coffee shop, I wipe the paint off my hands and rush over to the table where my mom, my sister, and Colette Russell are sitting, looking guilty as fuck.

"What happened?" I growl.

I had been watching, contemplating whether or not to jump in. Obviously, I should have jumped.

Mom is the first one to speak up. "Oh, she'll be fine, *mon chou*. She just got a little spooked, is all."

"Don't cabbage me. I've been working for months trying to get Thea to trust me, and you three just fucked it up in mere minutes." I've never spoken to my family like this, but I'm fuming.

Bex sighs. "JuJu—"

"No." I slam my hand down on the table, causing all three of them to jump. "She's it. I—"

The guys rush over, Anders putting a protective hand on my chest. "Woah, take a breath."

My hands come up, and I look around to see that everyone is as surprised by my reaction as I am.

"Julien, come walk with me." Dad says it with such finality, I go.

Scrubbing my hand over my face, I barely contain the aggravated groan I want to let out.

We walk down the sidewalk in silence. It only takes a few moments for me to regret the way I handled that. "I should go apologize," I say.

"You will," Dad assures, coming across in a way that shows me he knows I will apologize because it's the right thing to do, not because he's telling me to do it. "But first, let's talk. What's going on? You've been on edge all night."

My hands come up behind my neck. "Fuck. I don't know. The stress of getting the shop up and running I think, and… I'm so fucking *terrified*."

"Of becoming a father?"

"Of losing her."

Dad hums and tucks his hands in his pockets. "Do you know what happens when you hold onto something too tight?" he finally asks.

I shake my head.

"You risk suffocating it."

I crush my palms into my eyes, but even with my eyes closed, all I see is her.

In my kitchen.

In my garden.

In my bed.

Dad's hands come around my wrists. "Loosen your grip, son. Something this precious needs a gentle touch. Patience. Tenderness."

"I've been patient!" I barely contain the scream that is begging to be let out.

"Yes, you have." He nods. "You've always had the patience of a saint. I'm surprised it's taken you this long for everything to come to a head, if I'm being honest. There's a lot going on Julien. Give yourself some grace. Give Thea some grace."

Inhaling deeply through my nose, I attempt to release some of the tension. Dad's right. I know he's right. It's why I didn't immediately run after Thea, knowing she'd need some space after whatever transpired during her conversation with my family.

I shake my body, jumping up and down a few times for good measure. "Thanks, Dad. I'm going to… I think I'm going to walk the block to cool down." He claps me on the shoulder before heading back to the coffee shop, giving me a reassuring smile when he goes.

Later that night, after everyone has left except for me, I finally let myself cry.

Morning has been coming entirely too soon lately. I'm moody because Thea isn't in my bed. Instead a black fluff ball has made himself comfortable on top of my pillow. I know better than to irritate the cat, so I slide carefully out of bed and make my way to the kitchen.

The one person I do not expect to run into is Hank Rose. A fresh wave of shame washes over me when I remember that he witnessed my little outburst last night.

"Morning, sir," I say. He responds by tipping his mug toward me. I can appreciate that he is a man of few words.

Leaning back against the counter, I open my mouth to assure him I'm not a hot-headed douche bag. Before I can get one word out, he holds up his hand to stop me.

"Don't bother with the pretty words, boy."

Definitely does not feel like a strong start.

"My daughter is lucky to have someone who will stand up for her the way you did last night. Maybe coulda gone 'bout it in a different way, but whatever gets the job done."

I stare at him in disbelief for so long, I swear I see his handlebar mustache twitch.

"I... You're not mad?" I finally ask.

He grimaces. "What would I be mad for?"

"The disrespectful way I spoke to my family, the moment I lost my temper and slammed my hand on the table, the—"

Hank scoffs. "You showed some emotion. Don't have to apologize to me for that, seems like you made your amends, as it is."

He ponders for a bit, staring out the window by the kitchen table. I start sweating in the amount of time it takes him to take a sip of coffee and say whatever it is he's about to say. Finally, he stands, places his mug in the kitchen sink, looks me dead in the eye, and says, "She'll come around."

Then he's gone.

I'm still standing there at a loss for words when Thea walks in.

"Oh! You're up early!" Her voice is strangely high-pitched.

I look at the clock and see that it's a perfectly normal time to be awake.

Clearing my throat, I say, "Listen, Thea—I don't know what was said at the table after I left but—"

She waves her hands haphazardly through the air. "Said? Nothing was said! Just girl talk, you know? Nothing to worry about."

I narrow my eyes at her. Redness is rising up her neck, a telltale sign that she's embarrassed. We stare at each other while Thea flashes through several different attempts at a smile. "It seems like there is something to worry about, actually."

"Ha! No. No, everything is fine! Don't you need to get to the shop? Big day tomorrow!"

I do need to get to the shop, but I need to get to the bottom of this even more.

"Thea, you're acting strange. Can we just talk about it, please?"

What can only be described as a cackle bursts forth. "Me? Strange? I'm totally normal, cool as a cucumber, easy breezy lemon squeeze-y! Wait, that's not the saying… Whatever! I'm—"

She puts her hand down in an effort to fake a casual lean, but instead of leaning against the countertop, her hand goes directly onto the top of my steaming mug of coffee, knocking it over and spilling it down the cabinets and onto the top of her feet.

"Fuck! Ow! Ow ow ow, it's hot!"

I don't even think before scooping her up and placing her on top of the counter, next to the sink. Running cool water, I navigate her feet under the faucet. The water runs over the top of her scarred and blistered toes, washing all the coffee away. Thankfully it only looks a little red and probably surprised her more than anything.

I turn the water off and then bracket her body with my arms, calming us both down with a deep breath. "Cool as a cucumber, huh, Rosie girl?"

She huffs a laugh, leaning her head onto my shoulder. "I guess I'm more so cool as a steaming hot cup of coffee."

"What did they say, Thea?"

She sighs. "They were only reiterating how serious you are about this. About us. I know you've been saying that, but it freaked me out to hear it from outsiders, too."

"I'm trying really hard not to push you into anything, Thea. I'm trying to be patient."

She pulls away and looks at me. "You are. You are making me feel secure. I'm trying really hard, too, even if it doesn't seem like it. The emotional scars are deep. They are invisible wounds that are having every opportunity to reopen as I live through such a traumatic time in my life again."

"You know it's different."

"I do know that, but it's hard to *really* know it."

"Mmm, yes we actually talk about that a lot in my family. We can know something here"—I tap her forehead—"but we don't always know it here." I tap her heart.

Relief washes over her face. "Yeah. Yeah, that's how I feel."

"I can respect that. I—" I want to tell her that I love her, but I know I can't. Not yet. "I have something I want to tell you, but I know you aren't ready."

Her eyes widen as she takes in what I want to communicate.

"Just know," I continue. "When you are ready to hear it. I'm ready to say it. Okay?"

"How are you so perfect?" she breathes.

"No one is perfect—I hate vegetables, remember? But, Thea… I believe people can be perfect for each other. You… you're perfect for me, and I'm doing my damndest to be perfect for you."

I dry her feet off and then help her down off the counter. "We have some finishing touches that we need to add today, and you have classes to teach, yes?"

Thea nods in confirmation.

"Come to the shop after class. Keep me and the boys company. I'm sure other family members will pop by, we can make them feel really awkward about bombarding you with emotional conversations."

She giggles, sweeter than any music I could ever make, and says, "I'd like that. Thank you, Jules. For everything."

All I can think about is how I'd do anything for her.

I am completely, entirely hers.

Chapter Thirty-Three
DON'T SCAR THE POOR KID
Thea

I WANT TO BE ALONE WITH YOU ♥
wishes

It's the morning of the grand opening. Bardot Brothers Coffee Co. will officially be in business. I think about the T-shirt I stole from Jules the first night we met, and I feel so... proud of him.

I feel proud of this man that has come to mean so much to me.

After thinking about it, I'm also a little bit proud of me. The girl I was six months ago would hardly recognize the woman I am today. She'd probably tell me to blink twice if I was caught in some sort of small-town cult.

All of a sudden I'm very focused on how many times I'm blinking.

"What's wrong with your face, Mama?" Chloe asks, bounding into the kitchen. Her pigtails are bouncing as she breaks into a dance. I think she's the most excited out of anyone to go to the grand opening today. Girl loves a party.

"Nothing, chicken. You about ready to go? Where's Pop?"

"I'm right here." Dad follows Chloe into the kitchen, adjusting his bolo tie.

Raising my eyebrows at him, I ask, "Fancy today, are we?"

Dad's less than impressed by my teasing. "Big day deserves a nice outfit."

"Let's go, let's go, let's go, pleaseeee!"

I laugh. "I think Chloe is going to combust if we don't leave."

When we arrive, we have to park down the block because there are already so many people in line waiting. Some students looking to get a peek at their new hang out spot and some townies that I've gotten to know in the last several months—Louie included.

At the very front of the line, Bex and Anders are arguing over the correct height of the ribbon that will be ceremoniously cut in a few minutes. An older woman with a camera around her neck and a large press badge that says *Sassafras Gazette* is frowning at them, furiously taking notes on her legal pad.

We slide past the three of them and walk into the coziest coffee shop I've ever seen. What used to be a run down facility with antiquated equipment has been replaced by several vignettes perfectly placed for intimate conversation, a wall full of bookshelves and assorted plants, and a wooden counter topped with a shiny new espresso machine.

In a nod to what used to be, the original sign that hung outside of the old shop is now hanging up behind the bar. *The Coffee Shop* joins a gallery wall of signage and art surrounding a hand painted logo for Bardot Brothers Coffee Co.

Underneath, my favorite Bardot brother is arranging a display of muffins that look just as decadent as he does.

I walk over and lean against the counter top. "Do you think one day we'll tell our son that he was conceived in this very spot?"

"I think if we ever feel like scarring the poor kid, that would be a good place to start," he jokes.

"It looks amazing in here."

He leans across, planting a kiss on my lips. "It does now that you're here."

"Get a room, you two!" Gabe calls from the storeroom. "Actually, don't. We've got a shop to open." He claps Jules on the back, a huge grin forming on both of their faces.

The entire Bardot family—and those of us who are family adjacent—gathers in front of the storefront, ready for the official opening. Jules is bracketed by his two brothers, a look of relief on his face. He's ready for this change, it's palpable. As the enormous scissors come down, everyone cheers. It's absolutely perfect.

Except, maybe the ribbon was just a *little* too low.

We made it a few hours before I could see Chloe starting to fade, and honestly I wasn't far behind her. It seemed like everything was running smoothly when we left. Ben almost lost his shit when Cole turned up with a date, but eventually he settled on making the poor guy insanely uncomfortable instead of spitting in his coffee.

Dad took Chloe home to rest, but I ended up going over to the studio to work on choreography. By the time I was ready to leave, the coffee shop was still incredibly busy, so I didn't bother going back in. I did, however, watch creepily from the front window, observing Jules in his element.

Someone else took the orders, but Jules was in charge of the actual drinks. He masterfully crafted lattes, cappuccinos, and americanos in the few minutes I stood there watching. His tattooed forearms continuously caught my attention as he wiped his hands on his black apron after every drink.

I'm pretty sure I was drooling the entire time.

But now, I'm back in Jules' bedroom, massaging my feet and calves with my handy dandy massage gun. It's become our little routine to spend an hour alone together before I inevitably pass out, only to wake up a few hours later and make my way back to my own room.

Chloe and Dad went to bed a while ago, but I've been waiting up for Jules because—*who am I?*—I want to hear all about his day.

Over the sound of the massage gun, I don't hear him come in, though. Instead, he scares the shit out of me when he knocks quietly on the bedroom door. Always so thoughtful, always asking for permission—even in his own damn house. Even in his own damn room.

"Come in," I call, clutching my chest to calm my racing heart.

He does just that, closing the door behind him.

Without a word, he comes in and collapses beside me on the bed. I brush his hair out of the part of his face that I can see.

"Long day?" I ask.

"Mmmm," is his only response, face too smushed in the pillow to say anything else.

"Need a massage?" I wave the tool uselessly in the air.

"Need you," he mumbles.

Oh. I can work with that.

He rolls over onto his side, smiling slightly as he takes me in. "What were you doing with this thing?"

Jules turns it back on, running it slowly up and down my thigh. "Ugh, I decided to go to the studio earlier, but now I'm paying the price."

"I know."

"You know…?"

"I mean, I saw you ogling me through the shop window earlier, looked like you'd been dancing for a while," he replies, adding a wink for good measure.

"I was not—" He turns the massager onto the lowest setting and digs it into my leg, effectively silencing me. "*Fuck*, that feels good. I'm so sore."

"I'd like to make you sore in other places." He looks up through a fan of thick eyelashes. "Please."

My hand finds the back of his head, tugging on the elastic holding his messy bun in place. "You're always so polite with me." I scratch my nails across his scalp. "Always such a good boy."

Yeah, second trimester has made me a certified horndog.

A rumble works its way up his chest as he climbs over me, the massage gun slowly inching higher and higher up my thigh.

"I can be a good boy if you promise to be quiet." His lips find the juncture of my neck, sucking lightly as he works his way down. At the same time, the massager finally reaches my clit, applying firm, consistent pressure through my shorts.

"I don't think this is one of the recommended uses from the manufacturer," I whimper, followed by an audible moan when it hits *just right*.

"Then they are really missing out," he replies.

The relentless vibrations are about to tip me over the edge, but right before I can get there, Jules pulls the massage gun away, much to my disdain. "Come back!"

He nips at my nipple through the loose T-shirt I'm wearing. "Some adjustments, first," he replies, helping me into a seated position. He makes quick work of removing my shirt and sports bra, then drags me to the edge of the bed, placing several pillows behind me so I'm not flat on my back.

Once he seems satisfied—I let him fuss over me to his heart's content—he kneels on the ground before me, propping my legs over his shoulders. "Where were we?" he asks before placing the massager directly back on my clit.

"Fuck!" I'm trying to be quiet but he's making it difficult.

"Shh, Rosie girl. Remember your promise."

"I didn't promise anything," I counter. In response he promptly removes the massager. "Noooo," I moan. "Fine, I can be—" I don't even finish before it's back, accompanied by a soft pinch to my nipple.

"Jules," I whisper. "I'm so close." He can tell, too. I see his hips working as he seeks some friction against the edge of the bed. His hair is hanging loose around his shoulders, and he looks like some sort of fallen angel. Ethereal. Worshipful.

It's that vision that sends me over the edge. My legs are like a vice around his head, my body convulsing with the sudden onslaught of pleasure. "That's it, baby. Ride it," he encourages.

And I do. But it's not long before I need *more*. "Your dick," I plead. "I need you."

Faster than I've ever seen him move, he's up and stripping, his clothes landing in a haphazard pile on the rug, my shorts quickly joining them. He's hard and thick, a portrait of pure masculinity.

I'm so wet from my first orgasm, Jules is easily able to slide deep inside me. He places my legs right back where they were before, the angle putting me at a loss for words. I can't tell if I'm still orgasming or if I'm on to a new one. Either way, this man does magical things to my body.

"Jules! Oh my God, Jules." I scrunch my eyes shut, overwhelmed by him.

"Eyes on me, Thea. I want you to see exactly who makes you feel this way."

He does. I know it's him. I know I'm absolutely ruined for anyone else. He pounds into me, his finger rubbing my clit in time. We are sweaty, manic, and absolutely feral for each other. With a few more thrusts, we are both falling into sexual oblivion. Now it's my turn to remind him to be quiet as a primal grunt rips from his throat.

Once we are both entirely wrung out, he collapses next to me, breathing heavily.

"Don't pass out, old man," I manage to mutter, though I'm feeling just as exhausted as he looks.

My sass earns me a swift smack to the pussy—something I enjoy far more than I should.

After we both clean up, I slide under the covers next to him, still completely naked. "Don't go back to your room," he mumbles, pulling my back flush against his front. "Stay with me."

I think about it for so long, his breath begins to even out. "Okay," I finally whisper, hoping he's fallen asleep and can't hear me. It's the coward's way out, I know.

To my surprise, his lips find my shoulder blade as he squeezes my hip. Well, I guess I can't escape now.

Not that I actually wanted to, anyway.

Chapter Thirty-Four
EVERYONE NEEDS THERAPY
Thea

FOREVER YOUNG
Bob Dylan

I'm rudely awoken from the best night's sleep of my life by a door being flung open, slamming loudly against the wall. I pop straight up in bed only to realize that my tits are out and proud this morning.

We are a pretty free-flowing family, but I certainly wasn't expecting my child to barge in on my nude form before—I check the clock—8 AM Quickly, I pull the duvet up to cover my chest.

"Eww! Why are you nakey, Mama?" Chloe yells, prancing into the room in her mismatched pajama set. We're going to have to start working on a little thing called boundaries with her.

I look around the room, hoping to find an answer to her question in the thin air surrounding me. "I—uhm…"

"It was hot last night, don't you think, Chlo?" Jules asks, rescuing me from my temporary mental loss.

Chloe shrugs. "I wasn't hot."

I nod, dazedly. "That's good, my little chicken. Why don't

you go put a show on, and Mama will be out there in just a second, okay?"

She looks at me, then at Jules, wheels turning quickly in her little head. Her eyes snap down to my belly, covered but obviously visible under the blanket, and then back to Jules again. "Is JuJu my new daddy?"

"No!" I immediately shout. "I mean…" Oh God. "This is an after-coffee conversation, okay, Chlo? But I promise I'll answer any questions you have."

She seems to deem that an acceptable answer, turning on her heels and skipping back out of the room as quickly as she came in. When she asked about Jules being her dad before I was able to evade her question, but it looks like my time is up.

Jules hops up, using a pillow to cover his *manhood*, and closes the door behind her. "I'll get a lock," he states, as if a four-year-old little blonde tornado didn't just ask if he was her father.

"Orrrr no more sleepovers," I reply.

His brows furrow. "I like the lock idea better."

I flop back against the pillows, burying my face in my hands. "God, that was embarrassing. I hope I didn't scar her for the rest of her life."

"Everyone should go to therapy, this might be her reason."

"That's not helping." I feel the bed move as Jules slides back in. His hands come up to mine and slowly tangle in a way that forces me to stop hiding and face him. I'm one hundred percent positive my face is tomato red; Jules' smirk is all the confirmation I need.

"I really do think a good lock and therapy is the way to go." He smiles sweetly down at me, his long hair hanging loose around us.

Fuck, I probably need therapy too. I say as much to Jules.

"I can get you some recommendations—Mom really pushed it for all of us and, with her job being what it is, she definitely will know who to connect you with," he says.

Sighing, I roll over to face him. "It's always been too

expensive for me to even consider, though I have nothing against actually going."

His gaze travels over my face, contemplating. "You won't like this but I'm happy to help you pay for something. There's a lot of transition going on right now, it could be helpful. There's also so many online options nowadays that are more affordable."

"I'll look into it," I promise. "But for now, I need to figure out what I'm going to tell Chloe."

"Do you want me to be a part of that conversation?" he asks, and I know he won't be offended either way.

Shaking my head, I answer, "No, I should be the one to do it. I don't really talk about her dad often, and I know she'll have more questions as she gets older."

Jules is silent for a long time, mulling over his next words. I can always tell when he's internally processing because his jaw begins to work and his stare gets even more intense than usual. My dad is the same way, so I've had years of practice waiting patiently while the men in my life figure out what to say. I busy myself by tracing the tattoos on Jules' arm.

"You never told me what song this was," I say, interrupting his silence.

He looks down at his arm. "It's *Forever Young* by Bob Dylan. Dad used to sing it to us before bed every night."

Wow, that is quite possibly the sweetest thing I've ever heard. "Your family is something else, Julien Bardot."

"They're your family now too. This little guy is forever binding you to the chaos." His hand comes to rest on my belly, and he smiles big enough that his eyes create little crinkles in the corners. "And Chloe, too. And Hank." Jules' tone turns more serious now. "I may not be Chloe's dad, but I will always treat her the exact same way that I treat this baby. I promise she will never be made to feel any less than because she isn't mine biologically."

Am I crying? I think I'm definitely crying. Sobbing, actually. A broken "Thank you," is all I manage to get out. Jules rubs my back, taking deep breaths that I eventually sync up to. With one more deep inhale, I say, "Okay, I really need to go talk to Chloe. We'll come back to this."

Jules plants a firm kiss on my forehead. "Whenever you're ready, Rosie girl."

After donning appropriate attire, and Jules bringing me a cup of coffee, I make my way to the living room where I find Chloe. Plopping down on the couch beside her, I say, "Hey, Chlo. Are you ready to talk?"

She pauses her show and then climbs into my lap. There's less and less room there for her recently, which makes me miss the days we could really cuddle. "The baby in here is my brother?" she asks.

"Mhmm." I push her morning hair out of her face so I can see her scrunched up little nose.

"And JuJu is my new daddy?" she continues.

"No, he's not, baby," I reply. She's confused and this is hard to explain. I know we'll probably have this conversation over and over again in the next several years. "Your dad and I met when Mama was younger. Sometimes people aren't ready to be mommies or daddies, and he wasn't ready."

"But you were ready to be a mommy," she states, matter of factly. "You are my favorite mommy. The best mommy!"

She gives me a big hug to punctuate that statement. I breathe her in, needing her freely given little-kid love. "Thank you, baby. I love being your mama, and I'm so glad that you are my Chloe. If you ever have any more questions, I am always here to answer them, okay?"

Chloe nods, snuggling even further onto my lap. "So why can't JuJu be my new daddy?"

"I..." I don't know how to answer that. "Maybe one day he can." I cringe because I don't want to get her hopes up, but Jules has made it abundantly clear that he views Chloe the same way he views the new baby.

She nods and then unpauses *Doc McStuffins*, her favorite

show at the moment, and I guess that's the end of the conversation. After a moment, Chloe begins explaining exactly what is happening on the TV, as if I can't see it. "Chlo, I can see the show. You don't have to give me a play-by-play."

She looks up at me like I'm crazy. "I'm not talking to you, Mama. I'm talking to my brother! He can't see the show, so I have to tell him what's happening."

Kid logic. I love it so much. "Carry on, then."

We watch the entire rest of the show like that. When the credits start running, Chloe speaks just loud enough for me to hear her over the theme song. "I wish JuJu was my dad."

I can't help but wish for the exact same thing.

Chapter Thirty-Five
SAGE ADVICE FROM ANDERS OLSSON
Jules

SAY LOVE
James TW

Week one of the reopened coffee shop has gone about as expected.

And by expected, I mean we broke seven mugs, way under-ordered coffee beans, and the light in the storage room keeps flickering.

I'm grateful that Bex and Anders were able to extend their trip a bit because I've needed their help while Mom and Dad watch the girls.

"Behind!" Bex calls to the completely oblivious Gabe who turns around instead of getting out of the way. The tray Bex was carrying flips out of her hand, landing with a loud crash on the tile floor.

Make that nine broken mugs.

"Gabe, what the fuck?" Bex looks pissed, and I can't blame her. Gabe's head has not been in the game lately, despite his insistence that he's fine, and it's driving all of us crazy. "I think that's my cue," she says, bending down to clean the mess. Bex is working a few hours a day much to all of our annoyance—the woman had a baby a month ago, she should be resting. But she insists she's fine and wants to "feel like a normal person every once in a while." Her words, not mine.

After what feels like the longest day yet, we finally lock up later that night, each one of us more exhausted than the next. We've been trying to rotate who does cleaning and prep for the next day so at least we can get some sleep, and tonight it's Anders and me on duty. Gabe and Ben get their things and file out, looking guilty for not staying.

"Go!" Anders shoos. "We'll be fine!"

We wipe down tables, sweep the floor, and restock ingredients, all in comfortable silence. Anders hums quietly to himself and sometimes I'll join in. It's nice to have another musical person around. Eventually Anders breaks the silence.

"How are you feeling about becoming a dad?" he asks.

"Fucking terrified."

He lets out a hearty laugh. "I would be more worried if you were feeling super confident. It's scary business keeping tiny humans alive."

"I get a small glimpse of that with Chloe, but she's the most self-sufficient kid I know."

Anders nods. "Yeah, El seemed so much bigger once we brought Molly home, but she's still only two. I'm more and more amazed by your parents every day. Four of you by the time Gabe was four—it's insane."

"Absolutely insane," I agree with a smile. "Any advice you want to pass along? You've supported Bex through two pregnancies and births. What have you learned along the way?"

He stops mopping and rests his chin on the top of the handle. "Hmmm. Well in pregnancy and early postpartum in particular, you are useless. It can feel like the baby only needs her, so the best thing for you to do would be to make sure she has everything she needs. I'm sure you already do that," he adds.

"I'm trying. I read the weekly updates on the What to Expect app. I cook protein rich meals for her. I'm trying to be aware of her needs, it just—it doesn't feel like enough sometimes."

Anders shakes his head. "Don't tell anyone I said this, especially not Gabe, but of all of the Bardot brothers this could have happened to… c'mon man, you were made to be a dad. A partner." He pauses for a moment. "And Thea… she's great. She's already a mom, a good one at that. She's been dealt a shitty hand, but now she has you. And all of us."

I pause considering what Anders is saying. "What if I fuck it up?"

"You might," he replies. "The two most important words you can say to anyone are 'I'm sorry.' You fuck up? You apologize. To Thea. To your kid. I don't think I ever heard my dad apologize to anyone. Now I make it my mission to be quick to apologize. It's the best way to show someone that you care."

"Yeah, I can do that." I'm saying it to reassure myself more than anyone.

"I'm telling you, Jules, when that baby is born, nothing else in the world is going to matter. I used to live feeling like I had to prove myself to everyone around me. Prove that I was good enough, talented enough. Now? I live to hear the sound of Elodie's laugh. I live to see Bex rocking Molly as she falls asleep on her chest. Those are the things that matter, none of the other shit."

I think about his words as we finish the last few tasks. When it's time to leave, I stop Anders, sticking out my hand for a handshake. He grabs it, pulling me into a big bear hug. "You're going to be a great dad, Jules," he says, clapping my shoulder when he finally releases me.

I nod and head toward my car. I stop before getting in and call out, "Hey, Anders. You're already a great dad. Thanks for all your help this week."

He gives me a salute and then he's off, headed back toward a family that loves him.

Maybe I can get there soon, too.

ENTIRELY YOURS

I run by Louie's on the way home to grab a bite to take home with me. Louie waves at me when I walk in and gestures for me to have a seat at the bar while he finishes up with a customer. While I'm waiting, I take a look around. Louie's hasn't changed much in the many years I've been coming here. There's nostalgia within these walls for thousands of people who have created memories here. I hope one day Bardot Brothers Coffee Co. feels just as nostalgic for anyone who visits.

Louie meanders over, pouring me a beer before I even ask for it. "You need something to eat?" he guesses. When I nod, he continues, "I heard the opening has been a success. When I've stopped by for my morning coffee, it sure has been packed."

"It's been good," I smile. "It's no Louie's, though."

He waves his dish rag around. "This old place? Falling apart." He winks. "Just like I like it."

I order a burger to go—Thea has finally allowed beef back in the house—checking to make sure next week's food order for the coffee shop has been placed while I wait.

When Louie drops a greasy paper bag in front of me, I get some cash out to pay so I can leave. I'm ready to get back to Thea. Louie's next words, however, stop me in my tracks. "I heard the apartment is ready. When's Thea moving back in?"

"The—what? I…" I stammer like a fool.

Louie looks at me like I've grown three heads. "The apartment, Jules. Upstairs? Kathy told me it's ready to go. Figured Thea and everyone would be moving back in soon."

"I…" *hadn't heard that*, is what I want to say. "I'll have to ask Thea. Been busy so we haven't discussed it yet. I-I should get back to her now, actually. Thanks, Louie." I lift the bag in my hand, waving it awkwardly in goodbye.

The apartment is ready.

The apartment is ready and Thea hasn't told me yet.

Maybe she doesn't know.

But if Louie knows, of course Thea knows.

I'm more than ready to bring it up to Thea when I get home, however I'm effectively silenced when I find her curled up, sound asleep in my bed.

Here. She belongs here, with me.

I debate waking her up to ask, but I know that wouldn't go over well. My concern will have to wait until tomorrow. Even though my body is tired, my mind is racing.

It takes a very long time for rest to find me, and when it does, I dream in vignettes of raising our family. Birthday parties, family dinners, more kids.

I want it all, and I want it with her.

Chapter Thirty-Six
SURELY WHAT?
Thea

FAKE
Lauv, Conan Gray

The apartment is ready.

The apartment is ready, and I need to tell Jules.

The apartment is ready, and I *don't want* to tell Jules.

Something is wrong with me. I've gotten comfortable here in this little unit we've built. That should terrify me, but for some reason it doesn't.

Jules has done everything right. But my brain keeps telling me that surely he has some flaw I'm not seeing.

Maybe I should ask his mom about a therapist recommendation…

I've been at the studio a lot this week while Dad watches Chloe. I know he's going to miss his little buddy when she starts kindergarten, but I also know he's ready to have some freedom back.

Summer dance classes have been going so well, I truly couldn't have asked for a better community to come into. We've been working on choreography for our first ever studio performance over Labor Day weekend. Sassafras apparently goes all out at their end of summer festival. I still have several things I need to do to prepare for the show and know that summer will be over in the blink of an eye—it always goes too fast!

During my lunch break, I decide to wander over to the local craft store. I want to see if there's a simple costume I could throw together. Maybe I can rope Jules and Dad into helping me make bows for all of the girls...

I'm so lost in thought about all of the bullet points on my to-do list, I don't even register my name being called until the third time she says it.

"Thea? Thea Rose? Is that you?" she asks.

I look around, trying to identify the source of the voice. And then I see her. "Melissa?"

Fuck. Melissa Howard. We danced together in the company at Ballet Boston. She is a few years older than me, and I am fully convinced she hates my guts.

"Oh my God!" She beelines across the street, a teenage girl on her heels. "Thea fucking Rose. What are you doing here?" Melissa eyes my stomach but has the decency not to say anything.

"I...I—"

Before I have a chance to gather my thoughts, Melissa continues. "Shoot, sorry! This is my sister, Olivia—she's visiting Hawthorne! I'm trying to convince her to join the ballet, but she wants to go to a four year university." Melissa rolls her eyes as if that is the dumbest idea she's ever heard. Olivia looks like she'd rather be anywhere else, which, honestly, same.

Melissa's hand reaches out and clutches my arm. "But really"—her look turns pitiful—"how have you been? Since, you know, everything?" She gestures vaguely toward me.

Which is confusing because she shouldn't know the reason I left the ballet. Guy was insistent that I kept Chloe a secret, eventually forcing me to leave the company for vague "personal reasons."

I cross my arms over my chest. "What do you mean 'everything'?"

"Oh, well of course Guy told me." She gives me a little pout and places her hand on her chest. That's when I notice it. A giant fucking rock on her left ring finger. Melissa doesn't miss a thing. She notices me noticing her ring and immediately shoves her hand into my face. "Isn't it gorgeous? He proposed last month."

"He?" My question comes out as a barely audible whisper, my eyes darting back and forth between Melissa and her sister.

"Yes, Guy proposed! I couldn't believe it, I was in complete shock! He did it at the end of a perfor—ow!" Olivia has correctly clocked the shock on my face and elbowed her sister in the side.

Melissa's hands come up to the side of her face as her mouth forms a perfect O. "Wait! You used to have a crush on him didn't you! I'm so sorry you had to find out this way."

She doesn't look sorry. She looks like the cat that ate the canary.

"But you obviously have moved on," she continues, looking down to where my hand is resting on my stomach. "Your first baby! Must be so exciting!"

"It's... It's not my first."

Finally, I'm able to catch Melissa by surprise. "Wow. You've been busier than I thought," she says. "How old is your... son? Daughter?"

"She's about to turn five."

"Five..." Melissa narrows her eyes as she attempts to do the math in her head. I see exactly when it clicks. "That's why you left the company."

Ding ding ding.

"So what was it Guy told you?" I ask.

She hesitates now, her confidence starting to wane. "He told me you had a mental breakdown. That you were obsessed with him so the board decided to let you go." She eyes her ring, looking as if her world is beginning to crumble the same way mine did five years ago. "I'm starting to think that wasn't actually what happened."

"What an asshole," Olivia pipes up. "I've never liked him." She directs that part toward me.

"Stop, Olivia! I'm sure there's a reason that's what he told me." Melissa is grasping at straws now.

I scoff. "There's definitely a reason he lied to you. That reason is about to turn five."

"Oh shit," Olivia says. Melissa's face is now white as a ghost.

"Look," I sigh, having had much longer to process this information than Melissa has. "I'm sorry you had to find out about it this way, and honestly, I don't care if you don't believe me. But I have to go. It was… well it wasn't good to see you, but I hope everything works out for y'all."

I turn on my heel and walk back toward the studio, completely forgetting my original destination.

Without realizing it, I stop when I get to the front of the coffee shop and watch Jules through the window. I'm staring absentmindedly when all of a sudden he's standing in the window staring back at me.

He's so handsome, I can hardly stand it. His hair is pulled back in his usual bun, loose pieces falling to frame his face. He's looking at me with such reverence. Such…*love.*

The realization hits me and I audibly gasp. Jules sees the change in my demeanor and pushes through the front door to meet me.

He bends down meeting my eyes, both hands coming to cradle the back of my elbows. "What's going on, Thea? Is everything alright? Is the baby…?"

"Baby is fine!" I don't want to let him keep worrying even though I am spiraling. "I'm fine!" Between the squeak in my voice and the disbelieving look Jules gives me, I know I'm not being very convincing. "I just realized… I realized… we need to plan Chloe's birthday party. Well, *I* need to plan it. I should go."

"I can help you plan," he replies, speaking to me as if I'm the one turning five.

I wave him off. "Oh you don't need to do that! I'm her mom."

He takes that like a blow to the face. Finally he lets go of my arms and stands up to his full height. "Ouch." He runs a hand over his scruff.

"That's not what I meant. I am just... I'm burdening you enough as it is."

This seems to piss him off even further. He takes my hand and pulls me into the empty dance studio. When we get inside he turns, pinning me up against the door. "Listen to me Thea—what's your middle name?"

A laugh bursts free because how have we not covered this yet? "Shirley."

"Surely what?"

My head falls onto his chest. "Shirley. That's my middle name."

Jules hand comes under my chin, forcing my eyes up to his. "Thea Shirley Rose. You are not a burden. Chloe is not a burden. Hank is not a burden. Understood?"

I nod.

"Words, Thea. Am I understood?"

"Yes, Julien. Understood." I stick my tongue out at him, and he returns my sass by nipping at my bottom lip. His hand slides to my ass, squeezing gently as he takes my mouth with his.

His kiss is a promise, a declaration.

He drags me further and further in with each swipe of his tongue against mine. After a few minutes my hands get a mind of their own, reaching down to unbutton Jules' jeans.

"Woah there, Rosie girl." He smirks. "Later, okay? I have to get back to work and so do you."

I groan, wanting to continue down the path we were going.

He laughs, planting one more kiss on my lips. "Have you eaten?"

I shake my head, realizing I haven't eaten *and* I never made it to the craft store.

"C'mon." We go back to the coffee shop where Jules fixes me a croissant sandwich and makes me sit down to drink an entire glass of water before he lets me leave.

Despite everything weighing on me—the apartment and running into Melissa—I spend the rest of the day with a smile on my face.

Chapter Thirty-Seven
FINISH UP, YOU TWO!
Jules

PARTY 4 U
Charli xcx

I swing by Ben and Gabe's apartment a few days later. I knock, waiting for one of them to answer while eyeing the door across the hall.

Thea still hasn't said anything about her place being ready, and, after some thought and a little more sleep, I'm not keen to bring it up in case she decides she wants to move back in. I have made it as clear as I can that what I want is for the Roses to stay exactly where they are, but ultimately it's up to her.

I'm lost in thought when the door swings open and—"Cole?"

"Julien. I was just leaving." She looks like her normal mixture of mildly annoyed and cleverly observant.

Ben runs up behind her, shouting, "Wait!"

"Fuck off, Benjamin," she calls, brushing past me, down the stairs, and out of sight.

We both stand there watching her for a moment. "What the hell was that about?"

"Nothing," he replies.

Exasperated, I walk into the apartment. "I'm getting really damn tired of people keeping things from me."

"Who else is keeping things from you?" Ben asks. But I don't want to get into it either so I wave him off.

"Right… so you want me to talk but you don't want to talk. I think there's a word for that…" he muses.

"Yeah, yeah. I'm a hypocrite. Got it. Can I get to why I even came over here to begin with?"

He winks. "It wasn't because you missed your favorite brother?"

"I heard that!" Gabe yells from the back.

"You come in here, too!" I call back. He wanders in wearing only his boxers. "Were you sleeping?" I check my watch. "At 5 PM?"

He stretches his arms up above his head. "I was trying to, but it was hard with Ben and Cole going at each other like cats and dogs."

Both of us turn to look at Ben expectantly. "Did you come here to inquire into my personal life or did you need something?" he diverts.

"Right." I clap. "I need something. Chloe turns five next week, and with all of the chaos going on, Thea hasn't been able to plan a party."

"Say no more," Ben exclaims. "I'm in."

———

Apparently Chloe had confided in Ben that she wanted a mermaid unicorn glitter party. Mom and Dad said we could use their backyard, so we immediately got to planning.

Since most of Chloe's friends currently consist of adults, we decided to go all out and do a birthday brunch-slash-tea party. Gabe planned the menu, Ben took over decorations, and I was in charge of finding a few gifts and making sure that Mayor Cattington could be in attendance—Chloe's only request.

I walk into the Bardot family backyard a week and a half later, juggling three present boxes and a cat carrier loaded up with a very unhappy cat, and stop in my tracks.

Strings of twinkle lights are crisscrossing the backyard. Glittery stars and rainbows hang from the tree branches, sparkling magnificently in the sunlight. One long table is set up, covered with a pink and purple sequined cloth. Themed plates, napkins, and cups line the table, alternating between mermaids and unicorns. Center pieces explode with flowers and little glitter stars that match the ones dangling from the trees.

"What the fuck?" I'm speechless. Gabe and Ben stand in the center of it all, grinning. Who are these two and what have they done with my goon-head brothers? "When did you two become professional party planners?"

"Isn't it amazing?" Gabe asks, bouncing on his toes.

"Fuck yeah, it's amazing. How did you pull it off, though?" I'm still having a hard time believing what I'm seeing.

Ben's face grows serious. "Chloe told me she's never had a real birthday party before. And fuck if that didn't break my heart. I wanted her to have something special. You asked, so we had to deliver."

This is why I love my family. They can be intrusive and overbearing, but they love well and they love hard.

"I'm going to have to hire you for a baby shower," I say, freeing my hands so I can pull them both into a group hug.

"Holy shit," I hear Thea utter behind me.

"Language, Ma—Oh. My. GOODNESS!" Chloe screams in excitement, following her mom into the backyard. Her enthusiasm is palpable as she jumps up and down, tugging on Thea's arm.

"How—I don't…" Thea's reaction matches mine. She steps further into the yard, taking the entire scene in. When she turns back around, her eyes are full of tears. "Thank you," she mouths, looking at the three of us.

"Well, I'll be damned." It's Hank Rose's turn to walk into the party. He gives us a wink and a nod, which is the equivalent of a kiss on the mouth coming from him.

A loud meow catches all of our attention. I unzip the carrier, letting Cat out to explore the set up, too. He immediately races over to Chloe, butting his head up against her leg. "This is the best day EVER!" she screeches, and I smile, knowing the day has just begun.

Gabe's menu consists of tea sandwiches, chicken nuggets, and a build your own mac and cheese bar. He got juice boxes for the kids—Bex and Anders came in, as well as a few girls Chloe met in her dance class—and mimosas for the adults. He even went so far as to find non-alcoholic champagne for Thea and Anders, who has been sober since before he and Bex started dating.

Chloe has been glowing all day, but Thea... Thea has been radiant. She's wearing a form fitting sundress that accentuates her growing belly. Her hair is down in loose waves, and she kicked off her shoes as soon as she got here. She looks like a goddess that has been accidentally placed here among the mere mortals. And what's better is that I can tell she's having a good time. She's been socializing with the other parents, pointing out new party details to Chloe, and sneaking bits of frosting off the cake when she thinks no one is looking.

But I'm always looking. I can't take my eyes off of her.

She notices me noticing her, and her cheeks flush prettily. She saunters over, sidling up next to me. "Think anyone will notice if we go missing for a few minutes?"

I raise my eyebrow at her. "And where exactly were you thinking of going?"

"This house has a lot of rooms. Pick one," she challenges.

I look around to make sure that everyone is otherwise occupied and then say, "Follow me." She bites her bottom lip and does what I say.

My fingers tangle with hers as I guide us toward the guest

bathroom off the kitchen. Close enough that we can hear if people start to look for us.

I close the door, flipping the lock so we won't be interrupted again. I pat the counter next to the sink, indicating she should hop up.

"Nope." She shakes her head and the coy lip bite is back. I'm confused until she sinks down to her knees.

"No, Thea. I-I can't let you…" She's ignoring me, instead unbuttoning my jeans with a determined look in her eye.

"Why not?" she asks. "I really, *really* want to." She looks up at me, lustful gaze turning suddenly earnest. "I won't keep going if you want me to stop, but if you're only saying no because I'm pregnant and you have some complex protecting my knees, then hand me a towel and enjoy the next ten minutes."

"I won't fucking last ten minutes," I grit out.

Her grin is wicked. "Perfect. Pass me that towel."

I reach over her head, grabbing one of the hand towels. Instead of passing it to her, I get down next to her, folding it in thirds to provide the maximum amount of cushion.

"Always taking care of me," she tuts. "Even when I'm trying to take care of you."

My hand finds the back of her head, tugging until she falls into me. She tastes like the frosting I caught her stealing. When I pull away, I tell her, "You don't have to do this."

She rolls her eyes at me. "Stand up, Julien. I'm so wet from the thought of getting my mouth around your cock, I should have worn underwear."

"You—you're not wearing underwear?" I choke out.

Thea's head moves side to side, a smirk playing along her full lips. She makes quick work of my pants and briefs once I stand, eager just like she said she would be. Her warm mouth slides over the tip of my cock and, I was right, this definitely won't take ten minutes. I'm dangerously close to coming down her throat already.

She pulls back, looks me in the eye, and she fucking spits right on the head. "Thea," I groan. "You're going to kill me."

"At least you'll go out with a bang," she teases, quickly getting back to work. She hums and takes me as far back as she can, her hand circling around the base. Each firm stroke of her hand in combination with the wet heat of her mouth, sends me higher and higher. Thea moans, vibrations working their way up my spine. I'm so close, I—

"Wait!" My hands sink back into her hair, pulling her off me with a *pop*. Her lips are swollen and wet, and fuck I didn't think she could get prettier.

"Was it bad?" Thea asks, a hint of shyness in her voice.

"Bad? Fuck no. Baby it was so *fucking* good, but I can't stop thinking about how you don't have any underwear on, and I want to fuck that sweet cunt." I bend down and take her lips in mine. "Please let me fuck you."

She nods, reluctantly. "You can suck me off again, I promise," I reassure her. That seems to make her feel better. She pops up, and spreads the towel out on the counter before she sits down. Now it's my turn to get on my knees. I slide my hands up her legs, squeezing slowly as I go, enjoying how it makes her head loll to the side. When I reach her hips I find that she was not lying to me.

Thea has no underwear on.

My restraint snaps. I shove her dress up, stand, and line myself up at her entrance. She also wasn't lying about how wet she is because I easily thrust in all the way to the hilt.

My hand comes up to cover her mouth right as she lets out another guttural moan. Our hips slap together creating a lewd soundtrack playing in the background. I'm not going to make it, I want her to come but I'm already so close to the edge. I remove my hand from her mouth and move it down to her clit, stroking firmly.

I hold it together until I begin to feel her tightening. And then, we both fall. She slaps her own hand over her mouth, and I bite my tongue to keep myself quiet. What a picture of debauchery we paint as we slowly make our way back down from the orgasm-induced high.

A little sweaty and a whole lot disheveled.

Knocking startles us both and I instinctively cover Thea.

"Finish up, you two! Almost time to sing Happy Birthday!" Mom calls through the door.

"Oh my God," Thea whispers, laughing and burying her face in my chest. "Once this baby is old enough to stay without me for a few days, we are taking a trip somewhere remote. Where no one can interrupt us."

Shock tumbles through me at her insinuation. The fact that she'd even be thinking about a future when she's been so scared to commit. "I'll start looking into locations," I half joke. Only, I'm not really joking at all because that actually sounds like a dream come true.

A weekend away with Thea? Sign me up.

Chapter Thirty-Eight
I DON'T EVEN NEED THERAPY
Thea

DANCE WITH ME
Tones & I

I'm riding a high after the party that Jules and his brothers planned for Chloe. When I think back to her last birthday party which consisted of me, Chloe, and Dad going to McDonald's so Chloe could play on the indoor playground, I want to cry.

I begged the universe for a change, and it seems like it is paying attention this time.

Maybe I don't actually need this appointment with Iris, the therapist Elaine recommended. Life is great, I'm handling everything surprisingly well, in my opinion.

I guess I'll go this once because it's already booked… but she'll probably pat me on the back and say I'm good to go.

Driving out to Iris' office, I get a chance to admire the town more than I usually do. My life right now consists of about one square mile, which I'm not mad about. I pass by the park where the Labor Day festival will be held, and where Jules took me on our date, and see the cute gazebo that would actually be a perfect stage. I make a mental note to ask about that later.

When I arrive at the office, I find a seat in the waiting room. They really have this calming thing down to an art—the lights are low, there's soft music playing, and the chairs are so cushy, I might never get up. I pick up a home decor magazine and start absentmindedly flipping through the pages. My mind starts to wander, thinking of a future where Jules and I are decorating his home, putting in some more feminine touches. Turning the room that I'm currently using, and I use that term loosely, into a nursery for baby boy. What theme would we do? Or no theme might be better so he can grow into it. I wonder if Jules would let me paint…

"Thea Rose?"

A tall, spindly woman is standing at the door to the waiting room eyeing me expectantly over her wire frame glasses. Seeing as I'm the only one currently in the waiting room, she doesn't bother looking around, instead holding the door open while I drag myself out of the cozy waiting-room chair.

"It's nice to meet you, Thea. Right this way." She motions down the hall to another room. This one has a large window with a cornflower-blue sofa underneath and a cream wingback chair directly across from it. There's a desk in the corner topped with books, notepads, and file folders. Iris' diplomas are framed and hung on the wall, along with some muted pieces of abstract art.

"Am I supposed to lie down?" I ask, moving toward the couch.

"Whatever makes you most comfortable," she replies. "But most people sit, if that's what you're asking." Her tone is kind, welcoming me into what she can obviously see is a new experience.

When I do take a seat, she asks, "What brings you in today?"

"Oh. Hmm. That's a hard question to answer. I… I guess I have a lot going on at the moment and my… well, I'm not really sure what he is to me. My baby daddy?" I laugh awkwardly. "He thought it might be a good idea to come in."

Iris smiles, taking a few notes on the pad in her lap. "What about you? Do you think it's a good idea to come in?"

I lean over trying to get a glimpse of what she's writing but her scrawl is loopy and difficult to read upside down. She notices, of course, and reassures, "Don't worry, I only keep notes for myself. Helps me remember things in my old age. If there's anything of significance that I write down, I'll be sure to tell you."

"Right..." I pause, thinking about her previous question. "I'm not sure if it's a good idea to come in. I feel good now, things are going well. And I've handled so much on my own over the course of my life, I guess I'm not sure if I need someone to help."

"Mmm." She nods. "Can you tell me a bit more about what you've been handling on your own?"

So, I do. I tell her about Chloe and the studio. About this new pregnancy. I tell Iris about moving to Boston from Texas after my grandmother passed away and about how my mom died when I was young so I don't even remember her. I tell her about how strange it's been to be enveloped by the Bardot family, so easily embraced by people who hardly know me.

I talk for so long, a little alarm goes off, and yet, I still feel like I have more to say. "Is that all the time we have?" I ask, worry creeping into my tone.

"That's my five minute warning," Iris replies. "I'm sorry, I should have told you about it when we started. Helps keep me on track."

Five minutes? We haven't even gotten to the therapy part of things yet. "Oh, okay. I..."

Iris looks at me through her glasses. She's very good at giving wait time, I see.

"I guess I should schedule my next appointment."

She gives me an approving smile. "I would love that."

ENTIRELY YOURS

On my drive home, I stop by the apartment. We only lived in it briefly, but it already feels so cramped and sterile in comparison to Jules' house. I walk into the empty living room, trying to picture moving back in with Dad, Chloe, and a newborn. I poke my head into my old bedroom and realize there's simply no way I can share with Chloe and the baby. Chloe loves Jules' house. She loves having a backyard for building fairy houses. She loves exploring with Cat and trying new recipes with Jules.

And then I'm supposed to—what? Bring her back to this tiny apartment with no outdoor space where she has to share a room with her mom and little brother. I remember the newborn stage, no way is she getting a good night's sleep that way.

Right there in the middle of the empty apartment, I make up my mind.

We're moving in with Jules.

I get back in my car and drive as quickly as possible back home. As soon as I turn on our street, I see that his car isn't there. I circle around and head toward the coffee shop instead, feeling a renewed sense of urgency.

What if he's changed his mind?

What if he doesn't want this anymore?

I park in front of the shop, waddle-running from the car to the front door as quickly as possible. I spot him as soon as I walk in. He's behind the bar, making a drink at the espresso machine. "Jules! I want to move in!" I shout from the entrance, not caring that the entire shop turns to look at me like I've lost the plot.

Ben appears next to Jules, who looks completely dumbstruck, and says, "Didn't you already do that?"

Jules' palm comes up to the side of Ben's face, pushing him away without ever breaking eye contact with me. He rounds the bar top and prowls toward me. He still hasn't said a word since my proclamation, and I can't tell if he's about to kiss me or steer me out of the shop so he can let me down easy.

When he finally gets within arms reach, one hand comes up to grasp my chin while the other circles around my waist. He dips me, taking my mouth in a cinema-worthy embrace that has my stomach erupting in butterflies. Vaguely, I hear the crowded coffee shop break in whoops and applause, but all I see is him, all I feel is him.

And nothing has ever felt so right.

Chapter Thirty-Nine
HOT VAMPIRES
Jules

DAY DREAMING
Jack & Jack

After what can only be described as the most successful five-year-old birthday party Sassafras has ever seen, I feel like I need to recruit my brothers to help plan a surprise baby shower for Thea.

She would never ask for one, but I see the way she lights up anytime someone pays her an inkling of attention, and it makes me want to lavish her in it. That, and we really have nothing for the baby so I'd love to pull friends and family together to celebrate.

When I get home from the shop that night, Thea is curled up in our bed—fuck I like the sound of that—playing a game on her phone.

I lean over to give her a kiss, enjoying the way she smiles sweetly up at me. "Already making yourself comfortable in here, are you?"

She sits up straight. "Oh my God, I just assumed. I can—I don't have to sleep in here. I can go back to the guest bedroom."

"Over my dead body," I grumble, planting more kisses down her neck.

She smirks. "Well, we can't have that, can we?"

I spend a moment debating whether or not to move all of her things into my bedroom now or crawl into bed and pull her close for a late night snuggle.

Snuggling wins. "How was your session today?" I ask. "You can tell me as much or as little as you want."

Thea turns, becoming my little spoon, guiding my hand down over her belly. "It was good, I think?" She huffs a laugh. "It's funny, when I was driving over there I kept thinking about how I didn't really have much to say, and then I ended up talking nonstop for forty-five minutes."

"That's good," I praise. "That means you felt comfortable enough to open up a bit to an objective third party. Everyone needs someone like that in their life. Someone who can listen."

Thea hums in agreement. "Oh! Did you feel that?"

"Feel what?"

She moves my hand down to the lower portion of her stomach and presses my hand in firmly. "Thea what—"

"Shh!" she interrupts. "Just… wait for it."

So I do. I wait quietly until— "Holy shit, is that him?"

Thea nods enthusiastically. "Yes! He's kicking!"

It's amazing. I've never felt anything close to this feeling before in my life, and I instantly know I would do anything to feel it again. The little guy doesn't make me wait long, giving another firm press that I can feel from the outside of Thea's stomach.

"Woah," I say. "He's an athlete."

Thea's laugh is melodic. "I remember Chloe was pretty much spinning in circles for my entire pregnancy, so if he's anything like her, we'll definitely need to sign him up for a way to get his energy out."

Keeping my hand firmly against her stomach so I don't miss

any more kicking, I push up and bend over so I can talk directly to my son. "Hey, bud. Go easy on your mom in there, okay?" He gives another hard kick. "Fuck, did you feel that?" I look over to Thea who is smiling sweetly, eyes brimming with tears.

"Yeah, I felt it." Her laugh is gurgled.

I grin right back, kissing her stomach before settling against the pillows again.

"Have you thought about any names?" I ask. It's something we haven't really talked about since finding out we were having a boy.

"A little…" she admits. "Boy names are so hard. Chloe was easy, it came to me pretty instantly when I found out she was a girl. But nothing has popped out at me like that with him."

We both lay there, lost in thought for a while. Naming a child seems like such a huge responsibility. That's what they'll be stuck with for the rest of their life—it's daunting.

"I think I'd like to include Henry, if possible. Maybe as a middle name?" Thea whispers.

I give her a reassuring squeeze. "I love that. Hank's real name?"

"Yeah. He's just done so much for me. He's an amazing father—I'd love to honor him in that way."

"Great, middle name decided."

She rolls over to face me. "Middle name decided," she echoes with a faint smile. "Now just the first… and last I guess. Did you have any thoughts on that?"

"Hmm. Well Bex and Anders hyphenated to Bardot-Olsson. It's a mouthful, but Anders felt like it was really important for their kids to know that they came from both families, not just his. Plus, he has some… interesting parents, so I don't think he was inclined to stick only to Olsson."

"How do you feel about hyphenating?" Thea asks. "It's not something a lot of people do where I'm from. It's kind of the whole 'ditch your maiden name when you get married' kind of vibe. You know, the patriarchy is extra strong in the south. Not that we are getting married! But, you know, for the baby." Her face flushes bright red.

"Yet."

"What?"

"We aren't getting married, yet."

Her laugh is more of a high-pitched screech. "Funny, Jules!"

But I'm not laughing, so she quickly sobers up. "You're... are you serious?"

I nod. "One day. I'm not in a rush." I shrug. "But this is it for me, Thea Rose. I'm not planning on ever doing any of this with anyone else. I've never loved anyone before you, and I don't want to love anyone after you."

It's not quite a confession, but I still don't know if she's ready for that.

Then Thea shocks the ever loving fuck out of me. Instead of running away, like I'm half expecting her to do, she tells me, "I think I might like that idea. I think I might... like *you*."

"Thank God." I smirk, leaning in for a taste of her. Our kiss is tender and drawn out, full of silent confessions. When I pull away, I lay my forehead against hers. "All that to say, I'm fine with hyphenating, taking your name, taking my name— whatever you want," I whisper.

She contemplates for a moment before, "I really want him to have the same last name as Chloe. I don't want them to ever feel intentionally separate from each other in any way."

"We can make that happen," I promise. "I'm not just in this for you and our baby, I'm in this for Chloe, too."

I watch as a single tear drips down the side of her nose. "I know you are." She sniffs. "And Cat too, obviously."

"Obviously," I tease.

"What about Brooks?"

"Brooks Henry Bardot-Rose... Rose-Bardot? Brooks Henry sounds regal."

"Hmm, you're right," she muses. "I've always liked the name Emmett."

"I like Emmett."

Her smile is mischievous. "It was the hot vampire's name in *Twilight*."

"We are not naming our child after a *Twilight* character," I guffaw.

Thea's reply is indignant. "Why not?"

I think about it for a moment. "You know what, I don't have a good reason."

She gives a triumphant smile. "Emmett it is."

"Let's let that simmer for a bit before making any rash decisions," I joke.

"Fine, we can let it simmer." She watches me for a moment, gaze piercing. "Thank you, Jules. For everything. You've changed our lives."

"You, Thea Rose, have changed my life much more than I've changed yours."

"Agree to disagree." She yawns. I smile and watch as she slowly drifts off to sleep.

I never actually agree to disagree with her.

―――

"Benoit, I need your help."

My twin continues to wipe down the countertop, looking up at me with a raised brow. "Am I not being helpful enough?"

I set down the tray of coffee mugs I have and look at him straight on. "You've been moody lately."

"I have *not*," he says, rather moodily. Now it's my turn to raise an eyebrow.

"Do you want to talk about it?" I lean my elbows on the bar, recognizing I haven't been giving him very much attention recently, especially given the fact that he and Thea moved back to Sassafras around the same time. I've been neglecting my twin.

He's been wearing his glasses a lot more, and his eyes look tired behind the lenses. His shoulders are slumped and his back slightly hunched.

Ben shrugs, sulking.

So, that's a yes.

"Ben, I know things have been busy here. Are you regretting your move? We can hire some more college students when school starts back up in the fall. It won't slow down here, but at least we can get some more help."

Ben shakes his head. "No, it's nothing with the shop. I love it here—I'm really glad I made the move." He stops, pondering how much more he wants to tell me. "It's Colette."

"Cole… What about her?"

"It's a long story, I wasn't expecting her to—"

"Benjamin!" Well, speak of the damn devil. Cole storms over to the both of us, looking as if it's a very real possibility that smoke is about to start streaming out of her ears. Her red hair halos around her head, creating the illusion that she's on fire. "What. Did. You. Do!" she screams.

I put my hands up and back away slowly, making a mental note to check back in with Ben later.

When I get to the storage room, I find Gabe. Great, I need his help too.

"Gabriel, I need your help."

"What can I do for you, brother?" Thank God he's in a better mood than Ben was.

"I want to plan a surprise baby shower for Thea. You and Ben did such a good job with Chloe's party, I figured you could help me with this."

Gabe slaps his hand on my back. "Of course. What if we did a co-ed shower? Someone at work did that recently, and that way we can 'shower' you, too." He does jazz hands as he says the word "shower" for extra emphasis.

"I don't hate the idea. I mean it will probably just be our family."

Gabe narrows his eyes. "That doesn't feel right. We should do it at Louie's, invite the whole town!"

The whole town?

"That seems like overkill…"

"No way," Gabe insists. "Leave it to me and Ben, it'll be the most memorable baby shower this town has ever seen."

That's exactly what I'm afraid of.

Chapter Forty
U UP?
Thea

BAD LIAR
Selena Gomez

Jules is being shady.

I'm trying not to read into it, but he's definitely been dodgy in the last week or so.

This morning I asked him if we should run into Boston to the big baby department store there, that way I can test a few things out before seeing if I can find them cheaper on Facebook marketplace or at the thrift store. He nodded but then suggested that we wait. When I pushed further to see if we could plan on next weekend, he pulled his hair out of his bun, retying it with a noncommittal, "Maybe." His nervous tick.

I thought he'd be excited about my enthusiasm for the baby, but maybe he's having second thoughts.

Dad isn't much better. I tried asking him if he'd go with me, but he replied with some lame excuse about his knee acting up so he'd better not drive that far. Before I had a chance to argue or suggest that I drive, he told me I shouldn't be behind the wheel when my belly is this big.

Men.

When I called Maggie to talk about it, she wasn't much help either. She's not here and she doesn't know Jules, so her advice was to take my shirt off and see how he reacts. Really helpful. That's why I end up texting Cole.

> You busy?

COLE
Why does that feel like a U up? text?

> I hope you're up, it's nine AM

COLE
Some people don't have any other beings depending on them to be awake on a Saturday morning

Some people like to sleep in and dream about ways to destroy the very annoying man child that won't leave them alone

> Trouble in paradise?

COLE
More like trouble in purgatory

> Sounds like you need a girls day

I've never been great at the whole "friends" thing, but Cole's I-don't-give-a-fuck attitude is actually rather comforting. I know that she'll always shoot me straight, and I won't have to guess what's on her mind.

COLE
I'm already in hell, might as well add some fuel to the fire

> Perfect, bringing Chloe
>
> See you in a bit!!!!

COLE

You better bring me coffee

Easy enough. I stop by Bardot Brothers Coffee Co., pick up two lattes and a chocolate milk, and make the drive from Jules' house to Cole's apartment.

Chloe pounds the door several times before I have a chance to stop her. Cole yanks the door open, her leg propped out to keep an elderly three legged terrier from escaping. The dog catches me by surprise.

"I didn't know you had a dog!" I tell her, handing her the coffee and reaching down to scoop up the mangled creature. "He's pretty pitiful looking."

"He's on his last leg." She does a *ba-dum-tss* at her terrible joke. "His name is Ernest."

The dog looks entirely too bouncy to be named Ernest, but I don't question Cole's naming abilities, especially since we've adopted a cat named Cat.

Chloe lets herself into Cole's apartment, looking around nosily. It's definitely not super kid-friendly with stacks of reference materials and textbooks scattered around the living room. A half-empty carafe of coffee is already sitting on the counter but looks like it might be a few days old.

I carry the terrier in behind Chloe and sit down on the green plaid loveseat. "It's very dark academia in here."

"Mmm. I hate that you hit the nail on the head so fast. Maybe I should hang up a disco ball, just to spice things up."

"A disco ball could brighten up the space," I agree.

We drink our lattes and watch as Chloe attempts to teach Ernest how to shake, giggling every time he tips off balance.

"So, why did you make me get out of bed on a Saturday

morning? I'm going to assume it's not because you wanted to watch the damn dog attempt to learn new tricks."

"Language!" Chloe shouts from the ground.

"Just wanted to get out of the house, that's all."

Cole eyes me over the top of her coffee cup, a look of disbelief etched across her features. "Chloe, can I show you the patio? Ernest loves to play out there."

Chloe nods enthusiastically, and Cole walks her over to the French door that separates us from a patio and small yard space. I watch as Ernest's tail swings side to side, waiting for Chloe to toss him the ball.

Once they are settled, Cole comes back in, plopping down on the chaise lounge across from me. "Alright, spill."

"It's nothing!" I don't sound even a little bit casual. "I just... Well, Jules and I moved in together."

Cole's confusion is evident. "Didn't you already live together?"

"That's what Ben said."

Her face screws up even more. "Blegh. Okay, so if you already lived together then how did you move in together?"

"Well, the plan was to move back into the apartment after they finished the repairs from the busted pipe. That took longer than expected and I got comfortable at Jules' place, and then I went back to visit the apartment when it was finally done and realized there was no way I was going to be able to bring a baby back there." My head falls back against the cushion. "It's more practical to live with Jules."

"It can be practical and also something you want, Thea. The two aren't mutually exclusive."

I don't know that I've looked at it that way. Most of my life I feel like I've had to choose between being practical or doing the thing that I want. I can't honestly think of a time when the two have coexisted.

"He moved all of my things into his room," I add. "It was really sweet."

"I'm telling you, Jules has always been my favorite Bardot. He's a really fucking good guy."

"I know…" Then I remember why I came over here in the first place. "He's being weird, though. Do you think he regrets moving me in?"

Cole's head sways side to side as she contemplates my words. "I can't see him going through all of this, sticking by you—and doing a damn good job of it—and then suddenly regretting it."

"Then how do you explain the behavior? I asked him to go baby shopping with me, and I couldn't get him to commit. I've shown him a couple of pieces of art that I thought would go well in the nursery, and nothing. He's pulling away."

"It's got to be something else," Cole states. "It makes no sense for him to turn on a dime like that."

"Maybe…" I pause for a beat. "Have you ever been to therapy?"

"Everyone should go to therapy," Cole replies. "Of course I've been."

"I've started going. Iris thinks I need to work on assuming positive intent in those around me." I groan. "Easier said than done. Okay great, so I assume that Jules is not pulling away, and then I'm left heartbroken when he does?"

Cole looks at me for a long moment. "Will it hurt any less if you assume that he will eventually pull away and then it does happen? Seems like it would really fucking suck either way."

I sit up and stare at her. "Say that again."

"If you assume that Jules is going to leave you, or whatever terrible thing you're telling yourself, and then he does, it's still going to hurt just as much as if you assume that he's never going to leave you and then he does. Plain and simple, it would hurt like hell if he left you." She shrugs. "So why not enjoy the time you do have together, however long that may be?"

"Damn. They aren't lying when they say with age comes wisdom."

Cole flips me off like I knew she would. "Fuck you, I'm not even thirty yet."

"But you're about to be." I wink. "We should go out and celebrate! Do you have other friends?"

"No." Cole responds.

"Just you and me, then. I heard Louie's does a mean karaoke night."

"How about I lock myself in this apartment the moment the clock strikes twelve on the eve of my birthday? Maybe I'll hit my head on a shelf, which will sprinkle magic glitter on me, and then I'll wake up as a thirteen year old."

"Did you just reverse the plot of *13 Going on 30*?"

"So what if I did?" She takes a sip of her latte. "Anything to avoid marrying him."

"Excuse me? Marrying who?" I'm not sure I heard her correctly.

Chloe bursts back in the room, saving Cole from having to answer my question. "We aren't done talking about this," I tell her in a harsh whisper.

The bitch ignores me, instead asking Chloe if she wants to give Ernest a treat. Of course, the answer is yes, and Cole shuffles quickly out of the room leaving me to wonder what the hell she was talking about.

In the following week, I work really hard on assuming positive intent with Jules. He's not making it easy on me though, avoiding any and all baby related questions.

He won't even talk to me about names, telling me he wants to keep simmering on it any time I bring it up. We even had an appointment with Dr. Mitchell this week. Jules was so excited to see the baby, hanging the new sonogram up on the fridge when we got home. I figured that might be a good time to ask him about names again. Instead, Jules suggested we make a grocery list for the week with "nutrient dense" foods.

I told him I only wanted to eat thirty cent ramen for the rest of the week.

Maybe I'm being a little pouty.

While driving to the studio for one of our last rehearsals before the Labor Day festival, I try some of the new grounding techniques Iris has taught me. I notice the feeling of the steering wheel beneath my fingers, the sound of cars passing by, the warmth of the bright sun soaking into my skin.

I only feel mildly better.

By the next weekend, I'm so high-strung, one poorly worded interaction could easily send me over the edge.

I'm halfway through curling my hair when the power goes out.

Oop. That'll do it.

Chapter Forty-One
BAD SURPRISES
Jules

8 LETTERS
Why Don't We

Keeping this baby shower from Thea has proven to me that I am the world's worst liar. I can tell Thea knows something is going on, but she hasn't outright asked me why I've been particularly on edge. In an effort not to ruin the surprise, I decided keeping my distance would be easiest.

I was wrong. It has not been easy.

I miss her.

Gabe, Ben, and I are currently at Louie's decorating for the shower later tonight. I'm glad it will finally be here so there won't be any secrets between me and Thea anymore.

She's got her studio's performance at the Sassafras Labor Day Festival this afternoon. Once we finish up decorating here, the plan is for me to go cheer on her dancers and then suggest to Thea that we grab a bite to eat at Louie's to celebrate what I'm sure will be an exciting day for her.

We looped everyone else in on the plan, except Chloe because I get the feeling she's an even worse liar than I am. I'm hanging a banner that says "Emmett Henry Rose-Bardot" across the wall when my phone starts ringing. Thea's name flashes across the screen, and I immediately answer.

"Thea? Everything okay?"

Her answering sob breaks my heart.

"Thea. Answer me, what's wrong?" Frantically, I hop off the stool I was standing on and start looking for my car keys. I can hear her crying through the line, making it difficult for me to focus on where the fuck I left my keys.

"The—" She takes a shuddering inhale. "Power is—" Another sob. "Out! And my hair—"

I only half listen to the rest of her sentence because I'm so damn relieved she and the baby are safe.

"Where's Hank?" I ask, interrupting her latest round of tears.

"He"—she sniffles—"went to pick up the ribbon for the bows. I was supposed to"—sniffle—"get them but I totally forgot."

"Okay, I'm going to send Gabe over to help you. The breaker probably tripped."

"Gabe?" she questions. "Why aren't you coming?"

"I—" *Shit.* I look around at the half-decorated bar. "I have to…"

"You know what," Thea interrupts. "Never mind, it doesn't matter." I can hear the anger in her voice, coming right alongside her earlier sadness.

"Thea—"

"Tell Gabe the front door is unlocked for him." And then she hangs up.

Fuck.

"What's going on?" Gabe asks, having heard my end of the conversation. "Where are you sending me?"

"The power went out at my house, Thea needs help getting it back on."

"On it." He salutes on his way out the door.

Ben comes over to help me finish hanging up the banner. "Why didn't you go over there?" he asks.

I run through several different answers in my mind. "I've been so close to spilling the beans on this entire party, I need to keep my distance as much as possible today so I don't fuck it up." I also know she's mad at me, and I don't really want her to have a reason to push me away. I need to give her some space to calm down.

"We should have thought about the fact that you're a shit liar before we decided to make this a surprise for Thea." Ben laughs. I'm glad someone thinks this is funny, meanwhile I'm over here crawling out of my skin in discomfort.

We get the banner hung up, and I hop down off the stool, annoyed that I'm not at the house helping Thea. "What else do we need to do?"

Louie walks in just then. "Wow, boys! Place looks great. Can't remember the last time it was this clean."

He's not wrong, we mopped God knows what off the floor and wiped down half of the table tops so far. The entire place isn't sticky anymore. Well, except for the corner booth—that one is a lost cause.

Ben puts his hands on his hips and looks around. "Yeah, it does look pretty good, doesn't it? We're going to put blue table cloths on all the tables, and I picked up a bunch of centerpieces from Harriet's. Jules, you have to be at the park in an hour and a half, correct?"

"Correct."

"Okay, let's finish cleaning where Gabe left off, and then we need to set up the rest of the decorations." Ben looks around the space with an assessing gaze.

Louie nods his head. "You both do that"—he points to the back—"I'm going to keep prepping food, but you let me know if you need anything else."

A little while later, the place has really started to come together. Ben is weirdly good at party planning. Gabe eventually comes back and confirms that the breaker tripped but lets me know that everyone was fine and Thea, though stressed, seemed relieved that she'd be able to finish her hair before the performance.

I look at my watch. "Speaking of the performance, I need to get going soon. I have to go back home and shower before I head to the park." I wipe my hands down my face—I'm so fucking exhausted. "Can you finish up without me?"

Ben and Gabe shoo me out the door. "Go," Ben says. "Enjoy the festival, we'll see you later tonight."

By the time I get home, Thea, Chloe, and Hank have already left. Cat greets me at the door, meowing and pushing up against my leg. He follows me to the bedroom, jumping up onto the bed when I flop down, stomach first.

I have thirty minutes before I need to leave, and it'll take me about ten to get ready. I scroll through my phone a bit—I'm not much of a doom scroller, but I can see the appeal of turning your brain off for a few minutes. Cattington and I start watching cat videos, he paws the screen any time another animal pops up. I make a mental note to show Chloe later, she'll get a kick out of that.

As I keep watching, my eyelids grow heavier. Unintentionally, I drift off in the middle of a video of a cat being adopted by a gorilla.

Thea is a goddess as she glides across the stage. Her hair flows around her face, haloing it in blonde waves. A long tulle skirt swishes when she turns, painting even more of an ethereal picture. I'm mesmerized by her, so much so I don't even register my phone buzzing in my hand.

The buzzing finally becomes incessant enough that Cat butts his head up against my cheek. Vaguely, the thought crosses my mind that Cat shouldn't be in this theater with me.

He should be at home. Yet, he continues head butting me while my phone shakes the entire seat, the entire room. The whole world.

I wake so suddenly, I nearly fall off the edge of the bed. *Fuck!*

What time is it? I look down at my phone, which is buzzing in my awake state too, "Mom" flashing across the screen. Quickly swiping, I answer her call.

"Julien, where are you?" she asks, trying to hold back disappointment, but I can hear it seeping through.

"I—fuck, I fell asleep." I stand, stepping into my shoes, not giving a single shit that I'm still disgusting from cleaning Louie's. "Have I missed it? I'm coming. I can be there in five minutes."

"The first dance is about to go on stage. Hurry, dear, but drive safe."

"I will. Is she—shit. Is she mad?" I don't have to clarify who I'm talking about.

Mom hesitates, which is all the answer I need. "She'll come around," she finally tells me.

I'm so pissed at myself. This show means so much to Thea—a foray into something absolutely terrifying that she has done completely on her own. "Five minutes," I repeat before hanging up.

Glancing in the mirror, I redo my bun and roll some deodorant on. It takes me four minutes to make it to the park, but it's so crowded, it takes an additional three to find a parking spot and sprint to the gazebo stage area. I am dripping in sweat, but I make it. Chloe's group is the last one to go so I haven't even missed her dance.

Thea is up near the front, and I can immediately tell something is wrong. She's working her way through the crowd, ducking to try to get a look under the folding chairs that have been set up.

Pushing through the people around me, I navigate the crowd toward her. She's growing more frantic by the second, obviously looking for something. When I'm a few feet away, I call her name.

Thea's eyes hit me like a sucker punch to the gut. Tears that had previously been held back, carve a quick path down her cheeks.

"I'm so sor—"

She holds up a hand to stop me. "Later," she rushes out, voice breaking. "I can't find Chloe."

Chapter Forty-Two
LOST & FOUND
Thea

LOST WITHOUT YOU
Fly by Midnight, Clara Mae

An hour earlier

Julien fucking Bardot is making it really hard for me to assume positive intent. When the breaker tripped and he sent Gabe, I about lost it all over again.

Nothing wrong with Gabe, obviously he was able to help me, but all I can focus on is why Jules didn't come over himself. No matter which way I try to see the situation, all I can read it as is avoidance. Which takes me down a really fun little spiral of anxious thoughts.

Dad is driving us over to the park, but I can feel his sideways glances every thirty seconds.

"What?" I finally spit out.

"Nothin'," he responds. "You just seem a little stressed, is all."

I wonder if it was the way my shoulders have become closely

acquainted with my ears or the way I've been rubbing figure eight patterns repeatedly across my stomach ever since I sat down.

Or maybe it's both.

"I'm fine." Glancing back at Chloe, I see that she's fully engrossed in the *National Geographic Kids* magazine that Cole gave her. I lower my voice so only Dad can hear. "Jules is being weird."

Dad takes his hand off the steering wheel to wave me off. "Thea, you're lookin' for trouble where there is none."

I consider that for a moment, pursing my lips. "Hmm, but what if there *is* trouble?"

He scoffs. "Trust me, that man looks at you like some prize heifer."

I roll my eyes at his Southern-isms. "I really don't appreciate that comparison right now."

"D'you know how much prize heifers go for? That was a compliment. Talk to the boy, Thea Shirley Rose. Quit gettin' your panties in a twist for no reason."

I slump in my chair. He's not wrong, but he's also not the picture of healthy communication either.

"This is hard without a mom," I confess. We talk about my mom every once in a while, and truly Dad did such an amazing job raising me, but sometimes I miss this thing I never actually had.

Dad's hand finds mine, giving it a little squeeze. "I know, honey. I wish more than anything that your mom was here to see how amazing you've become. To see that little one back there." He nods toward the back seat. "I'm not dim enough to think I could ever replace having her here."

"I don't need you to replace her. You are a great dad and a phenomenal Pop. It's just hard when I don't have someone who has been through this before."

He hums in understanding. "I reckon Elaine would be more

than happy to talk to you about anything goin' on, if you wanted."

"Maybe after the show," I concede. "Maybe I'll talk to both her and Jules after the show."

We arrive at the park, and it's a whirlwind of tiny dancers asking where they are supposed to be. Chloe tugs on my shirt, pointing at all of the different vendors and games they have set up at the festival. "Can I go look, Mama?" she asks.

"Let's get through the performance, and then I promise we can walk around, okay?"

She nods in agreement, though her little eyes continue to wander over to the booth with giant stuffed animals displayed in every available nook.

We continue over to the stage area, with Chloe lagging behind. I can tell she's pouting about not being able to explore, but we don't have time. I have a few parents helping out, and Dad is able to pass out the light blue ribbons we got for all of the girls. Everyone was instructed to wear a black leotard, black ballet skirt, and pink tights. It's simple, and next year maybe we can come up with little costumes, but seeing everyone together might just make me cry tears of joy.

I did it. I fucking did it. I opened my own studio, dancers showed up, and now we are performing for an actual audience.

So what if the audience is ninety-five percent parents, grandparents, and siblings, and five percent random townspeople that happened to be at the festival today and stopped to watch the show.

It's a flurry of making sure the dancers are sitting in the right order, the music is working, and all students are accounted for. I don't even realize Jules isn't there until Elaine finds me.

She kisses me on both cheeks. "How's my cabbage? I'm excited for you!"

"Oh, I'm fine," I lie. "Ready to go on in…" I look at my watch, realizing we only have five minutes. "Soon. Is Jules with you?"

Her brows furrow. "No, dear. I assumed he'd come with you. Do you want me to call him?"

He's not here? I'm in such shock that all I can do is nod. If I think about it too much, I will cry, and today is not about him. It's about me. This studio. I won't let another stupid man take up unnecessary space in my mind.

Elaine gives my arms a squeeze, turning to mutter something to Hugo who has joined us. "I-I've got to go," I say. "Thank you for being here."

I wander back over to the stage, spiraling quickly. The first group is lined up—ten girls who have been taking intermediate ballet—and the older gentleman who has been helping with sound hands me a microphone.

"What's this for?"

He gives me a look that says *What do you think?* but is polite enough to say, "Thought you might want to introduce yourself and your group."

Right, right. That's probably a good idea.

My feet feel like they're moving through syrup as I take each of the three steps up onto the stage. Public speaking has never really been my forte, hence the dancing which can be done without a single word.

Turning to the crowd, my mouth immediately dries up. There are a lot more people here than I thought. "Uhm, hi!" I squeak. "My name is Thea, and I'm the owner of Whirlwind Dance Studio. We opened up at the beginning of the summer, and these kids have amazed me with their talent."

I take a deep breath before continuing. "I wanted to create a space to foster a love of dance for people of all ages. Fall registration will open soon, but for now enjoy this performance from each of our current classes. Okay, I think that's everything... I'm not used to doing the talking," I joke, garnering a few pity laughs. "Enjoy the show!"

The intermediate class files onto the makeshift stage as I file off. The music starts and my anxiety eases a fraction. The first dance is perfect—everyone remembers the steps, thank God, and their beaming smiles tell me they are having fun, too. Next up is the beginner elementary class, which will be followed by the preschool group.

I'm watching the beginners when I feel a tap on my shoulder. "Miss Thea?" One of the moms who was helping with the preschool class stands behind me, her eyes wide.

"What's wrong?" I ask, assuming one of the students needs to go potty right before they're supposed to go on.

"It's Chloe," she says, and my entire body goes rigid. "We can't find her."

Without responding, my body immediately jumps into action. I start looking under chairs, scanning the groups of dancers, and circle the gazebo to make sure she didn't find a patch of clovers or something to lure her away—there's no way she's gone far. Adrenaline is the only thing keeping me from screaming right now, my heart in my throat makes me feel like I'm going to choke. *Fuck, fuck, fuck* is on repeat in my head, so loud I only barely register the last dance finishing.

"Thea!" I know that voice. I stand up to see Jules pushing his way toward me. "I'm so sor—"

"Later," I say, hearing all of the emotions I've been bottling up coming out in that single word. "I can't find Chloe."

His face goes white with a muttered, "Shit." He begins looking in all of the places I've already checked, just as frantic as I am. When he quickly comes up emptyhanded, I think I might actually throw up. He wraps his hands around my forearms, looking me dead in the eye. "She's here, let me just—" Jules hops up onto the gazebo stage now that the beginner ballet dance has finished. He takes the mic from the polite older man, turning it on so everyone can hear him.

"Hello, everyone. Sorry to interrupt this wonderful performance. We are missing a dancer and would really appreciate your help finding her. She's about this tall"—he indicates down by his thigh—"bright blonde hair, and goes by Chloe."

The entire crowd springs up to help—it's mostly parents, so I know they understand the visceral fear I'm feeling.

The festival is surrounded by chained fencing so there is only one way in and out, but the park is large and there are several different attractions set up for her to wander off to. Hugo grasps my arm, letting me know he's going to stand by the exit and make sure she doesn't walk out. I hadn't even thought of that, and my anxiety level is now off the charts.

What if she's gone? What if we can't find her?

Jules is back at my side now. "We're going to find her," he reassures, reading my mind. We fan out, and I'm panic-walking, yelling Chloe's name over and over again. I see Ben, Gabe, and Elaine doing the same thing. Cole's fiery hair catches my eye too.

Dad finds me, guilt written across his face. "It's my fault, I should've kept an eye on her," he confesses.

"No, she was supposed to stay with the class mom," I reply, my heart still thumping wildly. "She knows better than to run off. Just, let's find her, okay?"

He nods and rushes off as well. What feels like an eternity passes until I hear, "We got her!"

Ben has Chloe in his arms with Cole and Jules on his heels. She's bawling, and it takes everything in me not to join her. Relief floods my entire nervous system when I take her from Ben, her body quickly molding to mine. I stroke her back as she soaks my shoulder with her tears. "Shh, shh, you're safe. Mama's here," I keep repeating, reminding myself just as much as I'm reminding her.

When she finally calms enough to speak, I ask her if she can tell me what happened. "I-I—" She hiccups. "I really wanted to see the stuffies!" she cries, pointing a finger toward the damn booth we passed when we first walked in. "And then there were *so* many games, I-I'm in trouble!"

I set her down and get on her level. "No, honey you aren't in trouble. I'm so, so glad you are safe. You scared us."

Big tear drops well in her eyes again. "I didn't mean to!" she wails.

In that moment, I'm so damn grateful she is here that I resolve to talk to her about the dangers of wandering off later, once we've all had a moment to calm down. My mind is still reeling and probably will be for a while.

I wipe Chloe's cheeks and ask her if she still wants to do her dance or if she'd rather watch. My brave girl still wants to dance, so she takes Dad's hand and they make their way back to the gazebo. Ben follows behind them, taking the initiative to make an announcement to the crowd that the show will be continuing.

My hands are still shaking as Jules takes a hesitant step toward me. "Are you okay?"

No, I'm not fucking okay. "You should have been here," I spit out. I know he isn't to blame, but I'm not thinking logically right now, and I need somewhere to aim my wrath.

To his credit, he shoves his hands into his pockets and says, "I know."

"She... she could've—" *been gone forever*. I can't bring myself to say it. "And now I look incompetent. Who is going to sign their kids up to take classes from a woman who can't even keep track of her own child?" My words are a harsh whisper.

"No one thinks you are incompetent, Thea. This could have happened to anyone."

"But it didn't," I counter. "It happened to me. And you weren't here."

He opens his mouth to reply but, quite honestly, I can't process anything he says right now, still doing everything in my power to hold myself together. "I need to go watch the rest of the show and make sure no one else escapes. I'll see you at home tonight."

I walk away wondering if I'm walking away for good.

Chapter Forty-Three
FICKLE THINGS, PART TWO
Jules

CRAZIER THINGS
Chelsea Cutler, Noah Kahan

Thea's words linger as she walks away from me. She's right, I should have been here, and I fucked up. I should have told her about the baby shower instead of hiding it from her, avoiding interacting with her in the hopes of keeping it a surprise.

I could see that she was stressed, but I didn't listen to my gut and try to alleviate that stress. I'm an idiot, and now she might not even come to the shower, and this will all be for naught.

Mom makes her way over to where I'm standing, frozen in the spot Thea left me.

"It'll be okay, *mon chou*."

"We should cancel the shower," I reply.

She ponders that for a moment. "Instead of continuing to make assumptions about what Thea would want, why don't you ask her."

Seems logical.

Chloe's performance is next, so Mom and I make our way back over to the stage to watch. She's adorable, up there performing with a huge grin, as if she didn't just scare the shit out of all of us. When she finishes, she turns and gives Thea two thumbs up which makes everyone in the crowd laugh.

After the last group performs, Thea makes her way back up on stage. She held herself together after Chloe was found, but I see the tension radiating from her body. She hides it well, coming across as calm and collected as she gives her final remarks.

"What a day," she starts. "I don't know about y'all, but I definitely wasn't expecting quite this much excitement during our first performance." She laughs but it's strained. The crowd, however, seems to be relieved at her nonchalance. "Thank you all for coming out to our first show! We look forward to many more in the future."

She smiles warmly at Dave, the town's resident AV tech, and then climbs down the steps to a waiting Hank and Chloe. They talk amongst themselves, Thea's eyes darting my way every few sentences. Finally, she leaves them and walks back over to me.

"Dad said something about going to Louie's, and when I said I wanted to go home, he said that I need to talk to you about it." She sighs, the weight of the world on her shoulders. "What's going on, Jules?" She looks exhausted.

"It's a baby shower. It was supposed to be a surprise, but I can call and cancel it right now. Everyone will understand."

"Everyone?" she asks.

My hands find my hair, like they usually do when I'm nervous. She clocks it immediately but doesn't say anything. "Ben and Gabe planned it. They might have been a bit overzealous when sending out invitations. I've been trying to keep it a secret, but I'm shit at secrets. It's why I've been avoiding you."

Thea chews on her nail, one arm crossed over her chest. Her shoulders seem to rise half an inch with every breath. It dawns on me then that she went into early labor with Chloe due to stress, and I'm easily contributing to excess stress in this pregnancy as well. "Every word that comes out of my mouth makes me realize just how royally I fucked this up. I... I wanted to surprise you, but..."

She rubs her brow. "Your intentions were good, Jules. I know that. I shouldn't be upset with you, but I am." Her eyes wander back over to Chloe, who takes that as a sign to join us.

"Pop told me!" She jumps up and down. "Can we go to Louie's to take a shower? Please!"

Her word mixup makes Thea smile. She looks like she would rather go home and sleep for five days, but instead she says, "Of course, Chlo. We have to go celebrate your baby brother, don't we?"

"We really don't have to," I whisper so Chloe doesn't hear.

"Yes. We do," Thea replies, without looking at me.

This is going to be fun.

"Is it me or is this the worst party anyone's ever been to?" Ben leans over, whispering in my ear.

Cole, from his other side, swats him across the chest. "Stop. It's not that bad."

It's pretty bad.

To most people, Thea probably looks like the glowing mother-to-be she's expected to be, graciously accepting gifts from townspeople and nibbling absentmindedly on a cookie shaped like a baby rattle. But to those of us who have grown to know her—really know her—she looks like she'd rather be anywhere else.

"Go over there," Cole hisses, eyes boring into me.

I look at Ben. "She's kind of scary."

He smirks—something I can't even begin to interpret right now—and says, "I know. I fucking love it."

Cole and I both groan at that.

I weave my way over to Thea, who is accepting yet another

knitted blanket from Harriet, the local florist. Seeing Harriet inspires me to grab one white and one red rose from a nearby centerpiece to bring to Thea. A feeble attempt at an apology.

"It's beautiful!" she coos. "Thank you so much, Harriet."

Harriet pats Thea's cheek and then turns to face me. "We are all so excited for you, Julien. You've always been the most responsible Bardot brother"—she peeks over my shoulder, where I'm sure Ben and Gabe are fucking around—"and you're going to be a great dad."

I give her a tight-lipped smile because I feel anything but responsible today. Actually, I do feel responsible, but responsible for Thea's frustration instead of her joy.

Harriet eyes the flowers in my hand. "Some of my best work and you plucked it right out of the centerpiece," she tuts.

I mutter an apology and lean into Thea as Harriet walks away. "Can we talk?" My hand finds the small of her back, and my stomach drops when I feel her tense up.

Bringing my hand back down, I shove it in my pocket instead. Thea's eyes are closed and she murmurs a quiet, "Sorry."

"It's fine, I just want to…" I don't know what I want. To rewind a few weeks and do all of this a little differently? To apologize for being late to the performance earlier? To beg her to trust me that it will never happen again?

Thea gets Chloe's attention and tells her to go find Hank. She quickly runs off, snatching another cookie as she goes—the adrenaline high from earlier obviously turning into a sugar high.

After a moment, Thea turns to me, her eyes not meeting mine. "Not here," she says, walking toward the exit. I follow her out onto the street and then into the door that leads to her old apartment. We hike up the stairs in silence and then stop in the hallway between her place and Ben's.

When she eventually looks me in the eye, I see so many mixed emotions, it's hard to latch onto one. "When I came to Sassafras eight months ago, my goal was to start over. Build a new life for Chloe and me. Fix some of the mistakes I'd made in the past." She pauses, contemplating, and I let her process. "I realize now that I was also running away, in a sense. From the mistakes I was trying to 'fix.' Away from people who made me feel so fucking worthless."

Her hand comes up to cover her mouth, eyes brimming with tears waiting for permission to spill. "And then you showed up. And I realized that some of the things from my past that I thought were mistakes—that people *told* me were—didn't have to be. They could be really beautiful accidents, instead."

She rubs her stomach absentmindedly. I want to touch her. I want to hold her more than I want my next breath.

"I've been working so hard on loving myself. Trusting myself... and trusting you. Though, you've never given me a reason not to, there have been others who ruined it for you. I—" Now the tears fall. "I'm mad at them honestly, not you. But my brain is so mixed up. Then losing Chloe today. I will never, *never* forget the feeling of sheer terror that took over me. And all I wanted was you there to help me." She hiccups. "Then that pissed me off."

She's full-on sobbing now.

"Let me touch you, please."

She holds up both hands to stop me. "No. No, I need to think. I can't fucking think around you. I—"

"Thea, please. I'm so sorry I hid the party from you. I will never forgive myself for making you doubt my feelings for you. It seemed—it doesn't matter, I will spend as long as I need to regaining your trust. And with Chloe—I should have been there and I'm fucking sick over it."

She shakes her head at me. "It's not that. I know you're sorry. Like I said earlier, I know you had good intentions. I just—my brain is scrambled, and I can feel four different stress knots forming in my back, and I just want to go home."

I step toward her, and she takes a devastating step back. "Yes, of course," I resign. "Let's go home."

"Actually." She winces. "I'd like to go alone. Can you and Dad get Chloe back home?"

"Whatever you need, Thea." I want her to need me.

Her feet carry her past me. I turn to the wall, banging my head against it a few times until a soft hand touches my arm. Keeping my forehead pressed to the wall, my eyes slide over to Thea. "Thank you," she mouths, planting a quick kiss on my shoulder before she's gone.

I spend the rest of the party mentally beating myself up over what I should have done. Replaying things I should have said. She warned me from day one that Roses were fickle, and right now I feel a bit like I overwatered or didn't tend the soil or some other melancholy metaphor.

My suspicions are confirmed when I find Thea fast asleep in the guest bedroom later that night.

Fuck.

Chapter Forty-Four
MANDATORY GIRLS DAY
Thea

LOVERS ON THE MOON
AJ Mitchell

The feeling of someone playing with my hair draws me out of sleep. I love that feeling—one I haven't experienced much since my grandma passed. It takes me a moment to realize it isn't Chloe, and it can't possibly be Grandmother.

"Good morning, my cabbage," Elaine's voice fully rouses me.

I roll toward where she's sitting on the edge of the bed. "No offense—" My voice has morning grogginess coating every word. "But what are you doing here?"

Her giggle is comforting and warm. "I thought we could have a girls day."

"A… girls day?" That sounds kind of nice.

Elaine hums in response.

Rubbing the sleep out of my eyes, I respond with a tentative, "Okay."

"Great!" She claps her hands together, and I have a feeling she wasn't going to take no for an answer. "Julien took Chloe to the park for Dadurday—well I guess technically it's Sunday

—but he made you coffee before he left." She picks up the coffee mug that I hadn't noticed was sitting on the bedside table.

I slept terribly in the guest room last night, and coffee sounds amazing right now. Elaine helps me into a seated position. "Take your time, I'll be in the living room when you're ready."

The first sip of coffee warms me from the inside out. Yesterday was a disaster. I still feel sick when I think about Chloe wandering around the festival on her own. She was probably gone for less than ten minutes, but the trauma of those ten minutes will stick with me for the rest of my life.

Of course, Chloe seems unfazed. *Kids.*

Then there's Jules. So many emotions were going rapid fire through my brain, I know I was unfair to him in response.

I enjoy my coffee—brewed to perfection, per usual—for a few more minutes before padding down the hall to the primary bathroom. I look as shitty as I feel. "Lovely," I murmur, turning the faucet on so I can wash my face. The splash of water works alongside the coffee in waking me up and fortunately, or unfortunately, the morning is bringing clarity I needed. The man made me a fucking banner with our son's name on it. A name he admitted needing to "simmer" on. And he hyphenated the last name with Rose first, something we had only touched on in passing, but he knew was important to me. I quickly finish getting ready and walk into the living room—a woman on a mission.

"I'm sorry, I need to go find Jules," I tell a waiting Elaine.

She smiles up at me. "After girls day, dear."

"Well, I—" She stops me with a look that I'm sure she used frequently while raising four children. "Yeah, okay. After girls day could work too."

"Wonderful," she replies. "Here's a breakfast sandwich. We're going to get our nails done."

"Is this like—I mean... are you going to lecture me on the top ten ways to satisfy your partner?"

Her smile turns mischievous. "Only if you want me to, *mon chou*."

Elaine doesn't wait for me to answer before she heads toward the front door. I trip over myself to follow. "What does that mean? I've heard you call your kids that before."

"It's a French term of endearment," she says over her shoulder. "Literally translates to 'my cabbage' which is why I switch back and forth. Hugo's mother used it frequently with him, so I picked it up when the kids were little. Had to add my own touch, though." She turns and winks at me.

"I love it," I say. "I call Chloe 'my chicken.'"

"I've heard!" We slide into the car before she continues. "Where did that come from?"

I think about it for a moment. "You know, I don't really remember. She was always on the go as a baby and toddler, from the moment she could crawl, I couldn't keep up with her. I used to say she was running around like a chicken with its head cut off—do people say that up here? Anyway, that eventually turned into calling her chicken, and here we are."

She smiles at that, and we continue to make small talk on the way to the nail salon.

"A manicure and pedicure for us both," Elaine tells the receptionist.

"Oh gosh, I should just do a manicure. My feet are disgusting from years of putting them through hell."

Elaine glances down at my sandaled feet, turns back to the receptionist, and says, "A manicure and pedicure for us both."

"You are," I say, "a force to be reckoned with, Elaine Bardot."

She looks at me with blatant sincerity. "That's the nicest thing you could have said to me."

I sit in the massage chair which feels very nice, I won't lie, and tell the tech to leave my callouses on. "I'll give you the pedicure," I concede, "but I need the callouses to dance."

"Fine, fine."

A comfortable silence descends. I enjoy being pampered,

something I'd never do for myself. Spending time with Elaine has me thinking about how I parent Chloe, but also time spent with my grandmother before she passed. I've wanted a mother figure in my life, I told Dad as much yesterday, and I'm thankful that Elaine is sort of forcing her love on me. Eventually, I break the silence by blurting out, "I don't have a mom."

Smooth transition, Thea.

"I mean, I do have a mom. Did. I don't remember her, though. I never had someone to give me motherly advice. Do you—do you have any?"

Elaine looks at me thoughtfully. "Julien was the perfect baby."

Of course he was.

"Ben, however," she continues. "He never slept. Gabe was only two years old when the twins were born, and I think I blacked out for most of their infancy. Truly, Thea, I'm so impressed by you. You are a wonderful mother to Chloe already—you don't need my advice."

"Thank you for saying that. I don't feel like a good mom." I sigh. "What kind of mom loses their kid in a public place?"

"Every kind of mom, dear. One time I left Bex on the front porch, fully strapped into her infant car seat. We drove halfway down the street before Jules said, 'Where's BB, Mama?' and I realized I had left her." She chuckles. "You've met her, she turned out fine."

"Oh my God," I chuckle. "Are you serious?"

"Yes!" she laughs. "I beat myself up over it for weeks! That's just part of motherhood. We mess up, we apologize, rinse and repeat. Your kids have to see you own your mistakes—that way they don't feel like they always have to be perfect. Whoever perpetuates the idea that parents never mess up, they're the issue here, not you. Take some of that pressure off of yourself."

And with her words, I truly do feel like she has taken a weight off my shoulders. "Thank you," I say. "I needed to hear that." I close my eyes, letting myself enjoy the hot water bubbling around my feet. "Tell me more about baby Jules."

"Julien… Julien has always been my quiet child. He's introspective in a way his brothers aren't. They were the class clowns, where he was content to sit back and observe. I think he and Bex are similar in that way, but Bex has really come into her own in her relationship with Anders. He's allowed her to find her footing and flourish into a wonderful adult—she would have done that on her own, but it's nice to have a supportive partner. Julien needs someone like that. He has an air of quiet confidence but doubts himself more than he'll let on. He's a caretaker but needs to be taken care of just as much as he needs to care for others. I'm sure you know all of this," she finishes.

I do, but I don't. I say as much to Elaine.

"That makes sense," Elaine tells me. "People are complex. Relationships, even more so. Knitting your life to someone else's —it's a brave thing to do."

"I am not feeling super brave lately," I admit. "Jules… I owe him an apology."

"Apologies are powerful things. If you both use them abundantly, you'll be just fine."

"I've never had a successful relationship before."

Elaine nods. "It only takes one."

"Elaine?"

"Yes, my cabbage?"

"I want him to be the one."

She gives me a full grin. "I'm happy to hear that."

"I need to tell him."

"After our girls day, dear."

I purse my lips and roll my eyes in exasperation. "Yes, ma'am."

We spend the rest of the morning wandering in and out of shops on Main Street, all the while an idea is forming…

At lunch, I bring it up to Elaine. "Do you think you could keep Jules out of the house for the rest of the day?" I ask.

Her joy is evident. "Consider it done."

I've planted myself on the floor of what was the guest bedroom. My job has become directing people instead of actually helping. Ben, Gabe, Cole, and Dad have been opening and organizing shower gifts, turning the room into the perfect little baby nursery.

Cole and I had a great time watching Ben and Gabe attempt to put together the crib before Dad got fed up with their shit and did it himself. They were then tasked with hauling the old bed out while Dad muttered something about them having more muscles than brains.

We hung the banner from last night over the crib, and it looks perfect. I rub my stomach, testing the name again. "Emmett Henry, how are you doing in there?"

"Did he respond?" Ben asks.

"You're an idiot," Cole responds.

My phone starts ringing, an unknown number with a Boston area code flashing across the screen. I struggle to get off the floor, waving my phone in the air as I leave the room. "I'm going to take this really quick."

I answer the phone when I get to the kitchen. "Hello?"

"Thea?" I know that voice. That voice sends shivers down my spine.

"What the fuck? Guy?"

"Yeah..." He pauses. "How're you, Thea? Haven't heard from you in a while."

Oh, fuck no.

"Are you high?" I hiss. "Why the fuck are you calling me. You made it very clear you don't want me, or your fucking daughter, in your life."

"I'm completely sober," he replies, completely ignoring the second half of my response. "I miss you, Thea."

"Abso-fucking-lutely not. You," I seethe, "do not get to call me from a random number after years of silence to tell me you *miss* me." I take a deep breath before continuing. "I ran into your fiancée the other day."

"She's not my fiancée anymore," he murmurs.

"Good for her," I spit.

I hear him stumbling around on the other end of the line, a car horn beeps in the background. As mad as I am at him, he's still Chloe's dad. "Where are you?" I ask.

"Boston."

No shit. "Get an Uber, Guy."

"I'm not drunk," he reiterates. "Just needed to get out of the apartment." He pauses for several moments before saying, "I want to meet her."

I know he's talking about Chloe. "After five fucking years?" I bite out. My hands are shaking, my whole body responding in anger to his audacity.

"Lis said you're pregnant again."

God, who knows what Melissa told him after we ran into each other.

"That's none of your business."

"Whose is it?"

"Also none of your fucking business," I hiss.

His heavy breathing is his only reply, and I realize I might never get this chance again. "You might think you want to meet her but—"

"I do," he cuts me off.

"Shut up, you asshole! It's my turn to talk," I yell. "You really fucked me up. You're a narcissistic jerk who lied to me and then abandoned me to raise a child on my own. I will probably never forgive you for that. It hurt so damn much." I clutch my chest, heart aching. "But," I continue, "I'm also so fucking glad you did it because now I have her. And she's perfect and beautiful, and nothing like you. I would go through hell all over again to be her mom. So, fuck you. And thank you. You lit my world on fire and without that, I wouldn't have been able to rise from the ashes. Now, lose this number."

And I hang up.

I take a deep breath, willing myself not to cry even as my heart breaks all over again. But when I turn around, my newfound friends—my new family—are standing in the doorway, watching me. Gabe starts a slow clap that Ben and Cole join in on.

"That," Cole says, throwing her arm over my shoulder, "was badass."

Finally, I do cry. A cathartic release. A shedding of years of anger. A renewal.

"When will Jules be here?"

Ben looks at his watch. "Ten minutes."

"Perfect."

And it really is.

My life.

My new family.

Him.

I'm ready for him now. Hopefully, he feels the same way.

Chapter Forty-Five
ENTIRELY YOURS
Jules

HEY STUPID, I LOVE YOU
JP Saxe

Today started with a text from Mom, essentially telling me to get my ass out of the house and to take Chloe with me.

No further explanation given.

I've learned over the years that when Elaine Bardot tells you to do something, you do it. So, when Chloe woke up, we went to get donuts and took them over to the park for a picnic like we've been doing most Saturday mornings. She was sad when we had to skip yesterday, so I'm glad Mom forced us out of the house today. She had a blast playing in the late summer sun for the better part of the morning, only arguing with me when I told her it was time to reapply sunscreen.

"Ben never makes me wear sunscreen," she whined.

"Ben is an irresponsible stupid head," I replied, to peels of laughter.

"I'm going to tell Mama you said that."

"She'll probably agree with me."

And then she asked me to push her on the swings.

I texted Mom an hour later asking if I was allowed to return to my own home. She promptly responded with no, but I could go to their house.

Dad was waiting when we arrived, all of the ingredients to make peanut butter and banana sandwiches out on the kitchen counter.

"GoGo!" Chloe calls, hopping up onto a bar stool. "What are we making?" She rubs her hands together in excitement.

"The Elvis special," Dad replies. Chloe has been very into *Lilo and Stitch* lately, so she knows exactly who he's talking about.

We play music over the bluetooth and make sandwiches, pausing for dance breaks when necessary. It's taken some time, but Chloe and I have built a mutual trust. I know I'm not her biological father, but I hope that she sees me as a father figure in her life as she grows up, and eventually, I hope we can make that official through adoption. I love her as much as I know I'll love Emmett when he's here. They're both a part of Thea, a piece of her heart. Loving all of her means I get a chance to love all of these tiny humans too. That makes me pretty damn lucky.

Eventually Mom comes home, but I'm still not allowed to go back to my house.

"Is she okay?" I ask. I miss her and I hate that I haven't been able to put my eyes on her today.

Mom's hand pats my cheek. "She's fine, *mon chou*."

"So I can go see her?" I ask.

"No," she replies, a sly smile crossing her face. "Not yet. We'll go back for dinner. Bex and Anders are coming in."

"Really?" That's surprising. "What for?"

"This and that," she says.

I untie my bun and re-tie it. "I love it when you're vague."

"Have I ever steered you wrong, my cabbage?"

No. No, she hasn't.

Several hours later, Mom, Dad, Chloe, and I are finally on our way back to my house. We pull up at the same time as Bex and

Anders, so I pop my head out of the window and call to Bex, "What are you doing here?"

She looks mildly offended. "Can't a girl visit her brothers?"

"No," I deadpan.

She gives me her signature eye roll and then continues unloading Molly from the car.

When I get to the front door, I'm greeted by the other two Bardot siblings. "What are you two doing here?" I repeat.

They shrug. "Thea called, we answered," Ben says.

A pang of jealousy hits me. Thea called them instead of me? She's slipping through my—

Ben hits me upside the head. "Stop spiraling and go inside."

"It's creepy when you do the weird twin telepathy thing," Gabe adds.

I ignore them both and push inside. Cole is there—another person in my house that is not the one I want to see. She doesn't mess around though, and just points to the guest room. "She's in there."

Jogging the last few steps, I push the door open to see a room that's been completely transformed.

I don't take a second look at it though, because there she is, standing smack dab in the middle, an apt metaphor for how she is also the center of my world. A blue dress flows over her stomach and swings slightly around her calves. Without waiting for her to say anything, I collapse to my knees in front of her, ready to beg for her to be mine.

She laughs and it's a balm to my aching heart. "Jules! Julien Bardot!" she admonishes. "What on earth are you doing?"

My arms wrap awkwardly around her middle, my face coming to the side of her round belly. "I'm sorry," I tell her again. I'll tell her over and over again until she forgives me.

Her fingers dig into my scalp, angling my head toward her. "Look at me," she commands.

"Anything for you," I breathe.

"I'm the one who is sorry," she starts, digging her nails in harder when I try to shake my head. "No, I am. You planned a beautiful event, and I got in my head—self-sabotage seems to be my strong suit. But Jules, I'm ready." She gets down on her knees so we are eye to eye. "I'm so fucking ready to be yours. Entirely yours."

I don't need to hear another word—we can talk later. I take her mouth in mine, savoring the way she melts into me. "Rosie girl, I missed you," I whisper, planting kisses across her face, down to her exposed shoulder.

"Jules," she moans. "Jules, wait. I have one more thing."

I stop, looking at her expectantly, searching her eyes to make sure this is real.

"Jules, I love you. I love you so much, and I'm sorry it's taken me this long to tell you, and I couldn't be happier to be having this baby with you. Emmett, Chloe, and I—we're… I can't believe our luck." She wipes under her eyes. "And all I fucking do now is cry, it's very annoying."

"Marry me."

She chokes on air. "Excuse me?"

"Marry me, Thea. I love you, too. I have pretty much since the moment I met you. I want you to be my wife. I want… everything."

Thea smiles, a hint of wonder in her eyes. "You are crazy," she huffs. "Let's have this baby first, yeah? Then we can talk."

I nuzzle back into her neck. "I'm going to keep asking until you say yes."

"One day, I'll say yes. I promise."

"I'm holding you to that."

She laughs. "Please do." She kisses me again, long and slow. "You didn't even look at the room."

So I do, though, I don't particularly want to look away from her. I look around and see they've put together the crib, dresser, and rocker. Floating bookshelves line the sliver of wall next to the window, overflowing with children's books. Over the crib, the banner from Louie's hangs, slightly lopsided but absolutely perfect.

"You still like that name?" Thea asks.

I fall back on my heels, cradling Thea's stomach in my hands. "Hi, Emmett," I whisper. "It's your daddy."

"Careful calling yourself that, Bardot."

I look up and give her a wink before turning my attention back to our baby. "I think Emmett is the perfect name for you. I can't wait to meet you." I lean a little closer. "Your mom is fucking gorgeous, by the way."

"Language," she teases.

"He'll hear worse out of this dirty mouth." I run my thumb over her lips, tugging slightly. "When are all of these people leaving our house?"

She winces at that. "I invited everyone for dinner since I wasn't the best sport at the shower yesterday. And, you know, Bardot Sunday dinner."

"Fine," I reply, replacing my thumb with my teeth. "But then I'm dragging you back to my bed and fucking you until sunrise."

"Yes, Daddy," she replies.

Fuck, I love her.

"Let's get this over with."

I help her stand, lacing her fingers in mine. Ready to start this chapter of our lives, together.

Chapter Forty-Six
TWO ENGAGEMENTS AND A FUNERAL
Thea

SOMEBODY TO YOU
The Vamps, Demi Lovato

In hindsight, dinner was a bad idea. I'm so horny, a strong breeze could make me come. Pair that with the looks Jules keeps giving me.

He knows. *He knows.*

It's like I told him I loved him and his restraint finally snapped. He just licked his fucking lips like a porn star.

Okay, so he was just eating dinner, but holy hell it was pornographic.

Conversation has continued around us, and everyone is either politely ignoring me panting like a dog in heat or they're completely oblivious.

I'm hoping it's the latter.

"So," Ben starts, looking between Bex and Anders. "Are you going to tell us why you're here?"

"For fuck's sake—sorry." She looks at Chloe, who has already narrowed her eyes at Bex's language. "We are—"

"We're moving back!" Anders cuts in, practically bouncing in his seat.

The room erupts. "Well, shit!" Gabe jumps up, engulfing Anders in the biggest bro hug I've ever seen. "Hell yeah! I've missed having my best friend around."

"And your sister," Bex adds. Gabe ignores her.

Elaine looks elated but also like she already knew the big news. "All my cabbages back together again!"

Anders claps Gabe on the back a few times before sitting back down next to his wife. "Hawthorne wants me to come back as an artist in residence, and we knew we couldn't refuse an offer to come back to Sassafras."

"That's amazing," Jules congratulates. "I'm happy for you both."

Bex covers his hands on top of the table. "Thanks, JuJu," she replies. "Added bonus: the girls will get to grow up close to their new cousins."

I don't miss that Bex said cousins, plural, and again I'm grateful for how the Bardot family has embraced both me and Chloe.

"Do you already have a house?" Gabe asks.

"Not yet," Anders says. "This has been in the works for a bit, but I had to figure out some contract stuff with *Hercules*, to make sure they could replace me. It was time, we did the whole New York thing, and we're ready to come home. We weren't sure if we were going to be able to make it work so we're staying at Elaine and Hugo's until we find a place."

"Hell yes," Gabe replies. "Sleepover at Mom and Dad's!"

Elaine looks like she might pass out, she's so excited.

Bex looks down at her phone. "Oh, Luci's FaceTiming! I told her and Riz to call me so I could tell them the news."

All eyes go to Gabe, and I make a mental note to ask Jules about that later.

"I'll just..." She excuses herself into the kitchen.

Ben stands, tapping his glass, unnecessarily given that we're already quiet. "I also have an announcement."

Cole, who is sitting directly across from him, says, "No. You don't."

"On the contrary, Collette. I absolutely do." His grin is a little maniacal.

I lean over to Jules and whisper, "Should we be worried?"

"Probably," he replies, with a smirk.

"As many of you know, Cole recently turned thirty," Ben continues.

"We are supposed to go celebrate!" I reply. "Cole! You've been avoiding me!"

"Birthdays are stupid." She's still staring daggers at Ben.

"Eloquent, as always, my dear."

I raise a brow at Cole, mouthing *"My dear?"* but she's not looking at me.

Ben is unperturbed. "Collette and I are—"

"No!" She pushes up from her chair, both hands planted firmly on the table.

Just then, Bex bursts back through the kitchen door. "Luci's engaged!"

"So," Ben calls out, "are we!" He tips his glass toward a fuming Cole, who has a death grip on her butter knife.

Jules reaches over and carefully removes the knife from Cole's hand, the rest of us too stunned to move.

Gabe doesn't say a word as he pushes back from the table and walks out. Every Bardot in the room winces. "Probably should have done that differently," Bex says, shooting Anders a frantic look.

He passes the baby to Elaine and tells her, "I got it, Baby Bardot. He just needs a minute." He then follows Gabe out of the room.

We sit in silence for a beat before Bex registers what Ben said. "Wait, you two are also engaged?" She points between Ben and Cole, confusion coloring her tone.

"No," Cole says at the same time Ben says, "Yes!"

"Benjamin!" Her eyes narrow. "I would *never* marry you."

"That's not what you said last night, Red." He looks extremely pleased with this barb, and after one look at Cole, he seems to have severely miscalculated. She shoves her chair back, storming to the doorway. Once she's there, she stops, taking a deep breath before turning around.

"I apologize for my swift exit, Mr. and Mrs. Bardot. I'll call you tomorrow"—she points at me before turning to Ben—"and fuck you." Then she's gone.

Ben finishes his drink. "I love when she's feisty," he declares before he, too, leaves.

The rest of us stare at each other in silence, unsure what to do next. "Y'all really know how to clear a room," Dad says, taking a sip of his beer, and effectively breaking the tension.

Hugo laughs. "Never a dull moment. But it has been a long day for a lot of people," he replies, eyeing Jules knowingly. "Let's clean up and then return the Rose-Bardot home to its natural state."

"Which really is only *slightly* less chaotic than its current state." Cat jumps into the middle of the table to punctuate my point.

It's another hour before everyone is gone, Chloe has gone through her bedtime routine, and Jules and I are finally alone.

We fall into bed, exhausted and yet utterly insatiable. Jules peppers kisses up and down my body, over my swollen belly, down to where I really want him. After an entire dinner of unintentional foreplay, it won't take me long to explode. His stubble scratches at my inner thighs as he licks and sucks and drives me fucking *wild*. I have a single thought before I fall into oblivion: *How did I manage to get* this *for the rest of my life?*

Jules lets me ride the waves then turns me onto all fours and slides in from behind. He curls over the top of me, keeping a steady pace as he traces my shoulder blades with his lips. "I love you, Rosie girl," he whispers into my spine before sitting up, gripping my hips, and pounding me until I see stars. He comes with a muffled grunt, falling onto the bed next to me afterwards.

"I love you, too," I say, kissing his sweaty forehead.

"Fuck, I like hearing that. Been waiting an eternity," he pants.

"An eternity, huh?"

"Yes, Thea." He gives me a serious look. "From the moment I first saw you in those red cowboy boots—we need to pull those back out, by the way—"

"They don't fit anymore," I whine, cursing my swollen feet.

"I'll buy you new ones. From the moment I stepped into that bar," he continues, "I was a goner."

Jules traces my body with his hand, from my shoulders down to my hips. "I still can't believe you're mine."

I wrap my hand around the rose tattoo on his wrist. "Fickle from the start." I sigh. "But you learned how to tame me."

He shakes his head. "Not tame—I'd never want to tame you. But I have learned how to care for you, and I'll happily continue learning how to do it even better, for as long as you'll let me."

"Hmm." I pretend to ponder. "How does forever sound?"

"Sounds pretty damn perfect," he replies.

Yeah, it really does.

Epilogue
HOW ABOUT FOREVER, ROSIE GIRL?
Jules

LONG RUN
Deacon, Nina Nesbitt

A little over one year later

"Don't worry, our party planning skills have only improved over the last year." Ben's voice comes through the line, his attempt at soothing me is not having the intended effect.

"Yes, but this party is really fucking important, Benoit," I reply, scratching under the chin of a very needy Cat.

He laughs, nonchalant per usual. "I know, Julien. You just get your family there, we'll take care of the rest. Got it?"

I mumble noncommittally and hang up the phone.

Thea saunters into the kitchen just then, a sleepy Emmett resting his head on her shoulder. He's rolly in all the right places. Quiet and contemplative, like his dad. At a year old, you can already see the wheels spinning in his head as he observes the world around him. The polar opposite of his sister who never stops talking, keeping us updated on all of the grade school gossip every night at dinner.

"Come here, bud." I reach out for my son, kissing his beautiful mother once he's in my arms. "Good morning, Rosie girl."

"Coffee," she replies.

"Already ready for you." I nod to the kitchen table where a steaming mug is waiting next to a full bouquet of burgundy roses.

"These for me, Julien?" she teases, picking up her coffee.

"Only ever for you, my love." I wrap my free arm around her, pressing a kiss to her forehead.

She leans against the counter and takes a sip, taking the two of us in.

"I can't believe he's one," she murmurs, a small smile cresting her lips.

I can't either. I wake up every morning, surprised to find this last year hasn't been a dream. "You ready for the party today?"

"Slightly worried about giving Ben and Gabe the full reins on this, but Chloe's party last year was absolutely perfect—I still don't know how they pulled that off."

"The exact thought I had this morning," I reply.

Chloe then comes bounding into the kitchen. "Uncle Babes" —yes, she's given them a combined nickname—"are great at parties!"

"Yes, they are, my chicken," Thea says, pushing Chloe's crazy bedhead off her forehead.

"Will Pop be there?" Chloe asks through a yawn.

Hank moved into Thea's old apartment a few months after Emmett was born. He came home one day and announced it was "high time" he lived on his own, and he moved out the next week.

"Pop wouldn't miss it for the world," Thea answers. "I think he even said something about bringing cupcakes."

Hank has also taken up baking in his free time.

Chloe's squeal of delight scares Cat, who jumps from the open window sill and scurries into the backyard. "Oops! I'll go get him," she continues before running out of the garden door behind him.

Thea sighs, taking another long drink from her coffee mug. "I love our chaos."

"Me too," I reply, joining her against the counter. "We should add to it."

She almost spits out her drink—this is the first time I'm bringing up this particular subject, though I did intentionally leave some space around the three roses I got tattooed over my heart after Emmett was born. "Julien Bardot! Have you lost your mind?"

"We have another room."

"'We have another room' he says," she scoffs, taking Emmett's little hand in hers. "I think your daddy is tempting fate after how perfect you are," she coos.

"Call me daddy again and I'll tempt fate all over our bedroom." My favorite blush creeps up her neck. "That'll never get old," I continue, running my finger across her flushed jawbone.

"Alright, TBD"—she only calls me that when she doesn't know what to do with me—"I need to get ready," she diverts. "But I think I'll enjoy my shower a little bit more now."

She winks at me on her way out of the room, peeling her shirt overhead as she goes.

"Low blow, Rosie girl," I call after her.

"Wish I could blow even lower," she calls back.

Fuck me.

I'll be counting down the hours until both kids are in bed and I can hold her to that.

A few hours later, we finally make it to Mom and Dad's for Emmett's first birthday party. The whole family is there, and Gabe and Ben decided on a farm theme so everyone is dressed up like vegetables, each one of my siblings donning a homemade cabbage costume. They look ridiculous.

"My cabbages!" Mom shouts as soon as we walk in. "Happy birthday to the littlest cabbage!" She takes Emmett out of his carseat, and I know we won't see him for a while. Thea follows after them and I head outside to find Ben.

"Is everything ready?" I ask, in lieu of greeting.

"Hello, brother. I'm fine, thanks for asking. The party *does* look great, you're right! Always so observant."

"Are you done?"

His shoulders slump. "Fine, yes I'm done, and yes, everything is ready." He pats his pocket, pumping his eyebrows at me. "Where's the birthday boy?"

"Mom grabbed him as soon as we walked in. Just so we're clear, you have the—"

"Thea!" Ben cuts me off. "Happy day of giving birth."

"Thank you, thank you!" she says, mock bowing. "The party looks fantastic! Y'all did another great job. The costumes are the cherry on top!"

Ben shoots me a pointed look as if to say, *See! Pleasantries aren't that hard!*

I ignore him, instead busying my hands with untying and retying my bun. Thea gives me a weird look when she catches the nervous habit, though. "You nervous, babe?"

Ben's eyes go wide, but he covers quickly. "I… I, uh, just told Jules I forgot the cake."

"I thought Dad was making cupcakes?" Her eyebrows furrow.

"He is!" Ben confirms. "But we thought a cake for Em to smash would be cute, too. Right, Jules?"

"Right..."

Thea waves us off. "It's fine! Cupcakes will do!"

Ben gives her finger guns. "Good call. I'm going to go…" He looks around in a desperate attempt to escape. "Go over there."

And then he's gone.

"Is it me or is Ben acting weirder than usual?" she whispers, leaning her head on my shoulder.

"He's always weird," I reply, hoping she doesn't notice how much I'm shaking.

We stand there like that while everyone files into the backyard. "Time to sing!" Chloe calls to the group. She's got a cupcake in her hand with an unlit candle poking out of the top. Mom carries Emmett over to his high chair, getting him settled before placing the cupcake in front of him. Once the candle is lit, we sing happy birthday to the boy who has brought infinite amounts of joy into my life. Between him, his sister, and his mom—I didn't know my heart, or my life, could be this full.

Thea stands next to Emmett, making sure he doesn't reach for the candle too soon. When the song is over, Ben slides something into my back pocket while everyone else watches Chloe coaching Emmett through how to blow out a candle. We all clap when she finally does it for him.

That's my cue.

"I have one more thing before we pass out cupcakes to everyone else." Thea and Chloe simultaneously pout at the loss of immediate sugar. "Thea, can you come here for a second."

She raises her brow but does what I ask. When her hand is in mine, I give it a little squeeze as she looks at me quizzically. "I've thought a lot about the night we met," I say. "How lucky I was that the hotel I booked happened to be across from the bar you were working at. How coincidental it was that you then moved here, of all places. How fortunate I am that you bought the studio next to the coffee shop."

Thea's eyes start to dart around, but mine are only on her. My thumb goes to her chin, gently guiding her back to me. "What's going on?" she whispers, her voice already sounding watery.

I reach into my back pocket and pull out my wallet. Inside is a scratch off. *The* scratch off. "I bought this that first night. I kept it with me, even after you left, some part of me knowing I would be seeing you again. Hoping I would be lucky enough to keep you."

"I can't believe you kept it," she whispers, a single tear falling. "You"—she takes the ticket out of my hand—"you don't need luck, though. Not with me."

"Well," I reply, taking the other item out of my pocket, "I kept it just in case… for this exact moment."

I pull out the ring, getting down on one knee. "Thea Shirley Rose, you have changed my life in so many ways. You've gifted me with two amazing kids and an unwavering love. I have wanted to marry you for entirely too long, and I can't go another day without calling you my wife. Put me out of my misery, please," I beg. "Marry me?"

She looks down at the scratch off and then tosses it over her shoulder. "Hell yes!" she cries, bouncing on her toes. "Now kiss me!"

And I do. Because I'm one step closer to being completely, entirely hers.

ACKNOWLEDGMENTS

Wow! We did it! This book challenged me in so many ways. After writing and publishing *Yours, Unexpectedly*, I knew book two was going to be difficult. All of a sudden, people were reading my writing. They had thoughts, feelings, and opinions—both good and bad. That comes with any work of art, right? You put yourself out there and have to be okay with everyone having access to a little piece of you. With a debut, you don't have that noise. With any subsequent novel, you have to figure out how to block out the noise... how to be happy with your work, no matter what anyone else is saying. And I am happy with Entirely Yours! It took me a while to get there, but in the end, I did—so shout out to me!

Always all of my love and thanks to my real life book boyfriend, Bryan. Someone asked me the other day what my husband thinks about his wife writing romance novels. I could honestly and enthusiastically say that he loves it. Thank you for always supporting me. I don't like to praise men, but you deserve it boo boo! Also, y'all have Bryan to thank for the playlist, so enjoy while listening!

To my daughters: It will be a long time before you ever read this. In fact, the other day Lainey asked me when I would write a book that she could read! One day, maybe you'll read this... maybe. Even if you don't, I hope you know how much of an inspiration you both are. Chloe was very much inspired by both of your feisty, spunky, silly attitudes and I hope that you are always unapologetically that way. You are my favorite Lainey and my favorite Emmy, forever and ever.

To my family: There's no way you're reading this, but I love you and am constantly grateful for the relationship I have with you. My own personal Bardot family.

To my friends: Erin and Lindsay, who I wouldn't want to do life without. Thanks for being bonus-moms to my girls! To the Margaritas, who constantly encourage me and make me laugh—Chili's and dongs 4eva. To my book club ladies, who never get mad at me when I don't read the book. To Neely, who is the best podcast co-host I could ever ask for!

Publishing takes a village (much like raising a child!), so I have a list of people to thank on that front. To my college friend Becca, who let me use the story of her Dad bringing Texas soil to put under the hospital bed so she would be born over Texas soil! That story always cracks me up. Thank you Isabelle, S.R. Clark, and Kelsey for creating the cover of my dreams! Thank you David and S.R. Clark for the special edition cover! Thank you to all of my alpha and beta readers (Vanessa, Wren, Jess, Kalie, Kelsey, Ange, Amber, Kelli, Bekah, Brittany, Bethany, and Emily) for seeing through the early draft muck and helping to create a wonderful final novel! Huge thanks to my author friends who get frantic question texts from me—Aimee, Jenn, Peyton, Ray, and DEG! Thank you Sadie for continually teaching me that I don't know how to use a comma! And thank you to everyone who has helped promote any of my work! Including Jess (Truly Yours Marketing), Rae (Booked with Rae), Joelle, and all of the supporters on bookstagram/booktok! I couldn't do it without you.

Finally, thank you to YOU! Thank you for reading and supporting my stories. I love you all big.

ABOUT THE AUTHOR

Rachel Lewis is a fresh voice in contemporary romance. With charmingly flawed characters and laugh-out-loud dialogue, Lewis' writing effortlessly blends witty banter, delightfully indulgent spice, and heartwarming found families that readers will want to call their own.

Beyond her own writing, Rachel co-hosts the popular "Welcome to the Smut Show" podcast, where she engages with writers and bookstagrammers about their love of romance novels.

Rachel is a mother of two crazy girls, wife of a crazy husband, and crazy for some 90's country hits. She is a nostalgic TV watcher, lover of fan-fic, and is always willing to try a new color in her hair.

Find her on all social media platforms @rachel_mlewis or learn more about her and shop merch at rachellewiswrites.com.